READERS' COMMENTS

"When I started to read *Fountain Street Heat,* I suspected a mild little story about a poor little black girl who eventually makes good in a white world. What a surprise! I soon discovered that the heat builds slowly - steadily - and with so much power I could feel it myself. I will read it again...."   *-Amazon reader*

Homecoming Queen is for all the women who wince and laugh when they see old photographs of themselves in go-go boots, and who still cry over old lovers. Hughes brings it all back - and then some.   *-Sherri Daley, author of* High Cotton

I am a voracious reader, yet I can count on one hand the stories that have touched me as *Homecoming Queen* did. *Fountain Street Heat* was every bit as engrossing. I highly recommend anything Linda Hughes writes!   *-Julie Alfano*

OTHER NOVELS BY LINDA HUGHES
Fountain Street Heat
Homecoming Queen
Tough Rocks
The House on Haven Island (coming soon)

NON-FICTION BOOKS BY LINDA HUGHES
LifeMaps for Midlife Women
Issues in Southern Education
Atlanta's Real Women
What We Talk About When We Talk: Stories From Women Over 60
(coming soon)

BECOMING JESSIE BELLE

a novel by
LINDA HUGHES

Margaret,
Enjoy!
Love,
Linda
9-10-14

DEEDS PUBLISHING | ATLANTA

Published by Deeds Publishing
Marietta, GA
www.deedspublishing.com

Printed in The United States of America

Library of Congress Cataloging-in-Publications Data is available upon request.

ISBN 978-1-937565-98-5

Books are available in quantity for promotional or premium use. For information, write Deeds Publishing, PO Box 682212, Marietta, GA 30068 or info@deedspublishing.com.

First Edition, 2014

10 9 8 7 6 5 4 3 2 1

Acknowledgments

My gratitude goes out to the Babcocks—Jan, Bob, and Mark—of Deeds Publishing for their contributions to this book. Most of all, I appreciate their continued faith in my work. They are wonderful to work with. Thank you also to Deborah Alexander, who prompted the idea for this story. And, as always, love to my husband Joe, and to my furry friends LuLu (our dog) and Lucy (the cat). Their *joi de vivre* keeps me going.

Becoming Jessie Belle is dedicated to my female ancestors, all of the women throughout the ages who made me.

Chapter 1

Jessie Belle knew she needed to keep her cool, but this pompous politician made her so hot under the collar she feared she just might blow a gasket. She took a deep breath and did her best to feign interest in the jerk who sat beside her.

"No, Jezzie Belle," he said, "The people of Yemen will never negotiate with pirates who kill men who are merely doing their jobs at sea. We're not like the United States, where many corporations have paid huge ransoms to those Samolian thugs. We refuse to give in to the demands of thieves, which would only serve to perpetuate this international problem."

Jessie Belle shook her head, swishing her shoulder-length auburn hair. She knew that played well for the camera, clearly signaling her irritation. She wondered if viewers could see the steam rolling out of her ears, too. It was bad enough that Consulate General Tuma blatantly denigrated her country—to a CNN worldwide audience, no less—but the way he leaned in over the newsdesk to invade her space and let "Jez-zie" roll off his tongue in a lurid hiss infuriated her. Even if viewers didn't get the clandestine message, she did. He was putting her in her place as a woman.

She entertained a delightful flash of a fantasy of bolting out of her chair, pointing down at him, and shouting, "You cocky male chauvinist pig, get your mud-slinging behind out of my studio!" But instead, her consummate professionalism reigned. She cast an expression of grave concern straight at him and in her most serious newscaster voice said, "But, Mr. Tuma, with all due respect, what about the lives of those innocent men working on that freighter? After all, Samolian pirates have a track record of slaughtering…"

"No. We will not negotiate."

He had interrupted her. Sure, these interview exchanges often became, in fact were expected to become, lively and sometimes even heated. But being rude to her, a top-rated newscaster on CNN? No-o-o, not as long as Jessie Belle Church had something to say about it. Consummate professionalism be hanged! She might be a proper Southern lady but namby-pamby Melanie Wilkes she was not. That goody-two-shoes from *Gone With the Wind* let everybody walk all over her.

The Consulate General opened his mouth to speak; with all of those perfectly veneered, big, white teeth she imagined that with a couple of xylophone hammers she could play a peppy rendition of *Dixie*; but she cut him off. "Well, in any case," she rushed to say, "we wish for the quick resolution of this most recent hijacking of a freighter off the coast of east Africa. Thank you, Consulate General Tuma, for being with us today."

She turned her body away from him, abruptly cutting off the interview. Looking into camera two she said, "And now it's almost time for me to say farewell. Thanks again for your Twitter comments. As always, you keep me tweeting with glee…" Her mind churned to come up with ad libs as she had sixty extra seconds, seeing that she'd cut short her final interview. That was an eternity of dead air in TV time, as boring as being on a never-ending bad blind date. She had to fill the void so her fans wouldn't want to break up with her.

She was aware of Gracie, the paper-thin production assistant who today wore a ghastly shapeless sack of a dress, quietly fetching that annoying man and thankfully leading him away. The air felt lighter once the big airbag was gone, so Jessie Belle lightened up and filled the time with more Twitter talk.

When the floor director cued ten seconds, she threw the camera her most charming grin, knowing that it dimpled her cheeks adorably. "This is Jessie Belle Church signing off for today. As always, remember that this world is too dangerous for anything but truth and too small for anything but love."

The moment the little red light on the camera clicked off, she popped up out of her chair. A nasty frown invaded her face as she ripped off her lavaliere mike, tore out her earpiece, and mumbled furiously to herself, "How dare he treat me as if I'm nothing? I earned my place at this newsdesk, thank you very much!"

It was true. She'd worked hard for her journalism degree at the University of Georgia before coming to CNN to slave away for two years as a production assistant and five more years as a field reporter. A year ago she'd been promoted to the newsdesk and had garnered rave reviews from audiences ever since.

Not only had she fought her way to the top of the business, she'd had to fight off her mama every step of the way. That was no mean feat, because if ever Scarlett O'Hara had actually tamped one of her demanding, dainty, little feet on solid earth, she'd come in the form of Jessie Belle's mama. Maisy Church just couldn't fathom why her precious little Southern Jessie Belle wanted to work. "Chi-i-ild," she'd say in her sugary Southern drawl, "we already have more money than God."

The question of God's financial status aside, Jessie Belle reveled at being in front of the camera. Of course she'd soon marry her wealthy boyfriend, Robert, which would help get her mama off her back, but she refused to give up working in television.

Like a bird preparing for the freedom of flight, she fluffed her feathers by lifting her chin, tossing her head, straightening her spine, running her hands down the sides of her trim physique, tugging on the bottom of her deep ocean blue Brunello Cucinelli silk sweater, and smoothing the front of her matching short skirt. Ignoring the snickers of the crew when she tottered by and stumbled in her ridiculously high Manolo Blahnik stiletto heels, she high-tailed it to her office.

Gracie was back by her side before she could get through her office door. "You're in deep doo-doo," the production assistant warned about the interview, nibbling at her cuticle as she spoke. "Harry's gonna have a cow. Another cow. He's already got a whole herd."

"I know, I know!" Jessie Belle relented as she scuttled inside and kicked off her shoes, flinging each foot so hard the little daggers flew across the room as if aiming for the kill. "Those things are *so* uncomfortable. I hate them."

"Getting mad at your dumb shoes, or even my incredibly comfortable shoes," Gracie chided, looking down at her own Birkenstocks, "isn't going to change the fact that you're in deep doo-doo with the boss."

Jessie Belle plopped down onto her overstuffed loveseat and buried her face into a toile throw pillow. "I know, I know. I'm sorry. I'm just so mad! That man annoyed me so much."

"What? I can't hear you." Gracie grabbed the pillow and tossed it across the room. "It sounded like you said, 'He anointed me so butch.'"

Jessie Belle moaned. "How long do you think before Harry calls me up?"

Both women jumped at the jangle of the telephone ring.

"No, Harry. Please! You can't do this to me." She despised the note of desperation in her own voice. But this was indeed a desperate situation.

"Well, darlin', actually I can. And I must. I just got off the phone with the big wigs upstairs," he said, pointing at the ceiling, "and they just got off the phone with Mr. Tuma, who called them on his cell phone, by the way, from our own lobby. He was very unhappy and suggested that our 'insolent' reporter might need to investigate in the field for a while. The brass agreed. They've had an idea for a story for a long time and just now decided it's perfect for you. You leave Monday morning."

Overweight and past sixty, Harry reminded Jessie Belle of the crusty old boss Lou Grant from the *Mary Tyler Moore Show* she used to see in reruns on TV when she was a kid. In typical Lou-like behavior, he sat on the edge of his desk, the hulk of his doughy body overflowing the sides, his arms crossed in determination.

"But, but…" she stalled, shuffling from foot to foot as she stood in front of her boss like a wayward kid in the principal's office. "But he was rude first!"

"You do know that you sound like a six-year-old child, don't you?"

"Ha-a-arry!" she whined. "You'd think the big kahunas upstairs," she said, jabbing a finger upward, "would stand up for me. I mean, I do have one of the highest ratings on the network."

He raised his bushy gray eyebrows and glared at her over the rim of the glasses perched halfway down his nose. "How could I forget? You remind me of your ratings every time something like this comes up. I know that audiences love your wit and Southern charm. I know they admire the *chutzpah* that got you to this point at such a young age. I also know that everyone loves your pretty face and reddish hair and that men love those tight sweaters." He twirled his finger around in the general direction of her chest. "And I also know that you are going on this trip."

"Oh, crimony! I don't believe this." Jessie Belle said between clenched teeth, pummeling her balled fists onto her hips.

"Don't you ever swear? Like, 'Oh, shit!' Go ahead, try it. Nobody has said 'crimony' since 1957." He'd often goaded her about this and knew it wouldn't do any good, which was why he enjoyed doing it.

She ignored the dare. After all, her mama said 'crimony' every time she was exasperated, so that was good enough for her. "But what about Robert?" she asked, hoping this new tack of mentioning her filthy rich, politically powerful boyfriend would rescue her. "You know I'm supposed to go to that charity ball with him next weekend in New York City. It'll be great PR for my show."

"This trip will be even better PR."

"No! I can't believe you'd let them do this to me because of one teensy-weensy little incident!" She twisted back and forth in frustration, her arms flailing spastically like a fish out of water.

"Jessie Belle," Harry stated flatly, shaking his head as he hefted himself off the desk. He wagged a finger at her. "There have been other incidences recently. They were already thinking of giving you a lesson in humility. What about the Martha Stewart episode, huh?"

"All I did was mention that her braised asparagus was a tad salty."

"She was on a tour for her new cookbook and was pissed as hell at your attitude."

"Then she needs to figure out how to cook braised asparagus! Have you ever had it the way she does it? I'm telling you, it's too salty. Besides, the audience loved watching someone finally stand up to the queen of the kitchen."

"Yes," he agreed. "And they'll love you on the road, too." He went around behind his desk and looked at some papers. "It's a special report on a National Geographic project, where they chart people's heritage based on their DNA. You'll be doing ten days on the road, following your biological heritage. They're calling it the 'Ancestry Quest.'

"By the way, a nurse will be coming to your office in a little while to swab your cheek for a DNA sample."

"What? My DNA? I already know my ancestry! Everybody in Georgia and half the people in the world know my ancestry!

My great-great-great-great grandfather was an earl in England, for goodness sake! King George the Second himself gave the earl's son, my great-great-great grandfather, William Church, a grant for the plantation land in the new colony of Georgia as a gift for services rendered to the Crown. What more does anybody need to know?"

"Oh," Harry said, grinning mischievously, "this goes much further back than that. You'll start in Africa."

"Africa?" She shook her head in disbelief. "Hello-o-o! I'm not African!" She swept her hands from her head to her toes in a dramatic gesture to illustrate her point.

"Well, according to this project," he said, poking at a paper on his desk, "everybody is."

"My Baptist preacher would love to take you to task on that!"

"Be that as it may, you'll start there and migrate to a new place each day, following the trail of your ancestors as they migrated out of Africa. But we won't know where that trail goes until we get your DNA results. So it'll be a surprise to us all. Won't that be fun?"

"It's poppycock!"

"Maybe even goddamned bullshit?"

She ignored his challenge to cuss but if ever she'd been tempted to do so this was it. "Who'll take my place at the desk while I'm gone? Have you even thought of that? You need me here, Harry."

"Oh, we'll have Bridget Barker fill in. She's been doing a good job out on the road; we'll pull her in for the duration."

"What? B-bridget B-barker? That blond bimbo birdbrain?"

"There you go, almost swearing. Good for you."

"I'm serious, Harry." She scurried up to his desk, placing her fists on it to lean toward him. "Why, she, she doesn't have enough experience behind the desk. She'll ruin my viewership!"

She straightened up, took a deep breath, and balled her fists again, as if ready to go for an upper cut.

"Nah, the viewers will tune in to see your special reports, because they'll be so goddamned exciting. Besides, it's been a year since you've been out on the road. It'll get you back to your roots, real journalism. Hell, even Diane Sawyer does it from time to time."

"She's old." Oops. The second those careless words slithered across her lips, Jessie Belle knew she'd sealed her fate. Harry would never side with her now that she'd denigrated the sacred love-of-his-life-from-afar.

"Jessie Belle Church! What did you say? Listen, little lady!" He clomped up to within inches of her and shook his finger in her face. "You'll be lucky to ever be half as good as she is! She's the best, the cream of the crop. She's got it all—brains, personality, talent. And those gams! My god, have you ever taken a gander at those legs?"

"Yes, I know. I'm sorry. I'm just upset. I love her, too. I do hope to be half as good as she is someday," she lied, believing, of course, that she was already as good, maybe even better. Which made this stupid road trip all the more stupid.

It was bad enough that she was being sent away like a chastised child, but the fact that Bridget Barker—that ruthlessly ambitious, back-stabbing, helium-boobed, bleached blonde—would be sitting in her chair just shoved a salt block into the wound.

"Tell me this isn't happening to me!" Jessie Belle wailed as she clamped her hands to her head and pulled on her hair.

Chapter 2

Clacka used a handful of soft, moist moss to stroke the thick tuft of wiry black hair on the top of her newborn baby boy's head. Her large earth-brown eyes open wide, she stared down at him where he laid on her still-swollen belly. He had just been placed there by the elder woman, the one they called "the bringer of life" because she had helped women give birth for as long as anyone could remember. The baby replied to his mother's glare with a squawk and returned her inspection with his own disbelieving dark eyes, blinking in protest at being thrust out of his blissful darkness. When he began to squirm and wail, Clacka nestled him into her sweaty bare breasts. He fell fast asleep, ignoring this bright new world that he did not understand.

The other ebony women, covered in animal skins that surrounded their waists and fell to their thighs, scampered around. One brought a hollowed gourd filled with water and the new mother drank greedily. She and the other women had been gathering fruit when the pain started, and Clacka had dropped the little round pieces of food and watched them roll away down the dirt path as she yelled to the women for help. She'd squatted and the baby came quickly.

As always while giving birth, Clacka was held by her mother, who sat behind her, cradling her daughter between her tree trunk legs. Clacka's head lolled in her mother's sagging breasts while sinewy arms reached around to brace her, holding her tight. She'd clenched her mother's hands so tightly during the final throes of the birth that her nails tore the flesh, but her mother uttered no complaints. This was the way that all mothers supported their daughters during childbirths. This was life.

The elder woman, the bringer of life, who sat on the ground at the foot of Clacka's spread legs, watched carefully as the blue cord that still connected the baby's belly with the inside of its mother turned white. "Ack!" she proclaimed, placing the human cord on top of a small rock she held in one hand and quickly cutting it with a sharp rock she grasped in her other hand. The cord split in two, falling away to spill thick, white juice onto Clacka's middle. With a flick of her stubby yet nimble fingers, the elder tied a knot in the cord where it attached to the child. "Cluh!" she commanded, pointing and motioning to a woman who hustled to use a wad of moss to wipe up the goo that had splattered onto the new mother's tummy.

Clacka's own mother then encircled her weary daughter's waist, maneuvered around the newborn that lay there, and massaged Clacka's belly with long deep strokes. Suddenly, a bundle of bloody flesh glided out of Clacka's body like the flesh of a fruit being squeezed out of its skin. She groaned in relief.

This caused the elder to bark more orders that resulted in one woman shuffling away with the revered afterbirth, which had fallen onto the large tree frond that had been placed underneath the young mother. As was done after all births, the rich green leaf that held the afterbirth was folded, each side carefully bent over the other to preserve the wet, red mass so that it could be placed on a boulder to dry in the sun and then, when it was ready, burned one night in a sacred fire of life. This ritual would bring good weather and good hunting until the next baby came, which looked to be that of one of the others, after a few more big moons.

Clacka looked back at her mother, who gave her a gap-toothed grin and nodded approval. Clacka was one of many children and her mother, although withered and old, remained strong. Comforted by the feeling of her mother's body around her and understanding that her own child had just been torn away from the warmth of its womb, Clacka protectively settled the infant more deeply into her chest.

Suddenly a noise in the brush announced the arrival of another and Clacka's little daughter burst out of the thick greenery. "Click! Click!" the child exclaimed, excitedly greeting her mother. Clacka looked up at her first child, who had been walking for many big moons now and could run like the wind on her tiny feet. Her second child, a boy, wasn't walking yet, but the elder assured her that he would be up and about any sunrise now, and that he would grow up to be a great hunter. This newborn was her third child and she knew she would have many more.

The little girl plopped down onto the dirt next to her mother and stroked the baby's hair. The infant woke up and his small, round mouth began to open and close like the tiny beak of a hungry baby bird. Instinctively, he turned his head into his mother's breast, latched onto a protruding nipple, and sucked.

Clacka tossed away the moss she still held in her hand and ran a finger down her daughter's cheek, knowing that the girl would one day also give birth to many babies.

She turned her attention back to her new baby boy and inspected his tiny body. All clean after the moss washing she'd given him, his dark skin glistened in the light of the sun, now high enough in the sky to break through the cover of the tall trees and to strike down upon them. She bent over him so that her body could shelter his little eyes from the sunlight, and looked him over. He had everything he needed: eyes, nose, mouth, ears, penis, and toes. He would make a good, strong man.

Suddenly, the father of her children came rushing out of the foliage. He stopped in his tracks, took in the scene, tossed his spear aside, and knelt his lean naked body down beside her. He spread his fingers wide to place his big rough hand on the infant's chest. The two parents looked deep into one another's eyes.

Then Clacka closed her eyes and lifted her face to the sky to take in the soothing heat of the sun. It was just like her life—full and warm. Her mother behind her, her mate in front of her, her children at hand, and the others in the near distance. She had everything she could ever need and felt content.

Chapter 3

Her wild moans jolted her awake. Embarrassed, Jessie Belle looked around to see if anyone else had heard her groaning in her sleep. She peered into the aisle, but the two men sitting up front weren't paying any attention to her. The roar of the engines on CNN's private Lear jet had apparently obliterated the sound.

Disbelieving, she glared at her stomach, where she clung to the front of her tight Rock and Republic designer jeans. "Oh!" she whispered, and snatched her hands away. Her tummy was flat as the proverbial buckwheat pancake, thanks to two hundred crunches a day during killer workouts in the network office's gym and a twelve-hundred-calorie-a-day diet. But the dream had been so real! She actually felt as if she'd had a baby! It seemed like her belly should be lumpy and mushy from having been pregnant.

How ridiculous. She didn't even want children. Chasing fidget midgets around Robert's beautiful, sprawling Buckhead estate, where they would undoubtedly live when they got married, was definitely not her idea of a dandy time. Thankfully, Robert didn't want any bawling brats, either. He said his two grown kids from his former marriage were more than enough.

That was one of the things she loved about him. He didn't care one whit that whatever that thing called "maternal instinct" was all about, whatever gene caused it, it had missed Jessie Belle Church as surely as it would have missed a rock. Thank goodness she had an older brother, Jeff, who'd done a fine job of meeting his family obligation of providing two sons to carry on the Church family name. Those egomaniacal little heathens afforded Jessie Belle the luxury of feeling no duty whatsoever to provide offspring for the sake of the family.

She thought of the night before, which she and Robert had spent together. Unconsciously, she ran her thumbs over the tips of her fingers as she savored the memory of gently stroking his thick, graying hair. Goodness gracious sakes alive, how she admired his face, still boyish even though he was forty-five. She loved the way he dressed during the day in meticulous Armani suits for work and spiffy Ralph Lauren duds for casual wear. But she loved him best when his toned naked body lay by her side. He always slept so soundly after having good sex. And the sex was always good.

He'd been surprised at first to learn that she'd only been intimate with two other men in her life, considering that she was twenty-nine years old when they met. There had been her boyfriend in college, the one she thought wanted to marry her but who, as it turned out, only wanted to bed what seemed to be the one and only virgin left at the University of Georgia. Unbeknownst to her, there was as much speculation around campus about her sexual status as there had once been about that of Queen Elizabeth the First. Like that redhead, Jessie Belle, UGA's homecoming queen in 2000, had also been dubbed "the virgin queen" and her sly boyfriend had gained celebrity status as the campus stud for undoing that. A low-down dog in her mind. Then in her mid-twenties she'd fallen head-over-heels for a news producer who was supposedly divorcing his wife but who, she discovered, was still living in holy matrimony at the same time he was boffing her. When she found out, she dumped him like yesterday's fish.

But Robert was different and she missed him horribly already. "Crimony!" she griped aloud, furious at Harry all over again for making her take this stupid trip. "I even bought that new dress just for the charity ball in New York next weekend and now I can't even go." She simmered with loathing for her boss, who she'd liked up to this point. But now not only had he insulted her by burdening her with menial work, he was making her miss a grand opportunity to strut her stuff in a cute, sparkly, black Prada number. *How could he be so cruel?*

Worse yet, she'd suspected that the New York weekend would have produced a Cartier diamond ring—the gorgeous, five-carat, marquis-cut stone set in platinum that she and Robert had looked at together the last time they'd visited the city. Now instead of showing off a big ring and announcing her engagement at a big soiree, she'd be sweating her buns off while schlepping through the hinterlands of the African jungle.

Great. Just dandy. Fine.

At least she felt certain that Robert would be dropping down on one knee before too long. And then they'd have a huge, fabulous, splashy wedding, to which she would not invite Harry. Then she'd move into Robert's exquisite 1930s mansion in the exclusive Buckhead area of Atlanta, he'd keep on buying companies and making money hand-over-fist, she'd continue to be a famous TV personality, they'd attend high society events all over the world, and they'd live happily ever after. So there, Harry! No way would she let a work assignment ruin her life. She couldn't help but grin broadly at the thought of her future.

A tinny rendition of *Georgia on My Mind* wafting up from her purse broke into her thoughts. She grabbed her Coach bag off the seat next to her and scavenged through a bunch of junk to come up with her iPhone. She glanced at the screen for caller ID, punched it on, and clamped it up to her ear.

"Hi, Mama!" she said, startled that she'd dreamt about having a baby and then been thinking of how she never wanted to have a baby, and it was her own mother. Maisy Church obliged her daughter to listen for a long while before she could get a word in edgewise. After some minutes, Jessie Belle was finally able to speak. "Yes, I know," she said. "Harry's *so* mean…. I'm on the plane now…. There are three of us." She angled her head into the aisle to get a look up front at the two men facing the bulkhead on either side of the aisle eight rows up. "I confess," she said, "I was already in the back here pretending to be asleep when they boarded the plane and then I really did fall asleep, so I haven't even said 'hi' yet. It looks like…" she said, taking another peek. "Oh yes! That's definitely Joe Hoffman. Remember him? One of the special report directors. I've worked with him before. He's short and has that little bald spot right on his crown… Ah-huh, the man from the upper peninsula of Michigan with the funny 'Yooper' accent. Sort of Scandinavian-German-Canadian. 'Yah,' 'eh,' and all that." She lilted the vowel sound at the end of each word to mimic the distinctive accent.

She guffawed, thinking of her own years of private speech lessons to get rid of her Southern accent so she could speak "Standard English" for television. Oh, she kept a twinge of her Southern accent for a touch of on-air charm, but was totally capable of turning it off. She no longer automatically expanded her vowels. "Atla-anta" had become "Atlanta," with a short "a" in the middle. "Geo-gia" was now "Georgia," with the "r" given its due. She could properly say "pardon" instead "pahden" and "butter" instead of "buddah." "Y'all," a vocabulary staple for any self-respecting Southerner, was gone with the wind. Except when she talked to her mama. Then it all blew back in.

Her mama asked about the second man, so Jessie Belle took yet another look to try to assess the other head up front. "Well," she said, "there has to be a cameraman, so that must be him. All I can see is the back of his head. He looks…" she said, mulling it over, "tall. Lots of unruly black hair. It's either a man or a gorilla. I can't tell which. Wouldn't surprise me if Harry sent a gorilla.

"But as far as I'm concerned, there's one person who's missing! Harry wouldn't even let me bring a stylist!" she groused.

A PERSONAL NOTE FROM

Margaret Berry

BECOMING JESSIE BELLE

"Can you imagine? I have to do my own hair and makeup every day! He said I'd look more 'authentic' this way. Ha! Makes me mad as a bee without honey is what it does. Bridget will look like a hot chick and I'll look like a ship rat."

Sometimes her mama drove Jessie Belle nuts with her blathering about marriage and grandbabies, but nobody else understood Jessie Bell's need for personal maintenance as well as that matriarch. After all, her mama was the one who had drilled it into her that a genuine Southern belle might as well turn up her toes to the undertaker as miss a weekly pedicure.

After fifteen minutes of woe-is-me bonding, her mama had to go get ready for bridge club. They called themselves "The Social Circle Ladies' Bridge and Tea Club," but Jessie Belle knew full well that the primary beverage to be consumed would not be sweet iced tea. Like many good Southern women, the matriarchs of Social Circle, Georgia, weren't about to let social status prohibit them from drinking their scotch whiskey.

"Y'all have fun. Tell the girls I said 'hi,'" Jessie Belle said. "And tell them to watch my stupid 'Where did Jessie Belle come from?' reports…. Thanks, Mama…. I love you, too. And give my love to Ida," she added, referring to her mother's African American housekeeper who'd been with the family for so long she'd started at a time when a woman in that position was called a Negro maid. "Talk to you tomorrah," Jessie Belle ended the call.

She punched out of the phone call, checked the time on the screen, and tossed the little gadget back into her purse. They'd been in the air for two hours and she'd slept most it.

After a brief spasm of fretting about that interloper back at the station, Bridget Barker, whose name she couldn't even think without a yelp and a growl, *Brid-get Bark!-er-er-errrr,* her mind meandered back to her dream. *Weird!* What was with all those weird natives who spoke that weird clucky language? And her feeling like she'd given birth to a baby? She shuddered and stroked her taut belly.

Determined to forget the nightmare and with nothing else to do, she glanced out the window. Below, the ocean stretched into forever. It was like looking at the sky on the ground. This was going to be one long flight.

Boredom settled in like reek on a wet towel left crumpled on the floor, so she pulled out her briefcase and took out the dossier Harry gave her when she left work on Friday evening.

She looked at the cover.

Genographic Project
National Geographic Society

She turned the page.

A Landmark Study of the Human Journey

"Where do you really come from? And how did you get to where you live today? DNA studies suggest that all humans today descend from a group of African ancestors who—about 60,000 years ago—began a remarkable journey.

"The Genographic Project is seeking to chart new knowledge about the migratory history of the human species by using sophisticated laboratory and computer analysis of DNA contributed by hundreds of thousands of people from around the world...."

For the next fifteen minutes she read, her head bent over the pages in fascination. It was more interesting than she'd expected. They traced "mitochondrial" DNA, that from the maternal side, as it was easiest to access. But the synopsis ended by recommending the Genographic website. Jessie Belle pulled out her iPad but soon discovered there wasn't good Wi-Fi reception over this stretch of the ocean, so she clamped it shut. She'd have to look at it later.

So now what? She popped her head into the aisle to see what the two guys up front were up to. They were still talking, each leaning into the aisle toward the other to be heard over the hum of the engines. Seeing that she was stuck here, whether she liked it or not, she decided she may as well go make nice.

She got up and started down the aisle but about halfway the jet hit a bump, which knocked her off her feet and into a seat. By the time she righted herself, the pilots' cabin door opened and the co-pilot's head poked out.

"No problem," he announced. "Just a little air pocket."

"Next time, ya know, warn us," Joe said, "so we can throw our arms in the air and scream in glee."

"Will do." The co-pilot saluted and disappeared behind the cabin door.

Jessie Belle started to rise but suddenly realized that her colleagues had been so focused on the co-pilot, they hadn't seen her. This was obvious when the no-name gorilla cameraman turned to Joe again and said, "So, what is she? Some kind of diva or something? I hate working with divas."

Jessie Belle ducked down. She was close enough now to hear most of what they were saying. Who did this guy with the Eastern European accent think he was, calling her a diva?

"Nah," Joe said. "Well, okay, yah. But she's a nice diva. Not a bitch diva like some of them, eh. Harry calls her the 'darlin' diva.' High maintenance for sure—old money and all that. Her dad's dead but her mom still lives on the old family plantation in Social Circle. I kid you not. There was an article about it once in the *AJC*. Said in the early 1800s the plantation was over 7,000 acres. The family made their fortune in cotton, with over six hundred slaves at any given time." He shook his head.

"Then her granddad and dad made another fortune in banking. Her mom's family goes way back, too, with more mullah. So Jessie Belle has money coming out of both ears. Which means she's only working because she loves her job."

"So she is a diva, a spoiled brat, and used to getting whatever she wants," the no-name gorilla said.

"Well, yah, maybe, but she's a really good kid," Joe said. "And very smart. Don't let that Southern belle thing fool you. She's got brains." He tapped his forehead with his forefinger.

Jessie Belle was crouched down with her shoulder pressed so tightly against the seat in front of her in her effort to hear that she almost fell over. She caught herself just in time. Who in heck did that no-name think he was, not only calling her a diva but a spoiled brat to boot? How dare he? Besides, did a spoiled rotten, true-blue diva get exiled to the hinterlands?

I think not!

No-name said something else. She couldn't understand it, considering the combination of plane noise and his Eastern European accent. Words rolled around in his mouth as if he were savoring wine.

Joe, on the other hand, with that Yooper accent, sounded like he couldn't wait to spit the words out. He said something else she didn't get either, which sounded like, "She's got rubber pants." Then it hit her. He'd said, "She's going with Robert Brentz."

Like a toddler tumbling out of a chair, she toppled into the aisle.

"Hey, Jessie Belle!" Joe said, looking back, half in concern and half in amusement. "You okay?" He fumbled with the laptop on his lap, trying to get it out of the way so he could come to her aid.

No-name looked back at her as if she were daft. But, after a quick appraisal of the situation, he signaled to Joe that he'd take care of it, methodically unfurled his rangy body to rise from his seat, strode the few steps to her side, and reached his plate-sized hand down in an offer to help her up.

"Ah, sure. I'm fine," she said, answering Joe's question as she looked up, way up, beyond long legs, past a tight torso, above broad shoulders, over a square jaw, and into the smoky gray eyes of the no-name stranger. He wore the typical cameraman outfit of scruffy shoes, old jeans, and a faded tee shirt. She didn't know what made her freeze and forget to extend her hand. But she thawed when he grabbed her by the wrist and unceremoniously yanked her up.

"Next time you eavesdrop, maybe you'd better use a seatbelt," he said.

"Ha ha. I wasn't eavesdropping. I was just, um, doing what investigative reporters naturally do. Listening in.

"I'm Jessie Belle, by the way, as you undoubtedly already know. The spoiled brat diva." Boldly, she looked up into his eyes as she extended her hand to shake.

A slight grin crossed his lips. She expected an apology, but instead he said, "And I'm Dragan Dlugitch, as you undoubtedly do *not* know." He pumped her hand once before letting go.

His stare unnerved her. He seemed—what was it? Intense? Condescending?

Whatever it was, she didn't like it.

"Dragon like the mythical monster?" she asked.

"No. *Dray*-gun. Just call me Dray. Although I suppose some have accused me of being a monster."

"And your last name is…what? Romanian?"

"Correct. Very good. Most Americans have no clue."

"Dah-*lu*-gitch. Did I say it right?"

"You did."

"Come on, Jessie Belle," Joe entreated. "Join us. Listen in first hand while we gossip about you. And you can give us the really good dirt, eh." He stood up, having finally lassoed control of his laptop, and moved over a seat to make room for her.

Jessie Belle slipped by Dray, uncomfortable that in the narrow aisle their bodies almost touched. She was relieved to sit down and grab Joe for a friendly hug. They exchanged greetings and he commented on her having been asleep when they boarded. She asked how his kids were, but all the while her mind swirled with the question of why she felt buck naked in the presence of that dragon man. The hair on the nape of her neck prickled at the sensation that his arrogant eyes bore into the back of her, no doubt undressing her, while she talked to Joe. When she looked back at him, though, he was looking the other way out the window, appearing to be totally lost in thought.

He's not even interested in me! Why not?

And why, she wondered, did she even ask that question?

Chapter 4

"There's no doubt she's an American hero!" Bridget Barker proclaimed.

Jessie Belle stared at the CNN newscast that blared from the laptop computer screen, her jaw hanging open.

"Our own Jessie Belle Church, who as you know is out on special assignment, saved a little girl's life today in Ethiopia…." Bridget continued, with what Jessie Belle knew to be a calculated look of appropriate pride. She felt certain her nemesis despised reporting this story. Jessie Belle hated to admit it, but Bridget did look good. In fact, with her perfectly coiffed fluffy hair and make-up artistically applied to perfection, she looked downright gorgeous, doggone it. And, worse yet, her reporting style was okay. For that, Jessie Belle hated her guts all the more.

"They did a great job with the whole piece!" Joe said. "Ya know, that footage you got of Jessie Belle is amazing, Dray. They're gonna play that up to make her the hero of all times. At least hero of the week. Eh?" He slapped Dray on the back.

Dray nodded but never looked away from the screen. Bridget was now doing voiceover for the video footage. There was Jessie Belle grabbing hold of an Ethiopian child and then protectively flinging her body over the little girl as they both fell to the ground while bullets whirled around them. Jessie Belle's hand covered the child's head and her adult body completely shielded the child's waif-like form. The little girl's head turned just enough to look at her protector and the camera zoomed in as Jessie Belle's lake blue eyes locked in with the terrified earth brown eyes of the child. It was the kind of spontaneous once-in-a-lifetime shot every videographer prays for.

"I swear," Jessie Belle said, "I'd never have remembered how I got onto the ground if I didn't see it. It all happened so fast!"

"I've never seen anybody move so fast!" Joe said. "The way you snatched that little girl up out of harm's way! That was amazing! Why, she just happened to be standing right there where those idiots started shooting. They didn't even care if they killed a child. Thank God you were there, Jessie Belle. Your motherly instinct sure did kick in!"

He had no idea, of course, how wrong he must be, but she wasn't about to admit that she'd never felt a drop of motherly anything. So what on earth made her put her own life on the line to protect that child when the squirmish between guerrilla rebels and local villagers broke out?

She had no idea.

Back on the screen soldiers suddenly appeared. Within seconds they shot and killed the rebels. Blood and gore filled the frame.

Jessie Belle turned away in disgust, only to notice that Dray stared at her.

"I didn't even know what the camera was catching," he said. "I was in the middle of shooting the villagers going about their daily business when the gunfire started. I hit the ground and rolled behind that well, and held onto my camera hoping to get the rebels. I didn't even realize there had been a child standing there. I should have helped."

"Hey," Joe said, "no apologies necessary. We all lived, and you got great footage of our hero here, accidentally or not. And the big brass is salivating over it. Besides, I'm the one who's supposed to serve and protect." They all knew that as a former CIA agent, Joe was expected to be as much bodyguard as director. "If anybody should apologize it should be me. I saw those assholes with guns barreling up in that rattle-trap truck, but too late. Damn! I miss the Agency and being able to travel with a gun. I really needed one this time. Thank God it all worked out and youse guys are okay.

"That little girl's parents will be grateful to you forever, Jessie Belle. I bet they would've been destroyed if anything had happened to their child."

Jessie Belle nodded, knowing that four-times divorced Joe, who paid alimony and child support to three of his exes, adored all of his five kids. He should know about parental love.

"Harry said they've already run this three times and it's huge," Joe said. "And they'll continue to use it as a teaser for the 'Ancestry Quest' story. The fact that we got caught in this raucous on our way to our original assignment just adds to the intrigue. Shows how determined we are to go through anything to nab the good stories for our viewers. At least, that's how they'll sell it. They'll repeat this every ten minutes for the rest of the day."

"And don't forget the YouTube hits," Dray noted.

"How's it feel to be a bona fide Bionic-Wonder-Super Woman heroine, eh?" Joe asked, patting Jessie Belle on the back.

She gnawed at her lower lip before answering. "I only did what anyone would have done in that situation. You always hear people say that. Now I understand. It's as if somebody else, somebody a lot braver, took over my body."

"Well, whoever it was, they did a great job!" Joe concluded.

She woke up in a pool of sweat. The small bed she slept on was concrete hard and the room was sweltering hot. This crude hotel in Addis Ababa, Ethiopia, wasn't exactly five star like she was used to. But it wasn't the discomfort alone that had awoken her. It was another haunting dream. This time she wasn't having a baby.

Instead, she saw the shadow of an ethereal, mysterious woman, a ghostly spirit, who smiled upon her. And she knew the apparition was pleased that Jessie Belle had saved that little girl today.

"Oh great," she groaned. "Now I've got a haint stalking me in the night. Just what I need."

She clasped her eyes shut in an effort to sleep, but slumber was as elusive as a ghost.

Chapter 5

"They're called the Bush People. They talk through an un-usual clicking sound. Thankfully, we'll have an excellent interpreter. No matter how much I try to learn the language, my tongue just can't do all of those clicks right."

Jessie Belle stared in disbelief at Edwin Sampson, the assis-tant director of the National Geographic Genographic Project who had joined them for the first day of their shoot. Her dream! Those people had used a strange clicking language, too. Clacka, ack, cluh. She flipped through her memory files to try to come up with more of their words, but that was all she could retrieve.

"Hey, Jessie Belle, you look like you've seen a ghost," Joe said.

His accidental accuracy startled Jessie Belle so much that her eyes blinked spastically. She caught herself and stopped.

"Pay attention, please," Joe continued. "This is important. We're gonna start filming soon. Didn't you get any sleep last night?"

"Oh, sorry," she mumbled. "No, I had a bad dream. I mean… well, never mind. I'm sorry, what were you saying?"

Edwin looked at her kindly and she got the impression that five years of studying indigenous people all over the world had built in him an enormous store of patience. She liked him, an-other surprise on this trip she hadn't wanted to take. He was about forty, an American scientist, good-looking, and dressed just like an explorer in old movies, in hiking boots, khaki safari shorts, a once-white tee shirt, a multi-pocketed khaki vest, and a jaunty straw fedora. Indiana Jones personified, viewers would eat him up.

Jessie Belle, Edwin, Joe, and Dray all huddled together around a battered old metal table that sat under a giant banyan tree. Even though the shade from the far-reaching branches and thick foliage felt like a gift from the gods, they all perspired as if they'd just run a marathon. Although she was dressed for the African heat in shorts, a tank top, and a wide-brimmed straw hat, sweat poured out of every pore of Jessie Belle's body. Joe and Dray, in shorts, tee shirts, and Atlanta Braves baseball caps, were drenched, too. It was over 100 degrees in the shade and they looked like what her mama called "stuck pigs."

"As far as we can tell," Edwin said, mopping his brow with a handkerchief, "the Bush People who live here are the most direct line from the oldest known human beings on earth. I know you want this all on camera, so that's all I'll tell you right now, but it's truly an amazing story!" His excitement over his work was contagious and Jessie Belle caught herself actually being a little excited, too.

"Jessie Belle," Joe said, "Edwin got your DNA results back this morning. Normally, it takes eight weeks but CNN has a little pull. So you'll hear the results on camera. I want the spontaneity of you hearing it for the first time. Now, remember that we'll be editing together pieces of your website video," he said, pointing at Edwin, "with pieces of live footage of you two shot here today with the Bush People," he said, pointing at Jessie Belle. "Then we'll include footage of just them, and Jessie Belle will do voice-over for that when we're done. The crew at home will draw up graphics, like maps, that will be added before the show airs. Any questions?"

Heads shook all around.

Jessie Belle dug into her backpack for a mirror and then wished she hadn't. Her hair had somehow managed to frizz, even in the absence of one iota of humidity, and stuck out like rusty scouring pads from underneath her hat. Her make-up had long since melted away. She dabbed on some pink lipstick and grimaced at her reflection in the mirror, knowing that was the best she was going to be able to do. Throwing her meager beauty accessories back into the bag, she looked down at her once-nice pink tank top, which clung to her damp body like a leach. Underneath, her bra felt surgically attached to her skin. Her cute safari shorts were already covered in a layer of dust. And her leather-sandaled feet were filthy. She looked down, wiggled her toes, and figured that at least the dirt helped hide the badly chipped polish on her toenails.

At this point in her life, this kind of thing normally annoyed the heck out of her. So why, she wondered, did she feel a sense of adventure? It reminded her of the old days, when she'd been a young cub reporter and everything had been new and exciting, before the days of fame and fortune. Was she actually starting to enjoy this stupid road trip? No! She refused to accept it. She'd worked hard to get above having to work out in the middle of no-man's-land in dirt and dust. She hated it!

For twenty minutes they followed a narrow walking trail away from their parked Jeep into what looked like barren wasteland. Then, suddenly, there stood the Bush People's village of mud huts.

Dray had been shooting the trek, sometimes from the front of the small band of hikers and sometimes from the back. When Jessie Belle first laid eyes on the village, he happened to be right beside her and the camera caught the light in her eyes and her gasp of surprise. She looked puzzled, then stunned.

The people, she realized in shock, looked just like the people in her dream! This just couldn't be.

Dray moved away to film the huts and inhabitants, and Edwin interrupted her thoughts. "Let me introduce you to the some of the villagers," he said.

Her mind swirled in disbelief as nearly naked men and topless women were introduced to her by the village interpreter. She felt like she was in some kind of messianic trance. How could she have foretold this? How had she known? She felt certain she'd never seen these people or heard about them on TV, and she'd certainly never thought of herself as being a seer who could look into the future. Or the past. She didn't even believe in psychics or fortune tellers or palm readers or mediums or voodooists or whatever the freaks were called. In fact, she steadfastly refused to believe in such malarkey.

"Tell me, what do you think your heritage is?" Edwin asked.

Joe had them sitting close together on two old tree stumps so they'd both be in the shot.

"Why, we come from the upper class in England," Jessie Belle said. "My ancestor was an earl. His son was given land in America with a Crown grant from the king himself."

"So, blue-bloods, would you say?" Edwin asked.

"Well, yes, that is how the Churches have been described."

"That's nice," Edwin said, "but that's just the last few hundred years. And only your father's side of the family. Have you ever thought about your total heritage? Much further back, including your mother's side. Remember there were thousands of years of ancestors on both sides. Long before England even had kings. A lot would have been going on in all that time. Have you ever wondered about that?"

"No," Jessie Belle admitted. "It never occurred to me."

"It doesn't to most people. Especially to Americans who have such short family histories to draw from. But our research indicates that we all—and I mean *all*—are derived from humans, as we know them today, who started out right here! On this very land!"

She looked down at the dirt beneath her dirty feet.

"So we could say," he continued, "that Ethiopia is the original Garden of Eden."

An image of her Baptist preacher taking umbrage at that last statement flashed across Jessie Belle's mind. She brushed the thought away. Her preacher could jump up and down, and shout "halleluiah" all he wanted, but he wasn't going to do her any good out here.

Unaware of her disbelief, Edwin went on. "For a long time the oldest human skeleton ever found was that of a woman nicknamed 'Lucy.' Her fossilized remains were found in this region about thirty-five years ago. She's estimated to have lived about 3.4 million years ago.

"But! Just recently the skeleton of another female was found near here, this one much older. It's 4.4 million years old! She's called 'Ardi' because the scientific name of her species is Ardipithecus Ramidus. She weighed about 110 pounds, was small-brained, and had an active sex life."

"They can actually tell all that from a mere bunch of fossilized bones that are over four million years old?" Jessie Belle asked, anticipating what her viewers would wonder.

"Yes, because the shape and position of her hip bones tells us that she bore many children. It's amazing what today's scientists can extrapolate from something that old!

"The people we are visiting here, the Bush People, are the closest thing we have today to those early humans. So studying them helps us understand how early people lived, how they survived, and what they believed in. We'll never know for sure, of course, but we can make some pretty decent educated guesses.

"One of the things we do know is that millions of years ago our ancient ancestors moved out of this region and eventually spread throughout the globe. Our research has allowed us to trace that migration and to map out how they dispersed around the world. Some groups went deeper into Africa, some went north on the Nile and out of Africa in different directions, and others went east over what is today called Asia. Some migrated into Europe. Eventually, human beings ended up all over the planet.

"Because some groups spent thousands of years in one place, their DNA would adjust and change, creating what we call 'markers.' So when a person today has a DNA test, we look for the primary markers that tell where their ancestors spent a lot of time."

He looked at Jessie Belle. "Are you ready to hear your DNA results?"

Dray zeroed in for a closer shot of her face. She smiled appropriately. "Sure! Give it to me," she said, whipping off her hat and tossing her frazzled hair.

"Your ancestors would have started here, like all of our ancestors did, and migrated north following the Nile. Everyone wants to believe their ancestor could have been Cleopatra but most of our ancestors would have moved through that area long before her time. They would have traveled together in small tribes and would have been hunters, gatherers, and fishermen."

Jessie Belle's mind veered off to an image of the regal Egyptian queen. Somebody must be the sovereign's descendent, so it was just as likely herself as anybody else. Maybe this was the majestic blood she felt flowing through her veins. Certainly the queen and she shared a love of high style, wealth, and fame. Jessie Belle mused that they'd have enjoyed sharing a girlie day playing with each other's makeup and clothes.

"When your ancestors went out of Africa," Edwin said, interrupting her fantasy, "they would have journeyed throughout the center of Europe and beyond. Your British heritage that you know about from your father's side would most likely be a combination of Celtic, Anglo-Saxon, Norman, and other common Brit inheritors from the European area.

"However, on your mother's side, your DNA shows us something quite different. You have a primary marker from what's called Haplo-Group V-87. That's Scandinavian." He stopped talking and waited for her reaction.

Jessie Belle stared at him in disbelief, forcing herself to close her gaping mouth. "Scandinavian? Like Vikings?" she queried. "No, I don't think so. I know British history and our earls came from Normandy in France."

And from the civilized French upper class, not from a bunch of pillaging, raping, murdering barbarians from way up North in the freezing cold.

A moving picture paraded through her imagination: A dirty, tattooed, long-haired Viking in animal skins and a horned hat, standing menacingly at the helm of a dragonship, shouting orders to slaughter everyone in their path. She shuddered.

"And," she went on, refusing to relent, "I'm pretty sure my mother's heritage is upper class British, too."

"That's not what your DNA says! That's what's so great about this project!" Edwin said, genuinely elated. "We think we know our heritage but we usually have no clue! DNA doesn't lie. You are Scandinavian. Yes, probably even Viking. Most likely, if your mother thinks of her heritage as British, her line is descended from Vikings who raided and settled in the British Isles from about 800 to 1100 AD. Isn't it exciting?"

She forced a smile for the camera. "Wow! Yes, how, um, interesting."

"Of course," he continued, "that's just part of your heritage. A predominant part that was easily evident in your DNA. But in reality, we all have combinations of ancestry we can't quickly trace. There's no telling what else is in there." He chuckled.

"Ha ha." Jessie Belle tried to make her laugh sound genuine but it came out like a little kid having been commanded to be polite to a dreaded, smelly, farting old aunt. "No telling," she echoed, having absolutely nothing original to say. "Vikings. Who knew?"

The diaphanous woman softly stroked Jessie Belle's brow, waking her from her deep sleep. Not afraid, as she'd met the woman before in her earlier dream, Jessie Belle lifted herself up, leaned back on her elbows, and looked up, fascinated by the apparition. Glittery fireflies flickered throughout the room, and reams of shimmery white gossamer fabric swirled around the ghost as she floated above Jessie Belle's bed.

Who are you? Jessie Belle asked, without having to speak the words.

I am the one who will help you become you.

I am me, Jessie Belle said, confused.

You are more than you know, the woman said, smiling kindly. Then she blew a sparkly kiss and languorously evaporated into the dark night, shards of glimmering light flickering out in her wake.

Chapter 6

What else could possibly go wrong on this stupid trip? Jessie Belle sulked.

She looked up at the towering monuments of Abu Simbel, the ancient temples built by the Egyptian pharaoh Ramesses II in the thirteenth century B.C., which was, by her calculation, a really, really long time ago. So long ago that she wasn't sure why it mattered. But it did, at least to the network honchos.

Since discovering the supposed migratory path of her ancient ancestors, the show's producers had drawn up an itinerary that included following that trail and examining who inhabited the most interesting of those spots today. Because her forebears would have followed the Nile downriver, which is north on this continent, that's what she and Joe and Dray were doing. This remote archaeological site on the Nile in southern Egypt was their first stop since flying out of Ethiopia.

She was cranky from the heat, hunger, and thirst and worried because she hadn't been able to reach Robert by phone since they'd left home. She was also utterly exhausted after a night of restlessness caused by a strange dream about the same ghost woman who'd appeared before. First the haint had seemed to be thanking her for saving that little girl's life in Ethiopia. Last night she'd seemed to be trying to get Jessie Belle to pay attention to something that didn't make any sense. She said she'd help Jessie

Belle become herself. How absurd. Jessie Belle not only knew herself inside and out, she had her whole life all planned. What more could there be?

The mystery had been haunting her all day, which really drove her crazy because the ghost woman had only been a silly dream, after all. At first the woman seemed as friendly as Casper the Friendly Ghost, Jessie Belle's favorite TV cartoon character when she'd been a little kid. But now, in the light of day, the spook of her dreams seemed sinister. More like the Ghost of Christmas Past. Most frightening, however, was why she let it trouble her. How could someone who didn't even exist unsettle her so?

And, as if in a grand scheme to pile more crap onto the dung heap of her life, after spending most of the day touring the monuments, which she reluctantly admitted to herself were indeed magnificent, the CNN private jet had decided to contract an unknown mechanical disease and cough. It kept making strange sputtering noises that concerned the pilots. Neither they nor the two Egyptian airport personnel on the short airstrip nearby could properly diagnose the problem.

So who knows how long we'll be stuck in this gosh-forsaken no-man's land?

Joe and Dray didn't seem to care, which annoyed her mightily. They were fascinated by the place. Now that most of the tourists had left, either in buses or chartered planes as there were no accommodations around here to stay the night, and the sun was setting, causing cascades of dusky light to shower the massive rock temples in a mysterious golden glow, Dray alternated between shooting video and taking still photos. Joe just kept milling around looking up, chanting over and over, "Oh my god! Look at that, eh! Oh my god! Look at that, eh!" He'd point in one direction and then another. His neck would certainly have a crick in it tonight from looking up all day.

Jessie Belle found a spot of shade and leaned against a rock, fanning herself with the brochure the tour guide had given her. She pulled a bottle of water out of her backpack and took a swig, but spit it out. The darned liquid had come to a boil in there. Hot as Hades. Even though long shadows inched their way across the desert sand and up the sides of the mammoth rock mound beside her, it offered little relief from the oppressive heat. She was sweating, once again, like a horse after the Kentucky derby. She wished somebody would show up with a hose and a brush to clean her up and cool her down.

She opened the brochure and started reading to refresh her memory about what the tour guide had said. This place had such a complicated history that it was impossible to take it all in at once. The two temples, the Great Temple of Ramesses (sometimes spelled Ramses) and the Small Temple of Hathor and Nefertari, had been carved into this mountainside by the pharaoh's African and Asian slaves to celebrate the winning of the Battle of Kadesh and to impress and intimidate the empire's neighbors. Hathor was a goddess and Nefertari was the pharaoh's queen.

Jessie Belle looked out over the sand at the temples. The Great Temple sat on the left with four three-story-tall statues of Ramesses and Nefertari sitting on either side of the door, which was an opening in the rock that led to the cavernous rooms inside. The Small Temple on the right had six figures, including the two royals and Hathor. Ramesses, as it turned out, had been a horny fellow, having two hundred wives and concubines. But it was evident here that Nefertari had been his favorite, as she was the one-and-only wife he had immortalized by his side in stone.

With the passage of time, the site had been abandoned and forgotten, only to be buried in the shifting sands. In the 1800s a Nubian boy led Swiss and Italian explorers to the stone carvings he'd seen sticking out of the desert floor. The dig was rich and deep, and the archaeologists reportedly named the site after the boy, Abu Simbel.

Most impressive was the fact that in the 1960s the whole shebang, enormous chunks of rock, had been cut into pieces, lifted up, and reassembled and inserted into a manmade mountain on higher ground in order to keep the site from being drowned in water when the Aswan High Dam went into operation on the Nile. It was impossible to imagine how such a feat was accomplished; but then, it was impossible to imagine how the whole thing had been built in the first place.

She looked around and didn't see anyone. Joe and Dray were not in sight. The tourists were all gone, and the tour guides in their flowing, white linen caftans had struck out across the desert in their battered vans, presumably headed for home. The evening shadows had lengthened, inching their way toward the open doors. It was spooky and intriguing at the same time, as if she and she alone were being invited to enter. She walked to the Great Temple and looked up at Ramesses II with his double crown that signified his rule over both north and south Egypt. Nefertari's crown stood tall and simple. Jessie Belle wondered how accurate the carvers were. If very, this queen had been a beautiful woman with a straight nose and arched eyebrows over large oval eyes.

I wonder if her great beauty is what brought her such privilege, Jessie Belle wondered. *Or was there more? Had a man who had all those women at his command chosen her above all others because he truly loved her? Did she love him?*

As if answers awaited her, she went to the temple door, hesitated for a moment, then stepped inside.

It was dark and dank now that evening was falling, and the four giant pillars that lined the Grand Hall, statues of Ramesses and the gods he worshipped, looked ominous. She rushed by them and entered the inner sanctuary.

Smaller but no less impressive were the sanctuary's four statues. One of Ramesses II, one of the sun god, one of the god of the rising sun, and one of the god of the underworld. Now this part of the tour guide's spiel she remembered: twice a year, on February 22 and October 22, the first rays of the days' light flooded through the front door, through the Great Hall, and into this chamber. It illuminated the first three statues, but not the last. The god of the underworld remained out of the reach of the light.

Transfixed by the dark statue of the underworld god, she couldn't resist staring at it. Thoughts of her nightmares suddenly deluged her mind, as if summoned by the frightening deity. She shivered and tried to pull her eyes away....

"Do you know…" Joe said, interrupting her trance.

Jessie Belle screamed and turned, lost her balance, and fell onto the legs of the god of the underworld. Realizing what she'd done, she screamed again, righted herself, fled past Joe, ran through the Great Hall, and shot out the door.

Joe was right on her heels. "Damn, I'm sorry, Jessie Belle. I didn't mean to scare you. Ya know? You okay?"

She gulped in air and managed to catch her breath. "Yeah, yeah. Whew! You really did scare me. I didn't know you were behind me."

"I'm sorry," he said again. "I thought you woulda heard me coming."

"What were you going to say? Do I know what?"

"Oh! Do you know how many movies have had scenes shot here? It's amazing! *The Spy Who Loves Me*. You know, James Bond. And *Death on the Nile*, then there was *Star Wars*, and *The Mummy Returns*. The things this place has seen in the last, oh, sixteen hundred years!"

"Where'd you learn that?"

"From the guy who's gonna drive us to Aswan, 'cuz our pilots won't take our plane up until they can fix it tomorrow and we've gotta keep moving."

Just then a beat-up old van pulled up and the Egyptian tour guide they'd had that day hopped out. "Get in," he said in a cheery British accent as he opened the wobbly panel door to the back seat. He was dressed in a long white linen caftan, looking calm, cool, and collected. Jessie Belle peered in the direction of the airstrip and saw their plane, as motionless as a dead bug. She looked up at the towering temples, now menacing monsters in the darkness. She even surveyed the endless stretch of desert sand behind her. What choice did she have? Yearning for her new storm red AMG Mercedes Benz convertible, with its pretty burl walnut wood trim and comfy cappuccino leather seats, and the luxurious black Rolls Royce limo within which Robert always squired her, she dolefully climbed into the rattle-trap old van.

Chapter 7

The sandstorm had raged for three days now and gave no sign of stopping. Karum covered her mouth with her rough wool shawl in defense against the assault, even though she was safely ensconced in the women's tent, the *o'hel*. It was only the sound of the pelting sand hitting the outside of the animal skin walls that made her reflexively seek further protection.

Sherina, the first wife of the *eesh*, their husband, reached out from where she sat next to Karum and gently held the girl's delicate wrist in her broad, calloused hand. Slowly, Sherina pulled Karum's hand down so that the shawl dropped from her face, revealing smooth olive-toned skin and full rosy lips.

"It's alright, my child," Sherina said, her mellow voice soothing. "The storm will go away by the time your baby comes. We will take good care of you and your infant. Remember that we are *a-hhots* now, sisters who take care of each other." She motioned to indicate the other woman in the tent. Tatia, like them, sat cross-legged on camel-skin rugs. Also pregnant and due in a couple of weeks, she nodded agreement.

Karum sat quietly and looked carefully at Sherina's hand, still clasping her wrist in her lap, with its veins like hard twigs and its dark spots that signified the beginnings of old age. For the first time it occurred to her that Sherina might be beyond her childbearing years. She looked up into the older woman's soft brown eyes, feeling bathed in their warmth. Then Sherina let go of Karum's wrist and tenderly stroked her cheek. Karum closed her eyes and reveled in the motherly gesture. She didn't want to be a mother; she only wanted to be with her own mother.

"Come. Eat," Sherina said. "You must keep up your strength."

The two older women commenced dipping pieces of flat bread into the augur of seasoned olive oil that sat in the middle of the floor. In between her bites of bread, Tatia also ate dried grapes, fresh nuts, and a pomegranate. Being with child had turned her into a ravenous eater. She had been thin as a skewer when they'd first met nine months ago but now she, like Karum, had a belly like a camel's hump.

"*A dank*," Karum whispered, thanking them, "but I am not hungry." It had taken her some time to get used to this strange language these people spoke, but now she was able to use many of their words to talk to them.

"Is it because you are afraid?" Tatia said, swallowing a chunk of fruit.

Karum considered lying, but decided it was too late for that. "Yes," she said, placing her hand on her protruding belly. "I am very afraid. I do not want to be an *eym*." She did not want to be a mother.

"Of course you are afraid," Sherina said. "It's your first child and you are so young. It is traditional to wait a while longer."

"My father could not wait. He had to trade me for the goat before my family starved. The sickness had come to his herd and all of his sheep died. So he had to find a way to feed my younger brothers and sisters." She knew they were well aware of her plight and how she had come to live with their nomadic tribe. But she'd fallen into such a deep depression that she retold the woeful tale for her own sake more than theirs.

"Shush, little one. Don't think about that now," Sherina said softly. "We know that being bedded by an old *eesh* like ours has been difficult for you. It was difficult for me, too, in the beginning. And he wasn't nearly so old or fat or greasy back then. We've never told you this," she said, looking at Tatia for approval and getting it with a nod, "but Tatia cried for three days the first time he bedded her. We thought you were very brave. You did not cry at all."

Tears sprang to Karum's eyes. They did not know that although they had not seen her cry before, she'd cried her eyes out.

"There, there," Sherina said, taking her last bite of bread and wiping her hands together to rid them of crumbs. "Don't cry now. You'll have fresh tears of joy when your baby is born!" She and Tatia smiled at each other and then at her, and Karum couldn't help but join them. A slight grin etched its way onto her troubled face.

They all looked up as a howl of wind caused the roof of their tent to flutter as if being beaten by the wings of a giant bird. The battering subsided, as did their momentary fear at losing their shelter. All was well now, but in their way of existence that could change in the blink of an eye.

Karum had many fears. Her companions had explained to her very carefully what was about to happen to her body, how the pains would come in waves and get worse and worse until the infant would poke its head out from between her legs. She did not want to feel the pain. She did not want her old, fat, greasy husband's child.

They had also told her that she would have to breathe to the rhythm of the *dumbek* drums. The men would sit outside the women's *o'hel*, beating the drums to remind her of the breathing. And she would have to push very hard when they told her to. She didn't want to push. Surely if she pushed that hard her innards would follow that baby right out of her.

And once the child came, they had told her, she would be happy and feel *a-hav* like none she had ever known. She would love the infant.

Sherina had said, "Then being bedded by our old husband will not seem so bad because it brought you a child of your own."

Karum did not admit it to them, because she did not want to disappoint these women who had been so kind to her, but she doubted that she would feel *a-hav* for the newborn. She had hated it since the moment she'd learned it was inside of her. She didn't see how its coming out of her body and causing her great pain would make her feel any better about it.

She looked at Sherina and Tatia and knew that, for their sakes, she would pretend to love it, just like they loved their children. Sherina had a son, the pride of his father, who was fifteen years old and had long since abandoned the woman's *o'hel* to be his father's steadfast companion. He was learning the ways of trading and had displayed a real talent for bartering. He seldom left his father's side, except when the old man was bedding a woman.

Sherina patted Karum's shoulder in a silent bid for her to stay seated, being so huge with child, while Sherina cleaned up the remnants of their meal. The older woman rose and went about her task, and Karum looked at her with wonder. Tall and graceful, her body had undoubtedly once been slim. Now she carried extra flesh, but a shadow of her former beauty lingered. Her features were gentle, belying her kind nature. She looked nothing like Karum's own mother but her soft gestures and concern for others were the same. Instead of filling the void created by the absence of her mother, however, it made Karum miss her mother all the more. Loneliness gripped her chest and sadness flooded her, as if an angry lion were wrenching out her heart with its teeth.

It made her wonder about Sherina's sadness at the loss of her second child. She'd born another child—one besides her son—a girl who would have been fourteen this year. When she was six years old, she died in a camel accident. The beast she was riding lost its footing and nearly fell, hurling the girl off its back to fall to the ground and crush her head on a rock. Sherina had talked about her daughter only once, in a raspy voice and with moist eyes that looked far away. The girl's death had broken her heart. After that, the old *eesh* insisted on having more children but two pregnancies, one right after the other, resulted in stillbirths. Sherina believed that her heart had been too sad to love them as they needed, so they had chosen to die and rise back up to the skies to be with the *a-do-nai*, their god.

Karum didn't believe in that strange idea that there was a creator up in the sky. Sherina talked about it often, but no such talk had ever occurred in the land of Karum's birth. Her people believed in the annual flooding of the Nile that provided rich earth for growing food, the rising and setting sun that made sheep and goats and children grow, and the importance of cleanliness so that no one would die of disease. There were others in her land, the rich pharaohs and their people, who worshipped ornate gods of the Nile and of the sun and of death, but her people were mere sheepherders who were too poor and who worked too hard to pay much attention to the strange ideas of wealthy pharaohs.

Tatia didn't seem to believe in one creator either, but Karum wasn't sure about that, as Tatia didn't talk to her as much as Sherina. With four young children running about most of the time, she was too busy. Tonight the young ones were in their father's *o-hel*, a tent that was much bigger and grander than that of the women, because their older brother had wanted to show them some tricks he'd learned from another wandering tribesman at the last oasis they'd stayed at. The tricks had something to do with colored stones that he would hide in his hands. It didn't sound interesting at all, but the children had been excited to go see what it was all about. Soon they would swaddle themselves in camel skins and fight the sandstorm to come back to the women's tent to sleep.

The older women, one about twenty years older and the other maybe ten years older than Karum, did not know that they had saved Karum's life. She had planned to kill herself after her father had left her here in exchange for a goat.

Tatia said, "I wanted to kill myself when I first came here." She gnawed nonchalantly at a fat nut, but her gaze bore into Karum. "Did you not want to do the same?"

Karum's mouth fell open in surprise. Had Tatia just been reading her mind?

"I know, you think I am reading your mind," Tatia said. "I don't know if that's what I do or if I just watch people very closely and read the signs in their eyes and faces. But I think you wanted to kill yourself just like I did.

"Bury that thought deep in the desert sand, Karum. It will do no good. Your child will need you. That's what I finally realized and I haven't thought of leaving them since."

Tatia stared at her so intently that Karum found that she couldn't pull her eyes away. Did Tatia mean only what she'd said?

Or was she foretelling the future?

Karum held the baby girl tight against her chest lest she drop the tiny little thing and break it. She didn't want that to happen.

Not yet.

Scurrying across the desert sand, the young mother repeatedly looked back over her shoulder in fear. Each glance brought a wave of relief that no one followed. Apparently she had been quiet enough.

The full moon shed light upon the path, although she'd never forget the way since doing it that one time. It had impressed her so much she could have done it in darkness as deep as sheep's blood. Besides, she'd walked it many times in her mind, rehearsing her plan over and over until the moment, this moment, had come when she could think of nothing else.

She huffed as she plodded up the dune, her bare feet sinking into the sand with each step. When she finally reached the dune's peak, she easily descended the other side. She paused to lean on the boulder at the bottom, where the dunes gave way to a rocky terrain.

She walked quickly to the edge of the precipice and peered over the edge. It was a long way down, with sharp-toothed rocks at the bottom that would surely impale anything that fell upon them. She'd realized that when she'd looked over the edge of this big cliff, that one time she'd dared to wander away from the women's *o-hel*. Her old, fat, greasy husband had beaten her when he'd spied her sneaking back, even though she'd thought she had craftily escaped his notice. Nothing, it seemed, escaped his notice. This gave her no doubt he'd find the bodies by the dawn of day. What satisfaction it gave her to imagine his distress upon losing some of his property!

She bent at her waist ever so slightly to look over the side again. Then she closed her eyes and took a step.

Unexpectedly, her toe caught on a pebble and she jerked backward. The unsteady motion caused the baby to cry. It was a cackle, really, not even the sound of a real living thing. Yet, Karum found herself pulling back its cover to look at its face. The feel of the shawl in her fingers, the one her distressed mother had made for her and had wrapped around her shoulders as both of them wailed when Karum was being hauled away, gave her pause. This shawl, she knew, meant she had been loved. Her heart was as surely joined with that of her mother as these strands of wool were woven together.

What was wrong with her, then, that she could not likewise feel *a-hav* for her baby?

The feelings that Sherina and Tatia had reassured her would come for her child had not come. It had been three days since she'd screamed and wished she would die during the horrors of childbirth, and yet the affection she was supposed to feel for this infant had simply never appeared.

She knew it never would.

The cackle came again and Karum looked down into huge brown eyes that caught a glint of moonlight and gleamed up at her.

She blinked. It was a real baby after all. So far she'd only been able to think of it as a thing. A thing that came from the *eesh* she hated more than she'd ever hated anyone in her life. From the first time he ripped her clothing off her and ran his chapped hands all over her soft naked skin, from the first time he stuck his rancid tongue into her sweet-breathed mouth, and from the first time he penetrated the most private part of her body with that crooked red stick of his, she'd wanted to kill him. She'd never figured out how to do that, but she did know how to do the next best thing. Kill what he believed belonged to him, showing him that it had never been his at all.

She fingered the shawl, now dirty and torn, and looked at the baby girl again. The little one's eyes were so bright, so…what was it? Hopeful? Suddenly, Karum wondered what her mother would want her to do. Then it came to her, like a wave of flood-water cresting the Nile, leaving in its path a fertile chance for life.

Quickly, she fled back to the women's *o'hel*, quietly entered, found her way in the dark, and placed the infant into the fold of sleeping Sherina's arm. Without hesitation, Karum once again left the tent.

Frantic now, she ran up the dune and let herself tumble down to roll in the sand on the other side, then bounded up and caught her balance when she reached the boulder. She stepped to the side of the cliff, curled her toes over the edge, spread her arms out wide, took a deep breath, and leaned her body forward….

Chapter 8

Jessie Belle screamed. It was an out-and-out bellow, not just the muffled cry one usually makes upon waking up from a startling nightmare.

Before she could collect her thoughts, there was a knock at her door.

"You okay in there?" It was Dray's voice. How in blazes had he got there so fast?

She stumbled out of bed and hurried to the door to answer, not wanting to holler and wake whomever in the hotel might still be asleep in spite of her shrill scream.

"Yeah, yeah. I'm, ah, I'm fine. Just a bad dream," she rasped through the door. "Go back to your room and get some sleep."

"Okay," she heard from the other side.

Geez. His room was right next to hers but his speedy response had been ridiculous. It gave her the creeps. What was he doing right outside her door? Was he stalking her?

Her squeamishness over that strange Romanian ebbed quickly, however, as the memory of the dream suddenly overwhelmed her again. Feeling dizzy, she shuffled into the bathroom, splashed cool water over her face, and dried it off with a thick Egyptian cotton towel. She glanced at herself in the mirror but in the black of night only big, spooky, frightened eyes glared back at her. She stared into those eyes, seeking an answer to the mystery of her dream.

What exactly had the story been about? She had to search her memory for all of the details, which surfaced as readily as boiling bubbles of oil. Usually she forgot her dreams as soon as she opened her eyes, but lately her dreams had lingered on like a clinging vapor. *It had been about a young Egyptian girl named Karum who despised her old, fat, greasy husband; her "eesh."* The women spoke a strange foreign tongue like none Jessie Belle had ever heard before, yet she understood every word. In fact, Jessie Belle had felt herself in that girl's body as if it had been her own body. She had known without a doubt that her body had born a child. She had felt herself falling, falling, falling to her own death!

It hadn't been the usual sensation of falling, the one that makes people jerk awake out of deep sleep, catching yourself in time so that you never hit bottom, whatever that might be. This had been different. Jessie Belle had sensed—what? Extraordinary peace? Exquisite bliss? Yes, but more, she decided. It had been sheer rapture! It had been a sensation of complete freedom from her physical body and from human emotion. From the ravages of life on earth.

No! Don't think like that, she commanded herself as she tore her eyes away from her own eerily shadowed image in the mirror, suddenly afraid of the retribution God might take for such a blasphemous thought. She buried her face in the towel. She wasn't a regular churchgoer anymore, but her years of Baptist upbringing had drilled into her the fact that God had a plan for each and every one of us, and if we ran into trials along the way, we were to face our tribulations and go on with living. We certainly were not to take the easy way out and escape through suicide. That would be denying God's gift of life.

She dropped the towel to the bathroom floor and went back into the bedroom. She and Dray and Joe were at the Mena House Oberoi, a historic palace resort outside of Cairo, right by the Great Pyramids of Giza, which they'd be filming tomorrow. Her exquisite room was a world away from the sparse digs she'd had in Ethiopia. Here there was an elaborately carved cedar bed with bright white Egyptian cotton sheets, fat down pillows, and a fuchsia paisley duvet coverlet. The bed's four tall posts were strewn with cascades of white gauze draping held back with silk tassels. The cedar nightstands on either side of the bed were inlaid with an intricate pattern of mother-of-pearl. A plush pink, purple, and green Persian carpet covered the floor. Two plump chairs were upholstered in bright patterned silk. The walls were a vibrant amber color, setting off every other hue in the room. And the enormous windows, which offered a spectacular view of the pyramids, were inset with Moroccan-designed grills, giving the entire space an exotic air.

Was it this alluring yet foreign atmosphere that had caused her to have another weird dream? Was being thrust into new environments somehow suddenly making her more sensitive to the feelings others might have had a long time ago? The ancient Ethiopian clicking-sound woman had been happy with her life and had cared about her loved ones. On the other hand, there was the girl who'd been born somewhere along the Nile but had been sold into a nomadic tribe. She was miserable in life but joyous in death.

Whatever the characters in Jessie Belle's dreams felt, she felt. It was exhausting and terrifying yet oddly enchanting at the same time. That was the most frightening part, the appeal. She was appalled at what her own demented mind came up with in her sleep but she was drawn to it, too, as if being lured by something she could not name or place. Something so alien to her that she had neither a name to call it nor a place to put it.

And the ghostly apparition of the woman who'd popped in a couple of times topped it all off.

"What's happening to me?" she wondered aloud. "Am I losing my mind?"

Fear rolled in like a heavy fog and oppressed her to the point of feeling like she couldn't breathe. She needed air!

Five minutes later, dressed in shorts and a tank top, she headed across the desert sand toward the pyramids. Earlier that evening she'd noticed that, even though these monuments were considered to be one of the great wonders of the world, teenagers, showing the same egocentrism as teenagers everywhere else in the world, saw them as a perfect place to talk on their cell phones, smoke, and make-out. They climbed up the big square blocks that were eaten away like giant stair steps, which was not visible from far away or in most pictures but was evident close-up. Up there, tucked into the ancient monoliths, they found niches where they participated in typical teen activities that made this their version of the wonder of the world.

Jessie Belle hadn't thought to bring her phone, wouldn't light up a filthy cigarette for the world, and didn't have Robert here to kiss on, unfortunately, but she did have an overwhelming desire to climb up onto those ancient stones. She needed to get up high where she could breathe, which would mean avoiding the yapping, cindering, hormonal juveniles. She needed to be alone, with no child-bearing dream figures or spooky ghosts around; she needed to think, although about what she had no clue.

In the end, she didn't think. She didn't try to reason it all out or put logic to it. Exhaustion overwhelmed her, rendering her brain unable to function. With her thighs drawn up to her chest and her arms wrapped around her knees, she sat way up in her nook, well away from any other human beings, and let her mind rest. She thought only about enjoying the hot but clear night air around her, the radiant moonlit and starlit sky above her, and the windswept patterns in the desert sand stretching into the horizon beneath her. It was all exquisite beyond words, grander than mere idioms could ever express. It was not to be thought about, but rather felt.

The saintly spirit didn't hover on this night. Instead, she sat at Jessie Belle's side in her cranny on the Great Pyramid, soothingly stroking Jessie Belle's hand.

Jessie Belle opened her eyes and smiled. "You look like an angel. What's your name?"

"What would you like to call me?" She folded her feathery hands into the lap of her shimmery pink gown, pleased that she'd been acknowledged.

Now that she was close by, Jessie Belle could see that the angelic woman looked to be middle-aged, the luminescent skin on her beautiful face reflecting as many stories as there are stars in the sky. "How about Star, because you're like a starry angel?"

"Oh! I like that! Yes, Star it will be. Although," she added, grinning mischievously, "I'm not sure anyone would ever have called me an 'angel.'" She cackled at the thought. "But, as you can see, I am a spirit."

"Why do you come to me, Star?"

"As I told you in my earlier visit, I've come to help you become you. You haven't done that yet and it's time, dear."

"I don't understand. How do you know what I'm supposed to be?"

"Oh, I don't! It's all a matter of choice—your choice. You've had many opportunities to become a fulfilled woman. It could have happened in lots of ways. But each time a path was offered, you ignored it and stayed with the one you're on. Like a horse with blinders on, as they say." She flapped her hands out on the sides of her head and bugged her eyes in a humorous illustration. Jessie Belle smiled at the realization that this spirit was a bit of a ham. "The problem is," Star said, leaning in to whisper her secret, causing her sweet breath to tickle Jessie Belle's cheek, "that path you've been on doesn't go anywhere. That doesn't have anything to do with your career. It has to do with the kind of woman you are." She leaned back and clapped her hands excitedly. "Thank goodness you're finally seeing other possibilities! Even if I did have to give you a jolt with that one nasty dream."

"Karum. Was she real?"

"Oh, yes. She's one of your ancestors. So sad, wasn't it? She didn't have the choices you have. Clacka was your ancestor, too. Such a simple but happy life. They're just two of the women who made you.

"And there will be more, nine in all. Each has a story to tell. They're hoping their stories will help you make decisions that will lead to your happiness. To being the best you.

"I'll see you again soon, Jessie Belle."

She blew a kiss and started to fade away.

"Wait!" Jessie Belle called out. "I know I've seen you before. I mean before you started coming to me like this in dreams. How do I know you?"

Star's vibrancy brightened. "I'm so happy that you remember!" she said. "I was with you when you were a child. You saw me all the time then. You called me your Starry Girl back then. I thought that was so cute."

"Of course! I remember now. Mama said you were my invisible, imaginary friend, and I kept insisting I could see you. And I could! Why did you ever go away?"

"Oh, I didn't. I've always been right here. You're the one who closed your mind to seeing me. It started the first time your mother entered you in a little girl beauty pageant. After that, you became so interested in clothes and hair and makeup you didn't pay attention to me anymore. I'm so glad you've chosen to let yourself see me again. That often happens when a person is at a crisis point in their life, and this trip certainly is a crisis to you. Your defenses have weakened with shards of doubt, so I've been able to slip right back in.

"I'll visit you again soon, dear."

She kissed Jessie Belle's forehead and drifted away. Jessie Belle savored the sensation of the delicate kiss and drifted into much-needed deep sleep.

Her eyes flew open. She'd fallen asleep. How long, she didn't know, but the moon had skated halfway across the night sky. And she'd had another one of those dreams of the mysterious spirit woman.

She blinked and looked around. Not nearly so many others were on the pyramid now; only a few cigarettes or cell phones blinked in the distance. She felt utterly alone, and it felt good.

Once again, she took in the beauty of this view from high up on the Great Pyramid, and shook her head to clear the disbelief that she'd actually fallen sound asleep in this rock-hard little niche. In spite of the strange dream, it had been a good sleep, although she felt certain her body would object as soon as she unwadded it and started moving its parts around.

She sat up, stretched her legs to let them dangle over the ledge, and lifted her arms up over her head. So far so good. She cocked her head from side to side. Not so good. Her neck was as stiff as a board. Oh well, it could be worse. She could be old and slow to come around.

Once more, she took in the magnificent view, but this time she wondered if the enigmatic environment was what had precipitated her last two dreams. The one she'd just had seemed so real. In her sleep, she'd readily accepted the apparition. But now that seemed at odds with the decision she's made before falling asleep, her vow not to let those weird dreams frighten or influence her in any way. She'd never in her life let anything intimidate her or stop her from accomplishing her goals, and she wasn't about to start now. No matter what she'd dreamt, she promised herself she'd put it out of her mind as soon as she woke up. At least, that had been her vow before falling asleep. Since the dream, however, her resolve wavered. After all, here she was mulling it over.

No! she quickly decided before she could give it any more thought. No more losing sleep over ridiculous imaginings. She'd fill her mind with other visions, like planning her wedding. That was it! Every time a weird dream interrupted her slumber, she'd just push it away and replace it with pleasant thoughts, like the elegant Vera Wang wedding gown she hankered for, the elaborate floral decorations for the church, and the fabulous reception they'd have at the exclusive Old Atlanta Club. Not to mention the wonderful life Robert and she would have together as man and wife. She smiled. Surely such fabulous daydreams could conquer those silly nightmares in no time.

She turned around to back down the stone monolith and scooched on her belly until her feet touched the next level of rock a few feet below. There she straightened herself up, rubbed her hands together to rid them of dust, and did it again and again until she'd shimmied her way to the bottom.

That's when she realized she was no longer alone.

A large, dark figure lingered in the shadows, sending a chill up her spine. She hesitated. Should she run, call for help from the few teens still up there, or confront the menace?

"Finally! I didn't think you'd ever come down."

The familiar voice both relieved and infuriated her.

"What the heck are you doing here?" she said to Dray as he stepped up beside her and matched her quick strides toward the hotel.

"More important," he countered, "what the hell are you doing out here alone in the middle of the night, in a foreign country no less? That's stupid and dangerous."

"It's none of your business what I'm doing out here! You're not my keeper."

"Well, actually, I am. Temporarily. Joe's responsible for your safety and he's not available tonight. He asked me to keep an eye out for you."

"Right! So that's why you were standing right outside my door when a bad dream woke me up?"

"Not that it's any of *your* business, but I just happened to be coming upstairs from a poker game in the lounge. That's where Joe is."

That stumped her for a minute. But she recuperated quickly.

"Huh! It's more like you're a stalker. You're creeping me out, if you really want to know."

"Did I say I give a bat's ass what you think? No, I did not."

"It's a 'rat's ass,' not a bat," she corrected him sarcastically.

"Bat's ass, rat's ass, who cares? I've got better things to do than babysit some diva reporter who wanders around in the middle of the night!"

"Oh, yeah, as if being a low-life cameraman makes you my boss! Get lost, bucko!"

"Bucko? What does this word mean?" He was really riled now, which made his accent invade his speech. It came out like, "Buck-oh? What does thees vert mean?"

"Hey," Jessie Belle shouted as they entered the lush lobby of the hotel, "if you can insult me, I can insult you right back!"

A Japanese couple who were checking in at the reception desk turned their heads to see what all the commotion was about. The man pointed, shook his head, and said something to his wife. She likewise shook her head at them.

Okay, Jessie Belle realized, this wasn't her best moment. Dray seemed to get it, too. They both fell silent, got into the elevator, rode up with their arms stubbornly folded over their chests, and said nary another word. Dray reached his room first and silently closed the door behind him. Jessie Belle started to slam hers, but caught it and shut it quietly.

Her usual stash of vim and vigor had been depleted. All she wanted now was to hit that big, soft bed and sleep the rest of the night away.

Chapter 9

"Rise and shine!" Joe hollered from outside her door. Startled out of blissful deep slumber, she opened one eye and grabbed her cell phone to check the time. 5 a.m.

"Go away!" she yelled as her head fell like a brick back into her cushy pillow.

"No can do. We've got an early start today. Remember? I told you yesterday. Gotta get this done before it gets too hot, eh."

"Yeah, yeah, yeah. I remember. I'm up!" She hadn't moved.

"Okay. See you in the lobby in fifteen."

"Right," she mumbled into her pillow.

Five minutes flew by and she stirred. "Oh, crimony. What am I doing on this stupid trip?" she asked the air. "That bimbo Bridget Barker is still in bed, won't be up for hours, and when she does finally get to the studio somebody else will make her look like a fabulous movie star. And I've got exactly nothin'. It's not fair."

She'd whined her way into the bathroom, where she spent less than ten minutes preparing for the day. She was indeed in the lobby on time. Joe seemed surprised. Dray looked sullen and turned his back on her as he talked into his cell phone.

"Who's he talking to?" she asked Joe. "One of his girlfriends?"

"Nah. His mother. She lives with him and his kids."

"What? He has kids?"

"Yah. Three of them."

"You're kidding! Three of those little ch-children people?" she stammered. "Don't they have a mother somewhere?"

"She's gone." Distracted, Joe stepped outside and started packing their gear into the hotel van that would transport them and all their stuff up to the Great Pyramid.

"Geez," Jessie Belle said to herself as she stole a glance back at Dray. "A thirty-something-year-old single dad with three kids whose wife left him and who still lives with his mother. Could a man possibly be any more of a loser than that?"

Dawn's first beam of prismed light reached out from the end of the earth, stretched across the boundless desert sand, and touched her face in an intimate invitation bidding her to open her eyes to the world. *What a strange way to think of a sunrise*, she thought, surprised at herself for this new perspective.

The relentless ray of sunlight, more intense now, held her attention. Shielding her eyes with her hand, she followed the shadows it left in the humps in the sand. Up and down, dark and light. Mesmerized, she felt the alluring pull of the tableau of the new day in front of her at the same time that she sensed the secure strength of the ancient sarcophagus in front of her. She thought about her venture up the pyramid's corroded side the night before. She'd felt compelled to connect with it, as if it was trying to tell her something.

"Cripes," she grumbled to herself. "Those weird dreams have really played tricks with my mind. As if a heap of crumbling rock could speak to me."

"Come on," Joe called out to her, dramatically motioning for her to come to the entrance of the Great Pyramid. "Let's see what this old wonder has to tell us!"

A few hours later they flew away from Cairo, having finally got back their private plane, with its hacking cough healed. Jessie Belle looked out the window and down at the three pyramids of Giza. What a beautiful sight! They must have been even more impressive, she thought, during the reigns of the pharaohs, looming strong and tall amidst endless stretches of dessert sand with a town of mud huts, sprawling homes, and a few palaces in the background. Today the city of Cairo, teeming with energy, smelling of Jasmine, and brimming with modern amenities, served as a backdrop.

They had taped all morning in and around the Great Pyramid, the resting place, their guide informed them, of a pharaoh named Khufu. Thus, the place was also known as the Pyramid of Khufu or the Pyramid of Cheops (Khufu in Greek). Built around 2560 BC, it once held the body of the ruler in an upper chamber, his queen in another chamber, and the traditional valued belongings the ancient Egyptians believed they would be able to use in the afterlife. None of that remained, however, as it had been robbed eons ago.

The taping inside had been difficult, as Dray had to stoop so as not to hit his head on the ceiling of the long, narrow passageway to the burial chamber, all the while walking backwards to shoot Jessie Belle and the guide. It hadn't been a pleasant experience for Dray and did nothing to brighten his already grumpy mood.

Outside, they got shots of Jessie Belle taking the requisite camel ride and waving at the camera. They also learned that the erosion of the exterior was not the result of thousands of years of weathering. During the Middle Ages, the Egyptians, poor but resourceful, stripped the limestone shell to build other buildings. Consequently, shops and homes all over the city had been found to contain casing limestone from the pyramids. Amazing as it was that the pyramids still stood after more than four thousand years, they would be in even better shape had they not been stripped of their exteriors. That's how good a job the paid skilled workers, probably about 200,000 of them working in a hierarchical system depending on skill level, and countless slaves as well, had done.

Jessie Belle continued to look out of the window of the plane. The glints of sunlight radiating off of the flowing water of the Nile made it look like the undulating scales of a reptile, like a snake languidly slithering out of sight. It made her think of Karum, the young mother who'd committed suicide in her dream. Strange that she even remembered the name. The girl had come from somewhere along the Nile, perhaps from around here?

No, she reminded herself. That girl had come from nowhere because she hadn't been real. So she put it out of her mind and forced her attention back to the task at hand. She took the travel itinerary out of her briefcase and studied it.

Later this afternoon they'd do a quick stop at an oasis in Jordan to trace the trail humans would most likely have taken as they spread out from Africa to other areas of the world. By evening they'd be in Salzburg, Austria, near their destination of Hallstat, in the Alps. Tomorrow they'd film there, then the next day they would move on to Oslo, Norway, home of those abhorrent Vikings. They'd spend two days taping there, as that was the crowning glory of her DNA results. After that they'd fly down to London, where Joe would do some work with the CNN London office, then over to Ireland, where Vikings had invaded and settled. It was from Ireland and Scotland that many people of Scandinavian ancestry came to America. Of course, it would never be known if this was exactly how Jessie Belle's ancestors came to be in America, but it was a good guess by Edwin Sampson, that ever-resourceful assistant director of the Genographic Project, who had mapped out this "Ancestry Quest" journey. The last day of the series would be shot at the family plantation in Social Circle, Georgia.

Her mother had been so excited at that news and at Joe's invitation to be interviewed about family history that she'd already started making the rounds to her masseuse, hair stylist, plastic surgeon, and personal stylist at Neiman Marcus. By the time a camera focused on her, she'd be calm, coifed, smooth-skinned, and well-dressed—the epitome of a Southern belle. In traditional Southern fashion, a façade would make certain the real story was not revealed.

The thought of her mother reminded Jessie Belle that she hadn't talked to her yet today. She grabbed her cell phone and dialed. No answer. She didn't bother to leave a message.

Then she automatically started to dial Robert's number, but hesitated. She'd tried countless times during the last few days, with total silence from his end. It was as if the phone was trying to reach outer space instead of Atlanta. She couldn't imagine what kind of business deal was keeping Robert so busy. What if he's been in a car accident or, goodness forbid, died! No, if he'd died she or one of the guys would have heard it on the news. It was as if Robert had fallen off the face of the earth. Trying him again might result in more disappointment. *Ever the masochist,* she punched in the number, only to get his answering service again. She hit the power button and threw the annoying little non-communication device into her purse.

"I want to be the one to tell her." There was no mistaking that voice. It was her one-and-only boss back in Atlanta, Harry. He and Joe were hooked up by Skype on the computer.

Jessie Belle stepped up behind Joe and looked over his shoulder at his laptop screen so she'd be in the shot. "Tell me what?" she asked.

Joe jumped, looking over his shoulder. "Damn! I didn't know you were in here." They were in his room at the Salzburg hotel.

"Your door was open," she said, "and I heard Harry say he wanted to tell me something." She glared into the camera spot on the laptop. "Tell me what?"

She watched Harry shift his weight in his chair, looking decidedly uncomfortable. Even on a little computer screen he looked big as an ox. "Listen, kid," he began. "I hate to be the bearer of bad news, but better me than the *National Enquirer*." He cleared his throat and tugged at his shirt collar. Jessie Belle had never seen him so nervous. The lug was usually steady as a sturdy tugboat. Her pulse quickened in her throat. "It's about Robert," Harry finally spit out. "He's been in the local news the last couple of days. It'll probably hit national pretty soon. Ah, hell, kid, I'm sorry but he's been seeing someone else since you left."

Her mind swirled in confusion. "What do you mean, 'since I left?' I've only been gone four days."

"I know. That's what makes this so shitty. Apparently, right after you left he and Bridget Barker ran into each other at a restaurant. They've been seen out together the last few nights. First my secretary told me, then it was in *Creative Loafing* today, and five minutes ago the janitor informed me it's all over Internet blogs. Something about your boyfriend taking Bridget replacing you literally. I'm so sorry. He's just no good. Any man who could be that ruthless is just no good. I hope you know that."

"He's seeing… *her*? *Her*?" she wailed. "You did this to me, Harry. I hate you! If you hadn't sent me on this stupid trip he'd still be with me!"

Harry leaned into the camera, causing his bulbous nose to look like a giant mushroom. "Now wait a minute, little lady. All I did was have you do your job. Robert Brentz is the asshole who did you wrong. I'm the good guy here! At least I had the *cajones* to tell you to your face. From what I hear, he hasn't even had the balls to do that. He's a scumbag, Jessie Belle. Good riddance to him, I say!"

"I don't care what you say! I hate your guts!" Jessie Belle stormed out of Joe's room, colliding with Dray on the way out.

"Well," Joe said into the camera. "That went well."

If anyone had ever forewarned Jessie Belle that this day in her life would come, she would have placed a million dollar bet that they were wrong. And she would have lost it all as surely as if she'd been a gambling addict who didn't know an ace from a jack. Or a jackass, as it turned out.

Here she was, hunched over a smelly bar table, slovenly drunk. Joe reached over to try to sweep a strand of her hair away from the pool of spilled beer it dipped into, but it fell back down to mop up some more of the sticky brew.

"An' zen he toll me he loved me," she slurred. "But he doshn't. He luffs her, Bridget Bark-er. Woof! Woof! She's a do-o-og. Get it?

"Yup. Robert toll me he loves me an' he doshn't." She shook her head spastically, to emphasize her point. "He's a big, fat, fucking fryer. I mean fyar. I mean li-ar.

"Oh no! I jus' said the f-word! I've never shaid that afore! I promised myself I'd never shay it. I'm such a horrible sinner! Now I'm goin' to he-e-ell!"

Buckets of tears streamed down her face, so Dray slid over more bar napkins. She grabbed one, swiped at her tears, noisily blew her nose, and tossed the gooey wad onto the pile on the floor.

"Hey! Barmaid!" she hollered, her attention suddenly diverted as she wildly swung the empty beer pitcher in the direction of the waitress. "We need more beer!

"Hey, that shounded jes like in the moofies, didn't it. 'Barmaid!' Ha! Funny, huh? Barmaid, barmaid, barmaid!"

Their waitress, a short but stealthy woman, came over and unhappily glared down at them with her hands on her hips. "Did you vant someting?" she asked in broken English.

"No," Joe reassured her. "Sorry. She's just a little drunk. Bring me the bill, please."

"Hey! Where you goin'?" Jessie Belle shouted after the woman. "Where's my schbeer?"

"You've had enough beer," Joe said. "We're going back to our rooms." He looked at Dray. "Sorry to have dragged you into this. I thought a few beers would help her drown her sorrows and all that. Who knew she'd be stinking drunk after sharing just a couple of pitchers?"

"It doesn't appear she's an experienced drinker," Dray noted seriously.

"Yah, my guess is this is the first time in her life she's ever been hammered. Her idea of getting shit-faced is probably half a glass of Dom Perignon at an art gallery opening. This dark German beer is a lot stronger than what we're used to. I'm even feeling a little tipsy. She'll sure feel it tomorrow."

The two men couldn't help but chortle at the thought.

The disgruntled waitress brought the bill and Joe threw down enough *der schein*, German bills, to include a healthy tip.

Jessie Belle, in the meantime, had been shredding napkins and reciting, "He luffs me, he luffs me not."

"Come on, Jessie Belle, time to go," Joe said as he and Dray stood up.

Jessie Belle didn't budge. She looked up at them and whimpered, "There's not going to be any Vera Wa-a-ang. I really wanted he-e-er."

"What's a Vera Wang?" Dray asked Joe.

"Hell if I know," Joe said. "Oh wait, I remember now. One of my wives used to talk about her. She's a woman who makes dresses. Wedding dresses."

"Oh, oh," Dray said. "We're falling into a whole new level of self-pity. We've got to get out of here."

With that, he and Joe each reached under one of her arms, pulled her up, and dragged her toward the door.

"Hey! Whatch you guys shink yer doin'?" Jessie Belle protested loudly while flapping her slack arms and kicking her rubbery feet in a futile attempt to free herself from their grasp. "Barmaid, where'sh my fucking beer? I want Wera Va-a-ang!"

Applause broke out behind them as patrons cheered their departure from the bar.

"You shmell nice," she said to Dray when he bent over her to place her head on her pillow. Joe had her feet; between the two of them they had no trouble lifting her slim frame onto her bed.

"What?" Dray said, surprised.

"You smell snice," she repeated groggily.

Dray backed away as Joe laughed. "She really is schnockered," Joe chided, "if she thinks you smell good. Let's get out of here before she says anything else idiotic."

Dray chuckled, and Joe took off her shoes and pulled a sheet over her, even though she still had her clothes on. The two men left Jessie Belle to sleep off her misery.

Jessie Belle thrust her feet in the air, battling the tangled covers. She'd tosseled so much they were wrapped around her legs like a mummy. She kicked and kicked until finally she was free.

Hot. She was so blasted hot! Without standing up, she tugged off her shorts and threw them on the floor. She had a vague memory of Joe and Dray bringing her up to bed a little while earlier.

Dray. That's what she'd do. She'd go have sex with him to make Robert jealous. So there!

She got up, padded out of her room, and was only mildly aware of some people in the hallway staring at her as she staggered a few doors down to Dray's room. She knocked loudly.

The door opened to a bare-chested Dray. It took him a second to take in the surprising scene in front of him. "Oh my god!" he said. He grabbed her arm, pulled her into his room, and slammed the door to block out the prying eyes in the hallway. "Jessie Belle, what are you doing here? Without any pants on!"

Jessie Belle looked down. "Oops." She pulled up her short tee shirt. "Oh wait, I've got these on." She pointed to the crotch of her silky red thong.

Dray stared down in disbelief, then twirled away, his hands in his hair. When he turned back toward her, a deep furrow etched his brow. "Jessie Belle, you can't be in my room. You especially can't be in my room with nothing on but a little tee shirt and a thongy thingy."

"Why not? How else are we going to have sex?" She giggled and lunged at him.

Reflexively, he blocked the assault with a side check, scampered to the far side of the bed, and grabbed a pillow to hold up in front of his exposed chest. "Sex! Oh my god, Jessie Belle, whatever made you think you and I should have sex?"

"You shmell nice. I like that." She staggered toward him and started to lift her shirt to pull it off over her head.

"No! No, don't do that!" He dropped the pillow and grabbed at her shirt, pulling it back down. "Keep that on!"

"Okay. Any way you like it."

"No, it's not what I like… I mean, it doesn't matter what I like. We're not having sex!"

Totally befuddled, her arms fell listlessly to her sides and she actually stomped one of her dainty bare feet. "Why not?" she whimpered. "What's wrong with me? Are you gay?" She brightened at the thought this was the cause of his rejection.

"No! I'm not gay. And nothing's wrong with you," he insisted, still defending himself with outstretched hands lest she attack him again. "In fact, sometimes there's too much right with you," he confessed, to himself as much as to her. "But I highly suspect the only reason you want to have sex with me is to make Robert jealous."

"Of course." She grinned like a happy hyena.

"I thought so. Well, as if that wasn't reason enough, I don't take advantage of drunk girls. Never have; never will. And you sure are drunk."

"Would you want to have sex with me if I was sh-sh…" She tried again. "Sober?"

Confusion crossed his face. "Well, um, that's a very big question. You're a very attractive woman. I'm a single, not gay, adult man. I like sex. A lot. But with you? That's a little crazy. You and I are just so…" he paused, searching for the word.

"Horny?"

"No! Not horny. Well, yeah, I haven't had a girlfriend in a couple of years, so I'm always horny. But that's not it. We're just so different."

"Oh yeah. I forgot. I'm a high class spoiled brat diva star and you're a lowly, lowly, lo-o-owly cameraman loser." She swayed and grabbed hold of the post on the footboard of the bed for balance.

"Well, I didn't think of it quite that way. Anyway, I'm sorry I ever started this name-calling thing. I reprimand my kids for doing that. Forgive me, okay? That was—how do you say it? Insufferably rude."

"And mean and lousy."

"Okay, okay. But in my defense, that's what I'd been told. That's what some of the folks at work call you behind your back."

"They do? Why?"

"Well, because you sort of are," he stated unapologetically.

"Oh."

"But mostly I said it because I was already annoyed with you."

"You didn't even know me yet. How could you have already been annoyed with me? Usually it takes a few minutes."

"Because I got called at the last minute to take this stupid trip," he said, perching rigidly on the opposite corner of the bed.

"Normally, I'd love an assignment like this. But last year I asked for a studio job so I could be home more with my kids. You and I never met because I took the early morning shift so I'd be there when they get home from school. With them, I have to plan ahead. This week was my little girl's first dance recital, and she was counting on me being there. I've broken her heart, and that breaks my heart. I was mad at you before I ever got on that plane because it's your fault we're on this trip in the first place."

"How do you know that?"

"Oh, everybody back at the studio knows that. Ever since that interview with the Consulate General of Yemen; that was the big, juicy gossip of the day. Even the janitor told me some of the details."

"Well, isn't that just peachy...." With that, Jessie Belle plowed face forward onto his bed, out cold.

Her eyes slitted open. A cement mixer churned in her stomach. Confused, she looked around. This wasn't her room, but she spied a nightlight in a bathroom and knew she had to head in that direction fast.

Out of nowhere, Dray appeared behind her as she wretched into the toilet, holding her hair back to protect it from the blow. When she finally finished with a ghastly dry heave, he handed her a dampened towel to wipe off her mouth. Carefully, he helped her up, led her to the sink, and held out a small cup of mint green liquid. "Here," he said. "Rinse out your mouth. You'll feel a lot better now."

Shaking uncontrollably, she did as he instructed. Swiping her mouth with the towel again, she said, "I can't believe what just happened. I'm so embarrassed."

"Don't worry about it. Remember, I've got kids. Children puke all the time."

An unexpected smile tried to grace her lips but was halted by a jackhammer that started grinding on her forehead. The resultant moan impelled Dray to lead her back to the bed, where he fluffed the pillows for her. He remained standing while she lowered herself onto the bed and slowly let her pounding head seek comfort, and then he covered her with the sheet. She noticed that he had on a tee shirt with his shorts now, recalling that he'd been shirtless earlier and had looked mighty good.

She faded out for a while and then roused.

"You okay now?" he asked as soon as she opened her eyes. He sat in the chair and had apparently been waiting for her to wake up. "Because if you are, we really do need to get you back to your room." He stood up and motioned toward the door, as anxious to get her out of his room as if it was the Dark Ages and she had leprosy.

Until he asked her to leave, it hadn't occurred to her to consider how she'd ended up in his room. Then it all hit like a bolt of lightning out of the blue. She stiffened and sat straight up.

"I came here and threw myself at you, didn't I?" she asked. It was at that moment she realized that she didn't have her shorts on. "Oh no! I did!" she answered herself. She felt around through the sheet he'd covered her with. Sure enough, there weren't any shorts on her body under there.

"It's okay," Dray said. "We didn't do anything. You were drunk is all. Nothing happened."

She didn't hear him, her mind too occupied with its own retribution. "Oh dear God! I'm a slut. A total slut!"

"No, you're not a total slut."

She blinked at him. "That means you think I am a slut, just not a *total* slut."

"No!" Frantically, he ran his fingers through his hair as if trying to grasp a helpful thought. He had enough experience with women to know there were some arguments a man could never win. He had to be careful here, as any answer would probably be the wrong answer. "You're not a slut at all."

As if the revelations of this day and night hadn't already been enough, as if her world hadn't already been rocked by one catastrophic earthquake after another, as if it all made any sense, Jessie Belle looked up into Dray Dlugitch's imploring, steely gray eyes; at his square-jawed, rugged face; and at his disheveled, dark hair; and thought she'd never seen a more handsome man in her life. She felt giddy as a goose, and this time it wasn't from booze.

Misreading her stare, he plugged ahead, "You were just drunk. It happens to the best of us."

"Yes, well, it never happened to me before," she murmured.

"There's a first time for everything. Right?"

"I need to go now." She pointed toward the door but didn't move.

"Okay. Want me to walk you back to your room?" He fidgeted, unsure of himself tonight for the first time she'd ever seen.

"No, I got here on my own accord; I'll make it back." She got off the bed, pulled the sheet loose, wrapped it around herself, and left his room. Clearly whatever attraction had just zapped through her entire body had not so much as tinged his pinky finger, let alone any other appendage.

He saw her as a childish spoiled brat. A diva. To seal the deal, he now saw her as a drunken slut. No wonder the guy thought of her as strychnine.

Unfortunately, she now saw him as the kind of man a woman could sink her heart into. She wished she'd never caught a glimpse of that because one broken heart a day was enough.

Chapter 10

Julia looked out over the sprawling vista of her Venezian vine-yards. Such a lovely sight! But her gaze didn't linger there; it stretched beyond, to the Adriatic Sea.

Her pale skin glistened in the hot morning sunlight while a balmy breeze from the sea caught her long, blond hair, causing it to escape its clasp and toss about in the air. Excited anticipation radiated from her exquisitely chiseled features.

He said he would come this month. "I'll return in the month of *Junio, mi amor*, when the camellias are in bloom. When your body is in bloom with our child! I can't wait to meet this new *infantuli* we've made!" He'd rubbed her burgeoning belly, kissed her passionately, and been off, as always, to sail the Mediterra-nean Sea. As the captain of a merchant ship, he traded his wares in the multitude of Roman Empire cities that scattered the coast from Gaul to the Middle East.

It was only the first day of the month, but ever hopeful, Julia scanned the horizon for his jaunty *carina,* his ship. She shielded her eyes from the glare of the sun and scanned the sparkling blue water. There were many ships, but none with a sail as colorful as his. It was not there. Not yet. But she knew it would soon appear. He would always come back to her. Of that she felt as sure as she was that the goddesses and gods watched over her.

"He's here!" Her younger brother, Cassius, shouted with glee. The nine-year-old boy adored his sister's *amator,* the man she loved. "Come! Look! I can see his *velum.*" He grabbed her hand and pulled her from her herb garden, leading her to the *portico* where she'd kept her own watch just an hour before. Cassius pointed dramatically. "There! I see his red and yellow and green striped *velum*!" Indeed, the colorful sails were unmistakable.

"Yes, I see it," she said. *Will the thrill of seeing that velum billowing in the wind ever diminish?* she wondered. It had been two years and still her heart did summersaults at the thought of being with Antonito. They'd met when she was fifteen and serving as an interpreter at the docks, a task she'd undertaken at first to serve her father's business and later out of courtesy to foreigners who struggled with the Venezian tongue. She didn't know why she so easily understood other languages, but she did. Perhaps it was because she'd visited her father's warehouse on the docks all of her life and had acquired an ear for the various dialects that gathered there, coming from the far reaches of the vast Roman Empire.

He had come from the far away land of Hispania. His language sounded exciting to her ears, throaty and sensual. His voice had first caught her attention. But it wasn't long before the rest of him did so as well. They had become lovers within two days of their first meeting.

Now, with her parents both dead and her being the head of the household, owner of the villa, master of the trade business, mother-figure for her little brother, and mother-to-be, she had quickly become a woman. But Antonito kept the frivolous girl inside of her alive. Even though he was twenty-two years older than she, he kept her young.

With her flowing, white robe fluttering in the breeze; her hair blowing about her face; and her big, ripe belly proudly on display, she portrayed a perfect picture of beauty.

"You are the most *bello femina* in the empire!" Antonito exclaimed the moment he saw her.

At being called a "beautiful woman," Julia giggled like a girl and let him sweep her up in his arms. "And you are the most *speciosus vir*!" she countered. He did indeed seem to be a more handsome man every time she saw him, with his thick dark hair that was streaked with silver, his vibrant pale blue eyes with the crinkles around the sides, and his powerfully built body. She couldn't wait to bed him!

Why was he talking to her about this when they could be enjoying *concubitalis* again? Languorously, Julia rolled over, exposing her full, naked breasts. He stopped talking and stared. She'd known that would work.

"I'll tell you about it later," he said, and went back to doing what they'd been doing for the last three hours.

"Julia, *mi amor*, I must tell you about the *sagrado vir* I've heard about. I know you've heard the name 'Jesus.' The man who was crucified thirty years ago at the hand of King Herod in Jerusalem. A following has built, and I was taken to a gathering while I was in Tyros in Syria. It was quite remarkable."

She couldn't understand why he insisted on telling her about this "sacred man" called Jesus. Everyone knew the rumors, of course, about the crazy man who'd claimed there is but one God and that he was a holy man who was the son of that God. So blasphemous was the belief that Emperor Augustus had declared it was illegal to speak his name anywhere in the Roman Empire.

She rose from the bed and walked across the room. His eyes never left her bare body as she poured two goblets of water and brought them back to the bed. She handed one to him and drank greedily from the other.

"I do not want to hear about this '*sagrado vir*.' He means nothing to me," she said, not unkindly.

"But he means everything me."

He went to his tunic, pulled an object from the pouch, brought it to her, and put it into her hand. She looked down on a small metal cross, a replica of the kind of cross used to crucify criminals and killers. But rather than its symbolism leaving her cold, it warmed her palm.

"This is a reminder of the life and death of Jesus Christ. This is a reminder of his teachings. A reminder that there is meaning to this life, one that brings us to loving one another in ways we've never known before."

So bold was his statement that Julia agreed to hear his story about the gathering of people who believed the preachings of this man called Jesus. Three hours later, she knew that her life had once again been irrevocably transformed by Antonito, the man she loved more than life itself.

Julia kneeled at her altar, put her hands together, bent her head, and prayed, just like Antonito had taught her to do. "Jesus, son of God; Mary, mother of Jesus; Mary Magdalene, wife of Jesus; and daughter of Jesus, hear my prayer…"

It took a few months to adjust to this different kind of prayer, but she'd come to treasure her moments of recitation. It had taken little time to convert her altar for the Roman gods and goddesses to one that included Jesus and the women who meant so much to him. According to Antonito, the women moved to Gaul, having left Palistina to escape those who wished to discredit the claims of Jesus and who might therefore harm his child.

She finished her prayer and surveyed her altar. Antonito hadn't been able to convince her to give up her Roman idols. She'd relied on them for too long to suddenly abandon them. There were small statues of Jupiter and Juno, King and Queen of the Roman gods. There were similar small renderings of Venus and Cupid, goddess and god of love. A dried grapevine had long laid on the back of the altar, in honor of Bacchus, god of wine, to encourage him to provide good crops each year. He'd been more accommodating some years than others, but overall he'd been extremely generous to her. After meeting Antonito, she'd added a large seashell for Neptune, god of the sea, to implore that god to keep her *amortorius* safe.

But now the small metal cross in honor of Jesus sat on a small alabaster pedestal in the center of the altar. Enchanted and inspired by the story of the humble man and how he'd come to be born and of the woman he'd married, his message that life was meant to be filled with love and understanding had reinforced her beliefs. He echoed her thoughts as though He'd been living inside her mind all of her life.

Jesus had been an outcast to Romans, just as she was an outcast in the social strata of Rome. Even though she was very wealthy and quite beautiful, she'd never been accepted in the privileged circles of her own community. Even as a girl, she was shunned by other girls and their mothers because she preferred going to the docks with her father to be part of all of the excitement the world brought to their feet rather than playing silly games with other children. To add to her infamy, she had recently born a child without the benefit of marriage. Indeed, she and Antonito could not marry because he was already married. He would never leave his wife and six children in Hispania. That didn't mean he loved her any less.

Besides, Julia couldn't think of one thing she needed a husband for. She was entirely capable of taking care of everything herself.

She heard the baby squawk and turned to find Antonito behind her, holding six-month-old Maggia. The sight of the two of them together, both with their shiny dark hair and bright blue eyes and big broad smiles, would never cease to amaze and delight Julia. She got up off her knees and hugged them hard.

"You do remember, don't you, *mi amor*," Antonito said, "that you must keep your worship of Jesus secret, as it is against the law. I'm a little worried that the cross I gave you is out in plain sight. I keep mine hidden in my deepest pouch."

"Oh, yes, I remember. But it seems you've forgotten that no one but you ever sees my altar, tucked away back here in my bedchamber. Besides, the cross can easily be hidden away."

"We will not hide our beliefs from Maggia, will we? We'll teach her to revere the sacred words of Jesus, to hold her worship safe in secret *aegis*, and to live the life of a blessed *femina*."

"*Vero*, that we will do."

Julia and Antonito kept their promise. And Maggia helped change the world.

Chapter 11

"Star, I'm so glad to see you! I have so many questions!"

"I suspected you would. That's why I came, dear." Now Star had on a shimmery, gossamer, lavender-colored gown. Tiny lavender-colored flowers freckled her silvery hair, and she smelled like lavender, too.

"I thought my dreams were supposed to be about my women ancestors," Jessie Belle said. "But I just dreamt about a woman named Julia, who wouldn't have been one. She was from ancient Venezia in northeastern Italy. They're telling me my ancestors were Celtic and Scandinavian. No Italians."

"Oh, my, that just goes to show how little 'they' know, doesn't it?" Star chuckled. "Today's scientists act as if early people never took side trips or got lost. Of course they did! Julia was indeed your ancestor."

Relieved, because she'd liked Julia so much, Jessie Belle asked, "What happened to her after my dream ended? It seemed like Maggia would become a Christian. Maybe one of the very first ones."

"Yes, it did seem like that, didn't it? But remember, everything isn't always as it seems. Maggia did practice Christianity for two reasons. She believed that Jesus had been a wonderful, loving man. And she wanted to please her father, Antonito, who came to be a devout Christian.

"By the way, a couple of months after your dream ended, Antonito's wife in Hispania died. She had been ill for a very long time. He had refused to abandon her in her time of need, even though many of his sea-faring mates had encouraged him to do so. Oh, she knew he must have someone else and she was glad. You see, she wanted him to be happy after she was gone. She'd actually always felt an attraction to other women and only had children with Antonito out of a sense of duty. He was such a trusting, manly man, he didn't figure that out for years. You know men! They just can't imagine that a woman wouldn't want them."

Star, Jessie Belle suddenly realized, was quite a girly gossip. Jessie Belle liked that. She was also liked learning that Maggia had known her father.

"Yes," Star excitedly continued her tale, "when his wife died, Antonito made Julia's villa his main residence, and she gave him her father's docks to run his business out of. Some of his children were old enough to choose to stay in Hispania, where Antonito visited them regularly. The youngest one, however, a bright boy of twelve, came with his father. He and Maggia married when she reached marrying age! That was fourteen back then. They were together until their deaths when they were quite old. They loved each other deeply."

"But, but," Jessie Belle objected without knowing exactly why. Then she came up with it. "Wasn't it odd for a half-brother and half-sister to marry?"

"Oh no, not back then. It was quite acceptable."

"Wow, that's hard to imagine. You said Maggia became a Christian. Earlier in my dream it ended with the knowledge that Maggia helped change the world. Was it because she kept Christianity alive when it was against the law?"

"Oh, my, no! It was because she helped keep goddess worship alive. She and others had to go underground, of course, but her mother had taught her well. Julia and Maggia loved Jesus, too, but saw him as one of many special people sent from the gods *and* goddesses. Oh, in the beginning, Christianity revered women like the Mother Mary, who wasn't considered to be a virgin at first, you know, as the idea is just too ludicrous for words. Besides, back them 'virgin' meant renewal each year, not the absence of ever having had sex. Nobody would have even thought of that! A virgin was a woman renewed and refreshed, which happened annually. And Christianity also respected Mary Magdalene, who was known to be Jesus's wife. But even in Maggia's time, arrogant men were already rewriting the story of Jesus's life. The Mother Mary became a silly virgin and Mary Magdalene became a mindless whore.

"Maggia thought Jesus would have been furious at how women were treated at the hands of his eventual followers. So she made sure that goddesses from all ages were not forgotten, including the Roman goddesses her mother had always worshipped. There was Vesta, the goddess of the home and hearth; Abundantia, the goddess of prosperity and abundance; and Diana, the goddess who helps women focus their attention. And, of course, she always included the Mother Mary and Mary Magdalene. Maggia's secret ceremonies, tucked away in the deep furrows of her vast vineyards, helped keep worship of females alive!"

Flabbergasted, Jessie Belle laid in silent thought. Finally, she said, "Did her husband know?"

"Oh, yes! They were both secret priests of goddess and god worship, side by side. They believed in total equality.

"Their descendants kept their faith alive until the Roman Empire fell, when the Huns and Goths and other savage vandals scattered people in all directions. After that, knowledge of the beliefs of people like your ancestors was lost, until now! Isn't it wonderful that you've been shown their story?"

Jessie Belle gnawed at her lower lip, unable to cipher so much information. Sounded like really old women's lib to her. But when she let her mind dig deeper, or maybe it was her soul, she knew it was more than that.

As if reading her mind, Star said, "Well, I think that's enough for tonight, dear. You look like you could use some more rest. Ta ta!" She kissed Jessie Belle's forehead and swirled away, leaving a trail of lavender-scented fairy dust behind.

Jessie Belle closed her eyes and fell fast asleep. Her mind had been taxed to its limit. Like a glass filled with too much wine, the overflow spilled out and meandered away, unable to be recouped. She couldn't think one more thought on this night.

Confusion roiled, a cacophony of dissonant thoughts bombarding each other in her head, competing for attention. *The Battle of Beliefs*, she thought. It made it nigh on impossible to wrangle a single cogent thought and harness it.

Jessie Belle stood on the balcony of her room, snuggled into the white terry cloth robe provided by the hotel and drinking a steaming cup of coffee. The view of the Alps was spectacular. And the view of the city of Salzburg, with its ancient cobblestone streets, medieval stone buildings, and Victorian street lights, was like a fantasy. It was touted as being one of the most romantic cities in the world. "Long walks and sweet talk. Salzburg is the perfect city for a romantic weekend away!" the hotel brochure insisted.

Fat lot of good that will do me, Jessie Belle thought.

She made another attempt at sorting out the mess that made up her life. Her emotions flip-flopped from fury and depression that Robert had so brutally dumped her to relief that she didn't have to deal with the rich snob anymore. Then they'd flip back again and she'd break out bawling over her loss. At one moment she felt jealous that Bridget Barker had stolen her job, at least temporarily, and her boyfriend, perhaps permanently, and in the next instant she didn't give a dang about that twit. To add to the havoc, she'd become hugely attracted to Dray, a total loser who hated her guts.

To top it all off, she thought she might be going crazy because of her weird dreams, then the next second felt joy that she had reconnected with her childhood spirit friend. The only problem with that was she didn't believe in spirits. She'd revel in the message of a dream then chastise herself for believing in the dream at all.

But the dream she'd had last night about Julia and Antonito had seemed different, even though it'd occurred while she'd been sleeping off a drunken stupor. Her doubts about the dreams were beginning to fade. Like that one pair of jeans she had at home that had been too stiff and tight at first but had slowly faded and softened, giving way to her body to eventually form a smooth second skin. Out of a hundred pairs of jeans in her closet, those were the ones she thought of as her real jeans, the ones she always grabbed when she cared more about comfort than show. Her dreams were like that. The doubt was fading and the dreams seemed like second nature. Compared to everything else in her life they seemed real. She had to admit to herself that regardless of whether they were insane psychotic episodes or true visions from the past, the lessons to be learned were profound.

She thought about Julia, an independent woman so long ago. Julia didn't try to mold herself into her society's definition of a woman. She created her own definition. Of course, it helped that she lived in an age when that was possible. Still, Jessie Belle admired her gumption. She couldn't help but notice that Julia loved a man who was outside her social status. Dray came to mind.

There was one more thing on her mind, but this she was not confused about. There was something she knew without a doubt that she needed to do.

Twenty minutes later a surprisingly refreshed and put-together Jessie Belle entered the Alpen Kaffeehaus and strode across the room. Every male head in the place popped up to get a gander at the beautiful young woman with the flowing auburn hair who wore a tight pink sweater and even tighter jeans. Joe and Dray, who sat in a back booth, were the last to notice her, but when they did, each froze with his coffee cup in midair. They looked like mechanical dolls in a carnival machine, their arms awkwardly suspended in the air like they were awaiting a coin in a coin slot.

"Good morning, gentlemen," she greeted them as she slipped in beside Joe.

Joe lowered his cup and said, "Wow, Jessie Belle, you look great, considering."

"Thank you. Must be the result of all the good care I got last night." She looked at Dray. He returned her gaze, but she found his eyes to be unreadable. He said nothing, instead regaining his ability to move, as if a quarter had been stuck in the slot, and taking a sip of his coffee.

"I want to thank you both for taking such good care of me," she said. "And, I want to apologize for my bad behavior."

"Eh, that's okay," Joe said, swatting the air dismissively. "No harm done."

"No, I want to apologize. I'm sorry I was such a pain in the derriere last night."

"What's 'derriere'?" Dray asked.

"French for ass," Joe said. "She doesn't want to 'ass' that because she thinks it's a bad word. The French version sounds better."

"I see," Dray said, shrugging his shoulders. "But if 'derriere' is French for 'ass,' in France you'd just be saying ass, so what difference does it make?"

He was teasing Jessie Belle and she knew it. The two men chortled as a waitress appeared with a cup of coffee for Jessie Belle and a fill-up for the men. They nodded their thanks, seeing that none of them spoke German.

"Anyway," Jessie Belle said, determined to speak her piece, "I am truly sorry. It was just a shock, one minute planning my wedding and then the next minute finding out, from my boss of all people, that there will be no wedding. I didn't handle it well and you two took the brunt of the fallout. I promise that for the rest of the trip I'll behave like a professional."

"Ah, hell," Joe said. "That was the most fun I've had in a long time. Besides, you handled it a lot better than I ever did. We got you to bed before you did too much damage, so don't worry about it."

She considered that for a moment. First of all, from his re-action it appeared that Dray had not told him about her very worst behavior. So Dray kept confidences, it seemed. Second of all, she considered that Joe had been divorced a number of times. "When you split up," she asked him, "did you usually want the divorces or were you brokenhearted by them?"

"Well, yah. I guess I'm just an old softie. The kind they write country songs about, cryin' in my beer and all that. Tore me up bad the first three times. By the last time, though, when I caught my wife in bed with the meter reader, I was sorta used to it by then."

"Still, it had to hurt."

Joe drank his coffee thoughtfully then said, "I've come to the conclusion that it isn't jealousy that makes us go crazy when somebody kicks us to the curb, at least not most of us reasonable people. It's grief, pure and simple. Grief not just for the loss of the relationship with the person, but also because our dreams are dead. Every picture we had in our heads of how we imagined our lives would be is suddenly obliterated. That's just plain hard on a person."

"At least you have your kids," Dray said.

"Youbetcha! Five of the greatest kids on earth. How they survived it all, I'll never know, but they seem to be relatively un-scathed by my pitiful track record, eh."

They drank their coffee in silence for a few moments. Jessie Belle sipped slowly, savoring the rich brew while she got up the nerve to ask a bold question. "Dray, what about your marriage? Did your wife leave you with the kids and did it break your heart, or did you leave her?"

Dray choked on his coffee. "What wife?" he asked.

"Well, the mother of your children. Joe said she was gone."

Joe sputtered, "Gone as in dead, Jessie Belle. And it wasn't his wife, it was his sister."

"Oh! I'm so sorry!" She couldn't believe she'd blown it with Dray again. Goodness gracious sakes alive! Would she ever be able to come up with an appropriate thing to say to this man? Apparently not.

Dray recovered from the momentary shock of having erroneously been married off. "It's okay. I can see where you got that idea," he said. "No, I've never been married. I thought I was getting married once, but she left when I adopted the kids. I took them when my sister and brother-in-law were killed in a car accident in Romania three years ago. I was already working in the States, so I brought the kids and my mother here to be with me. I couldn't do it without my mom. She's really the one who takes care of us all."

Jessie Belle stared at him. *Great. This is just great*, she thought. *Now I like him more than ever. A man who would take in his deceased sister's children. What woman wouldn't fall in love with that? And I don't even like children!*

"You gonna eat anything? Want a pasty or something?" Joe asked.

"No," she said. "I'm not up for that yet. I'll grab a snack in a little while."

"Okay, then! Let's hit it. We've gotta drive around the mountain and get to work!"

And I've got a lot of work to do on my life, Jessie Belle thought as they left to begin another day of tracing the life journeys of her ancestors.

"Hallstat is one of the richest finds on earth in terms of Celtic heritage," the professor said, sweeping her arm to indicate the valley below, which held a crystal clear lake in the palm of its cupped hand. The professor, Joe, Dray, and Jessie Belle stood at a lookout point on the side of the road. The view mesmerized. The valley bottom held the verdant aqua lake then curved up to vaulted, lush green slopes, which gave way to massive blue-gray mountains that soared to pristine white snow-capped peaks.

Jessie Belle listened intently, amazed at the subject matter experts the network had come up with on such short notice. The professor, a trim blonde who appeared to be in her thirties wearing nice jeans and a pretty sweater, was a doctor of anthropology at the University of Salzburg. Although she was Austrian, her English was excellent.

"Now, of course," she said to Jessie Belle, then to the camera, revealing her adroitness at media presentation, "your heritage, according to your DNA, is rife with Scandinavian contribution. So your Scandinavian ancestors would have traveled through this area long before the Celts. The humans who ended up in Norway and Sweden and Finland, on the long journey out of Africa, would have come through here many, many thousands of years ago. At least by 11,000 BCE, during the Paleolithic Period. The Celts, on the other hand, originated from a group we call Indo-Europeans that came in about 600 BCE, during the Iron Age, from somewhere out on the plains of Eurasia.

"But even though the Indo-Europeans who became the Celts were here later, they're important to your heritage because anyone who has British heritage, which I understand is the part you knew about from your family's most recent past, is very likely to have some Celtic heritage. Those Scandinavian Vikings would have swept down into Great Britain, raiding and pillaging and, yes, raping, and then eventually mingling peacefully with the original inhabitants, including the Celts. So you're actually looking at more than one aspect of your heritage here, because the humans who became Vikings probably came through here and later the Celts came through here, too."

She thrust her arm out, palm up, to emphasize the magnificent view of mountain, dale, and lake. "Look at this earth! Who knows who all has passed over this very land upon which we stand? The earliest humans probably came from that direction," she said, pointing south. "The Indo-Europeans would have come from that direction." She pointed at the mountainous terrain on the eastern side of the valley. "And we just came from Salzburg," she added, pointing behind her to the west. "That wasn't here back then, of course. No coffee shops or pubs. Can you imagine?" She chuckled. "Shall we proceed?"

They got back into their cars and drove down the winding road to the anthropological dig.

Jessie Belle did her best to take in everything the professor said, but much like listening to lectures when she'd been in college, she had a hard time focusing. The place was too beautiful to be talked about, she decided. It was another of those places that needed to be felt. As much as she'd liked the professor to begin with, eventually she wished she'd simply shut up. Just like in college. She'd actually fallen asleep in a lecture hall once and been awakened by the snap of a finger on the back of her head. A fellow student had saved her from the professor's wrath as the old codger headed up the aisle in her direction.

But Joe and Dray were so enchanted with this academic windbag they didn't seem at all inclined to tell the blabby little thing to cease and desist. It especially annoyed Jessie Belle that the woman openly flirted with Dray. And he, although busy filming, seemed to like it. Now that chapped Jessie Belle's derriere no end. Not that she had a claim on him, but she still didn't like someone else try to dig in her claws.

What Jessie Belle got out of the tour was that the Celts had been a loosely organized band of many tribes. They were highly advanced for their time, especially in metal working, making weapons, farm implements, and jewelry that displayed uniquely artistic designs. The professor showed them photos of a swirly circle design that had been especially popular, being found on hundreds of pieces of gold jewelry like delicately crafted torcs, neck rings that were often inset with gems. Tired as she was, Jessie Belle had to admit that the jewelry was beautiful.

But after that, she lost interest completely. Maybe it was the fact that this whirlwind assignment was starting to wear her out, or the reality that she was jealous of the professor for playing the coquet with Dray, or most likely it was the actuality that her body was working off its first, and avowed last, dreadful hangover. In any case, Jessie Belle ambled away from the little troupe and found a secluded spot by a nearby stream. Sitting down on a rock, she pulled off her shoes and rubbed her sore feet. Why she thought it a good idea to bring couture wedge footwear on a trip like this, she didn't know. Cute, yes. Comfortable, no. She dangled her bare feet into the cool water. *Ah, heavenly!* She wondered if she'd had an ancestor who'd sat here, just like this, enjoying the tranquility of this very same spot.

"Jessie Belle! Jessie Belle!" Her eyes flew open. Just like the thump on the back of her head in class, Joe's voice knocked off her nap. She sat up. Her feet still languished in the stream and her head had rested on a mossy little mound beside the rock upon which she had perched. It was time to leave wonderland and go back to the real world. Whatever that was.

In the car on the way back to the hotel, Joe and Dray buzzed with excited chatter about the day's shoot, while Jessie Belle sat like a mannequin in the backseat. When they reached the hotel, they invited her to join them for dinner, but she declined. She wasn't up for food, which would require action on the part of her still roiling stomach, or conversation, which would call for an awakening of her comatose brain. She booked a massage with the hotel masseuse and after a good rubdown went straight to bed.

Chapter 12

Her feet were fat.

And she hated her *schuhs*.

Brunhild looked down, having to use her hands to hold in her fat belly, which over the years had spread out like a sack of grain, in order to see her ugly feet. She didn't know why she was suddenly interested in them but there they were, swollen dead piglets at the ends of her stubby legs. Her worn leather *schuhs*, riddled with holes and splattered with ale, were ugly, too. Everything about her was ugly. That was the one thing in life she knew for sure. It had been years since she'd been a young girl who would gaze at her pleasing reflection in the stream, but she didn't need to see her reflection to know that the once pretty girl who had assumed that her face and body would always stay the same had turned into a fat slob. Her pleasantly pink skin had turned into a ruddy mess and shiny long brown hair had become a bland tangle of rope. When she'd last taken a bath, she couldn't even remember. She despised her body too much to see it bare. The stench of her own perspiration and sweat didn't even bother her much anymore, it merely mingled with the wretched smell of the stupid men and even more stupid *hures* she had to endure every day. It had been months since she'd even bothered to wash her apron and the rough, brown wool had become stiff as a frozen corpse. She slid a finger over the fabric but snatched her hand away. It felt so horrible that she couldn't believe she even wore it. There had been a time when she would have been appalled at such squalor.

But life had beaten Brunhild down until she no longer cared about such things. Or, at least, she no longer allowed herself to think about how she might still care about such things. Thinking too much only brought her pain. So it was surprising that she'd granted herself these few moments of solitude. But, today she felt unusually contemplative, as if her mind was trying to tell her something she didn't quite understand. As if something important was about to happen.

She touched her cheek, remembering that it, too, used to be soft. As always these days, surprise caught her when her cheek met her hand long before it should. Her puffy face must be ugliest of all, she guessed. In the last ten years, what had once been comely had turned into a misshapen mass, like bread dough punched down and rising back up in all the wrong places to form a twisted, sagging loaf of bad bread. It was her husband who always did the punching.

She sat on a wooden barrel out behind the *ale haus*, for some reason not afraid, as usual, that her husband Etzel would come along and slug her in the mouth for her laziness. She peered into the back door of the mud brick hovel that served as the village drinking place, and saw that the beast was so busy laughing with a group of drunkards that he hadn't even noticed yet that she was gone. What did they find so funny? Whatever it was, she knew it would not be funny to her.

Hrodwulf scampered up from behind her and barked, "What are you doing here, you fat *kuh*? Get up and go to work!" Only seven years old and he already imitated his father, calling her a big animal that is good for nothing but milk and meat. No child, Brunhild thought, should ever talk to his mother that way. But with four boys who were all as cruel as their sire, she'd given up long ago trying to gain any respect from her own family. For a moment she feared that Hrodwulf would run inside to tell on her, but his gang of bully buddies called from down the dirt path and he ran to join them in their never-ending mischief.

She hated them all! All of the men in her life. It had taken her some years to admit, but four times she had given birth to pure evil. Any male seed of Etzel's could come to no other end.

Leaning forward, she glanced inside again. There, in the back of the room, washing tankards in a bowl of grimy water, was her only hope, her only salvation for thinking her own life had not been a total loss. Five-year-old Griselda—a thin, plain child with hair like sotten straw—did her chore without complaint. Unlike her favored brothers, she was required to work. And unlike her brothers, she was kind to her mother. Brunhild loved the child and longed to give her a better life. But there was no such thing to be had.

"What are you doing, you lazy, fat *kuh*?"

She'd been so focused on Griselda that Brunhild had failed to notice that Etzel had left the group of men, disappeared along the side wall, and then suddenly appeared at the back door. He slugged her in the face.

Her fingers traced to her swollen cheek. This time she'd lost a tooth, which had bled mightily, so the inside of her mouth hurt as much as the outside of her cheek. Don't *denken*, she told herself. Keep *beschaftigt* so you don't *denken*. Keep busy so you don't think. She could not let herself think about it. It would do no good.

From a shelf she took down a long, wooden bowl and went out back to pull pork off of the skewered carcass that roasted over a fire pit. But as she went to place the bowl on a rock beside the fire, her hands would not move. She stood there staring into the roughly hewn bowl as tears sprang to her eyes. This was the bowl Etzel had thrown the fetus into and placed on display on the rock, to remind her not to get pregnant again. That was after he'd kicked her bulging belly and slapped her sobbing face until she'd miscarried the child, which had been big enough to be able to tell it had been another daughter. That had been a year ago and Brunhild still mourned the loss of that infant girl. If it had been a boy and lived, she would have mourned that, too.

Etzel had insisted she not remove the bowl with the decaying, stinking fetus in it. It broke her heart that it laid out there alone in the dark of night. She sobbed on the day a torrent of rain fell and made the little rotting mass float around in circles. And she got another beating for begging her husband to bury the poor, innocent, unborn babe. Then one morning, after a week had passed, she arose to find the dried up fetus in the fire pit. The bowl had been put back on the shelf in the *ale haus*.

This all had been his punishment to her for the misdeed of getting pregnant. She knew, of course, how babies were made. But, unlike Etzel, she felt certain it wasn't all her fault when she conceived. That didn't matter anymore, anyway. Etzel had never hesitated to bed the *hures* who hung around the *ale haus* and since that pregnancy hadn't laid a hand, or thankfully anything else, on her.

Her tears splattered into the bowl, stirring her back to the moment. She balanced the thing on her hip and pulled at the pork. Don't *denken*, she told herself. Keep busy so you don't *denken*. Stay busy so you don't think, she repeated over and over like a prayer.

Hurriedly, she took the meat into the men and then delivered tankard after tankard of ale to tables full of noisy bums. The place was packed. The men, sitting on short stools around small wood tables, were all up in arms about the invading barbarian tribes from the north that had been swooping into Germanic villages and raiding them for anything they could find. Rumor was they killed the men, raped the women, and kidnapped the children to raise them as slaves. Of course, this gossip had been about for years, but now it swirled into a furious storm because a refugee had just arrived, saying that the day before the Barbars had hit his settlement in the next valley. The protection from battle that came with being sheltered in a mountain dale had been shattered.

Brunhild looked at the angry horde in front of her, glared at her monster of a husband, thought of her four evil sons, and determined that there could be no more ruthless barbarians than those right here.

The meat was quickly devoured as the men shouted fighting plans with their mouths full, so she picked up the empty bowl, only to realize that she held it in her hands right above the back of her husband's head as he sat on a stool. The bowl was a sturdy piece of roughly carved wood, heavy enough to deliver a fatal blow. She stood there, unmoving, the weapon hovering in the air, her gaze focused on her target, the balding top of Etzel's head. It was odd how the thought came to her. She didn't feel angry; she didn't feel vengeful; she didn't feel out of control. She only felt a sudden urge to murder the bastard. She raised the bowl higher, higher….

Screaming from outside jerked everyone's attention to the front door. Everyone's but Brunhild's. With all her might, she thrust her weapon downward just as Etzel bolted off of his stool. With a loud crash, the wood split apart on the edge of the table, spewing splinters in all directions. One hit Etzel in the neck. Stunned, he reached up to pull it out. The look of shock on his face as he swiped at the trickle of blood that appeared, the look that turned to total disbelief as he realized what she'd tried to do, warmed her heart. He took a step toward her.

Just then a man ran into the *ale haus*, screaming, "They're here! They're here! The Barbars are here! Grab a weapon and fight!" Another man grabbed Etzel's arm and gave him a knife, one that Brunhild felt certain he would have used on her had he not been carried along by the throng as it tumbled out the front door and into the street.

"Griselda! Griselda!" Fear grabbed Brunhild by the throat as she tried to find her daughter. Everyone was gone now, having taken any weapon-like object they could find and running out to fight the invaders. How some thought they'd fend off spears and arrows with ale tankards, she didn't know and didn't care. All she cared about was her girl. In their haste, the mob had overturned the table, flooded the dirt floor with spilt ale, and left the room in shambles. Griselda's little table with her washing bowl was broken and in pieces on the floor, the murky water slithering out around it. "Griselda! Where are you?" Brunhild screamed frantically.

"*Mutter.* Here."

How she heard the frail voice over the wild din now coming from outside, she did not know. It felt as though she heard it with her heart instead of her ears.

She turned to find her daughter cowering in a corner. "There you are!" the mother wailed, enveloping her child in her arms and huddling with her in the dark, dank corner in the back of the room.

How much time had passed, she did not know, but it seemed like an eternity. Night had fallen. Things had quieted down outside, but she could tell the Barbars had not yet left. From her corner hiding place, where she hovered protectively over her daughter, Brunhild had been able to piece together what had happened outside just by listening. First there had been a thunder of hoof beats, the loudest, most terrifying sound she'd ever heard in her life. But, surprisingly, there had been little sound of battle. She didn't know what a battle sounded like, one having never before occurred in her village, but she imagined they were usually noisy, with slashing swords and whizzing arrows. Seeing that the victims had been mostly unarmed, however, this battle had apparently been quick, and except for an agonizing death cry each time a man was slaughtered, rather quiet.

Then it sounded as if the invaders were getting down from their horses, drinking from the village well, and shouting at each other in a brusque language she did not understand. She heard things being dragged around, as if bags of grain and other items were being taken from people's huts. Then shrill wailing began. Women being raped, she supposed. It didn't sound like the children crying were being attacked in any way, as their moans were long and loud with no sharp intakes of breath that would indicate physical pain. No, they were crying out of fear. She clung to Griselda, who had miraculously fallen asleep after hours of sobbing herself.

Exhausted, Brunhild had almost nodded off when a monstrous figure appeared in the front door, looming over the room. She opened her eyes wide, squinted, and settled on staring in awe. It was the largest horse she'd ever seen in her life, with a large man atop it. Dawn's early rays billowed in from behind, making it seem as if the beast and its rider floated on air as they strode right into the room and came to a stop before her.

The big man stared down at them, causing Brunhild to instinctively shove Griselda behind her.

When she finally boldly looked up into his eyes, they surprised her. Not blood-thirsty, not evil, not lustful, not even angry, they were the weary eyes of an old barbarian warrior who was tired. It was as simple as that.

He gestured for her to stand. Slowly, Brunhild rose to her feet. They glared at one another in silence for a long moment until she said, "I won't go without *mein tochter*." She pointed toward Griselda. Although he didn't understand her words, he knew her intent and nodded. Indeed, she would not go without her daughter.

Gently, she lifted the child up and he took her in his strong arms, setting her on the horse in front of him. He reached down for Brunhild. She grabbed a stool and, with the lightness of the svelte girl she'd once been, hopped up onto it. The big barbarian had no trouble with her heft as he pulled her up behind him, where she settled in with her arms around his rotund waist.

The war horse's enormous hooves, each one as large as the heavy wooden bowl Brunhild had tried to murder her husband with, poked through the debris scattered about the earthen floor and sauntered out the door. When the bright dawning light hit Brunhild she shielded her eyes, only to see that Etzel lay dead right in front of them. A misty ray of morning sun struck his crumpled body, as if offering her a glorious gift. The best part of the alms was that the bastard's head had been lobbed off.

The horse stepped over the corpse and kicked the head in the process, causing it to tumble down the path as casually as a loose melon. Brunhild watched it loll down the dusty lane, rolling from the stubbly chin to the malicious eyes to the ruddy bald spot on the top of its head to the bloody severed neck. When it stopped upright, its wide lifeless eyes still held a shocked look of disbelief.

The warhorse walked past the bodiless head.

Brunhild spit in its eye.

The barbarian warrior halted his beast and turned to look at her. She smiled. Surprise crossed his wizened face, followed by understanding, then amusement. He smiled back.

He turned his giant steed toward the north and they rode off, never to return.

Chapter 13

Brunhild had been her ancestor, one of the women who had made her. Of that Jessie Belle felt certain. A young Brunhild, undoubtedly a Celt, had sat by that same stream near Hallstat where Jessie Belle had soothed her feet. Perhaps the girl from times gone by had even splashed her toes in the water in the very same way as her descendant. But that would only have been possible before Brunhild married. After she married she'd been treated no better than a beast.

Jessie Belle shuttered at the thought, but was brought out of her reverie by Joe.

"Well," he said. "we've gotta skedaddle and catch that flight to Oslo."

She chugged the rest of her coffee and got up to go. The three of them were in their Salzburg hotel restaurant again and had just finished a healthy breakfast of thick slabs of ham, eggs fried with hunks of bleu cheese on top, and pumpernickel toast slathered in farm-fresh butter. Jessie Belle could feel her arteries corroding already.

Having lost the privilege of using the company jet, which had been called to another assignment for a few days, they were on their way to the airport to take a commercial flight to Norway. None of them were looking forward to the experience after being spoiled by the luxury of the private flying accommodations.

Jessie Belle hadn't been in her cramped middle coach seat for fifteen minutes when she fell fast asleep, partly in defense against the jabbering woman next to her and partly because she hoped that letting herself doze would produce a visit from Star. She had so many questions about Brunhild!

Sure enough, Star granted her wish and appeared. This time the spirit looked anything but angelic in a rather campy get-up fit for an adult film version of *Heidi*. Apparently in honor of their visit to the Alps, she wore a low-cut dress that allowed for a view of ample cleavage, revealing her own round mounds. On the other end, the gathered skirt was so short it was a miracle the valley between her legs wasn't visible. Incongruously, the frock had child-like puffy short sleeves and the fabric was blue with white dots. She also wore a white apron. Her silvery hair was in long braids that coiled around her head.

Jessie Belle grinned at the spectacle. "You about to cook a meal?" she asked.

Star chuckled and smoothed her apron. "No, of course not. But it is a fetching touch, isn't it? I just love dressing up! I don't know why you humans, especially you women, take clothes so seriously and wear things that are so uncomfortable. You have so many rules about what you 'should' wear and so much of what you put on is so dumb! I mean, those high heels! Here you are, given the gift of feet so you can walk around and you destroy them. It doesn't make any sense. You should have more fun with your clothes! And with your body! Only wear things that don't hurt you.

"Ah, but you didn't want to see me for that, did you? You have some questions about Brunhild. Well! You'll be pleased to know that she lived a happy life with the Barbars. The old warrior who took her and Griselda away died not long after they met back up with the tribe. But he was good to the two of them, needing a nurse more than anything. Brunhild knew how to brew crude ale, so she honed her skills in order to give the old man something that would comfort him in his last days. He went into the afterworld totally plastered! Thank goodness! Otherwise the pain of his old wounds would have been too much to bear.

"Then Brunhild became very popular with the whole tribe. Turned out everyone liked her brew. She and the tanner became fast friends, and for years afterward he kept her in nice, soft, well-crafted, leather shoes. And she kept him supplied with ale. It was a perfect trade. Never again did she have to work in *schuhs* she hated. It sounds like a small thing, but it was very important to her.

"Hey! Maybe that's where your love of shoes comes from. But really, dear, take a tip from Brunhild and wear something more sensible.

"Anyway, you probably want to know about Griselda, too. She grew up to be as good a brewer as her mother. They worked side-by-side until Brunhild died at a ripe old age. Griselda married and had four children, every one of them nice to their mother and grandmother.

"So sometimes, Jessie Belle, life does have a happy ending. It did for Brunhild and Griselda. It can for you, too. It's up to you.

"*Auf wiedersehen*, dear!" Star proclaimed. From her short stay in Austria, Jessie Belle recognized the phrase as German for "goodbye." Before she could get a word in, Star disappeared.

Oh well, at least she didn't yodel goodbye.

Jessie Belle roused from her nap feeling surprisingly refreshed. The yappy woman next to her by the aisle was shouting over the roar of the jet engines at a bored-looking old woman across the aisle. The fellow on her other side, by the window, had also taken the cowardly way out and was snoozing, his jaw hanging open. But he jolted awake when the plane hit an air pocket and bounced around like ping pong ball in a tornado. Then the landing felt like the ping pong ball had suddenly fallen out of the twister and barreled to the ground. It clearly wasn't the pilot's best effort.

The jostle to get out of the big metal tube seemed to take longer than usual. Joe, Dray, and she had been scattered throughout the plane, with her in the back. She could see tall Dray's head, bobbing above the other passengers, but couldn't spy short Joe. Eventually, however, the three of them met up at baggage claim.

"Oslo, eh!" Joe said. "Never been here. Have you?"

Both Jessie Belle and Dray shook their heads.

They rolled their bags out to their rental car, including all of the equipment Joe and Dray had to lug around. Once inside the sleek, black Saab, Joe asked, "Who wants lunch?"

"I do," Dray said.

"I don't," Jessie Belle said. "The minute we hit that hotel I'm finding me a hair and nail salon. And after having my hair done, and a manicure and pedicure, I'm going to go buy me some nice new shoes!"

Jessie Belle admired her new shoes. She'd surprised herself by purchasing some moderately priced, flat sandals with a brand name she'd never heard and could not pronounce. They were so cute, though! Soft, forest green leather, they had adorable leather flowers down the center strap on the top. They looked especially good with her fresh pedicure and pale pink polish. Best of all, these shoes were the most comfortable things she'd had on her feet in ages. She loved them!

Her cell phone rang, so she hopped up from the chair in her hotel room and shuffled through her purse, coming up with it after a number of persistent rings. Glancing at caller ID, she moaned, "Uh-oh. I'm in trouble."

She hit the button, clapped it up to the side of her head, and said, as cheerily as possible, "Hi, Mama!"

Forty-five minutes later, her mama finally having run out of steam, they said goodbye. Jessie Belle threw the pesky phone back into her purse, plopped back down into the chair, flung her legs up over the arm, and once again admired her new shoes.

The conversation on the phone had not gone well, just as she'd known it wouldn't. That was why she'd avoiding calling Mama to tell her about Robert breaking up with her. She'd known Mama would eventually hear about it on TV, at the beauty salon, or at bridge club. But she hoped to put it off as long as possible. Leave it to old gossipy Gloria at bridge to tell her all about it, calling it "Robert's big dump."

"You have to come home right now and get him back, Jessie Belle!" her mother had demanded, as if that was all there was to it.

Melancholy settled in again. No boyfriend. No Vera Wang wedding gown. No Buckhead mansion.

At least I have my new shoes, she thought, contemplating her pretty feet.

"So we spend tomorrow here tooling around the fjords and the next day in Oslo at the Viking Ship Museum, where we'll see a real Viking dragonship," Joe said, pointing out their route on a map of the area. The three of them sat in a close circle around the small table in Jessie Belle's room. "We'll finish in Oslo in time to fly to London on a commercial flight that evening," Joe continued. "Dray and I work in the London office that night. The next day I work at the office while you two have a day off. Remember what that is? It's fun. You'll love it. That evening we fly to Dublin, where we'll visit the sites and meet with our old friend Edwin Sampson. Our dear assistant director of the National Geographic Genographic Project who so dramatically announced the results of your DNA." Joe nodded at Jessie Belle. "Turns out viewers loved him, what with his Indiana Jones persona and all. So our guys want him back. He's still doing his research in Africa, but they've agreed to fly him up to be part of our final show over here. Then we get our private jet back and fly home, and do the last show at your mother's plantation."

"I'm sure Mama still wants to do that," Jessie Belle said. "She loves nothing more than publicity. But it turns out she's a little upset with me right now over 'Robert's big dump,' as she and her friends call it. That kind of publicity does not sit well with her. So she's going to be a little frosty toward me. You might want to keep that in mind when you plan the interview with her."

"Thanks for the tip," Joe said.

"Why is she upset with you?" Dray asked. "You didn't do anything. It was all his doing."

"Not according to my mama. She thinks that if I weren't so involved with my career in journalism I could concentrate on a woman's real career, marriage. In her mind it's my fault because I left town and left the poor boy unattended."

"That's insane," Dray insisted.

"I never claimed my mama is sane."

"Hey, I almost hate to mention this," Joe chimed in, "but the truth of the matter is that all of this break-up publicity has done nothing but boost the ratings of our segments. Viewers, perverse little critters that they are, apparently love seeing the new girlfriend introduce spots that focus on the old girlfriend. Consequently, ratings have been through the roof. Jessie Belle, your fans are more glued to their sets than ever. They're very vocal, as it turns out, and they've jammed the CNN blog with hate mail for Bridget. On the other hand, she has some followers, too. So the end result is more combined viewers than ever.

"Back at the station they're calling it 'The Battle of the Bombshell Babes.' No offense intended by me, Jessie Belle. Just repeating what I've heard. The janitor has a pool going; everybody's betting on who'll end up with Robert in the end."

"Great. That's just great," Jessie Belle said, resigned to the notoriety this had brought her.

"Well, okay, then, let's get some rest," Joe said. "It's been a long trip and we're on the last leg."

As they left her room, Dray sort of smiled at her. It made her feel like a teenager.

"Argh! I can't sleep for beans!" Jessie Belle complained to herself.

She'd fallen asleep for a few hours, awakened, tossed about for an hour and, even being as exhausted as she was, couldn't seem to muster up any more slumber. She got up, threw on some clothes, and left the room. Perhaps, she'd decided, a snack would help.

Plodding barefoot down the hall toward the vending machines, counting the unfamiliar Euro coins in her hand as she went, she was surprised to hear Dray's voice. She stopped and listened more closely. Yes, it was him, talking all lovey-dovey to someone. There was no mistaking that sound, even though she'd certainly never heard him talk like that to her.

As stealthily as possible, she followed the voice. It came from behind a door that stood slightly ajar. She reached out to push the door, thought better of it, then went ahead and shoved it open just a tad. She could only see a crack of the room, but there he was, clad in his boxer shorts and a tee shirt. The memory of her earlier drunken debacle in his room flooded back. He'd been in his boxers then, too. Once again, the sight did not disappoint. He was sitting in front of his laptop, which was on a desk that was positioned sideways from her, talking on his webcam with someone. Obviously, it was someone he cared for a great deal. Even loved, it seemed.

"Yes, honey, I miss you more and more every day. But it won't be long now before I'll be back home."

A soft female voice said something that Jessie Belle couldn't quite hear. Where was this person anyway? It was the middle of the night. Oh, she realized, it was late evening in Atlanta. Just before bedtime. That must be it—he had a girlfriend in Atlanta. Of course he did. He'd told her he didn't, but like all men he lied as easily as he breathed.

He responded to what the woman said. "Of course we'll go to Bruster's as soon as I get home. Just like I promised. Double cherry ice cream sodas for us both."

Crimony, Jessie Belle thought, *an ice cream shop. That's his girlfriend's idea of a welcome home activity? Even I could do better than that. I'd at least go for dinner at Bones.* She tried to get a look at the computer screen but it was turned too far out of her view. She clamored to see what the woman looked like. Probably tall with legs up to her neck, long dark hair down to her waist, and sexy allure dripping all over the place.

"Okay, sweetie. You go to bed now. I'm sending lots of hugs and kisses." He blew kisses into the camera. "Remember, I love you more."

"No! I love *you* more." This time the voice was loud enough that Jessie Belle could hear it clearly. It was followed by a distinctly childish giggle. There was no mistaking the chirp of a little girl. It must be his niece, Jessie Belle realized, his adopted daughter. How old was she? Seven? Yes, seven. A flash of shame struck over the suspicions she'd just had about the female.

"No," Dray insisted, "I love *you* more." This was apparently a game they knew well. "Now, please go get your grandma. Good night, honey."

"Okay." There was a pause, then a final echoing declaration, as if the child was walking away from the computer. "I love you more…"

Dray's chuckle reverberated through the room and landed like a symphony on Jessie Belle's ears. How was it possible for this big, burly galoot to be so sweet?

"Hi, ma!" he said. "How's it going over there today?"

She couldn't hear his mother's response, other than to ascertain that the Romanian accent was much more pronounced than her son's.

"Yeah, everything's going well here," Dray said. "It won't be long and I'll be home. It sure was great talking to all the kids tonight. Everybody's behaving, I presume?"

Whatever his mother said made him laugh heartily. This was a family that enjoyed each other's company. Jessie Belle thought of her own mother and suddenly felt surprisingly lonely. Not because seeing her mama would give her comfort but because seeing her mama would not give her comfort.

"Sure. Bye, Ma. I love you, too."

As Dray clicked out of webcam mode and started to shut down his laptop, Jessie Belle tip-toed back to her room, knowing she was falling head over heels for a man who couldn't be more wrong for her.

Chapter 14

Erika grabbed her sable fur wrap and thrust it around her bare shoulders. A cool breeze from this northern sea had meandered into her cubby and surrounded her naked body, cloaking her in a sudden chill.

Leif lay in peaceful slumber at her side. He'd been sleeping so soundly when she'd come to him in the middle of the night, she suspected that when he awoke he wouldn't know if their love-making had been a dream or real.

Nothing, my love, could be more real than this.

She kissed his broad forehead and lingered over his handsome face, taking in its pleasure in the moonlight. He smelled as fresh as a waterfall, seeing that the day before he'd taken his weekly bath, as was customary for Vikings. She'd bedded many a man in her time on earth, but none like Leif. He was a shipwright and sailor, and was her one true love. Of that, she felt certain. Never would they part.

Her long copper braids fell forward and grazed his chest as she looked down on him, causing his muscular body to stir ever so slightly. She sat up, pulled up his fur covering, and tucked it under his chin to protect him from the nippy night air. He shifted again, only to fall back into deep repose.

Her own fur wrap slipped down, exposing the image of the snake that encircled her upper left arm. The waning moon gave off an eerie blue light that caused the black outline of the serpent to appear to jump off of Erika's chalk white skin. From its single head, the snake's long body split in two, the dual shanks intertwining and circling Erika's sinewy arm until meeting up again at its singular tail near her elbow. Even in the dim light, Erika could see the serpent spinning its magic, making certain that no matter where Erika journeyed to in the physical world, she would always return to her own true self. She smiled upon her serpent protector and then pulled up her wrap.

She arose, stretched her tall body, and walked the few steps to the side of the longship—her longship—the *Freyja*. She'd named it after her idol, the Nordic goddess of celebration and passion. Those were two aspects of life that Erika never wanted to lose! She'd certainly kept them alive on her craft, which had been given to her by her *far*, her father Erik Bloodtooth, when she had been seventeen years old. Here she was, two years later, the only woman to have ever captained her own Viking longship *drekar*, or what the hated English called a "dragonship" because they believed it was shaped like a monster.

Many, especially her *mor*, her mother, had vehemently condemned the idea of Erika having her own vessel. But her *far* had proven himself correct in thinking his only daughter had as much *släss*, bravery, in her as any of his seven sons. After all, the first time she'd ever joined an invasion expedition was when she'd been a mere seven years old, the time she'd stowed away in his ship and no one knew she was on board until they were well out to sea. Her *mor*, a weak woman as far as Erika was concerned, had not known for six months, when the treasure-laden longships proudly returned home to Norway, if her child was dead or alive.

The thrill of that first raid had left an imprint on Erika's heart as surely as if it had been branded with the hot iron of body art. She'd known since then that being master of her own ship was all that she ever wanted to do.

Indeed, the *spebarn* she bore the summer that she turned seventeen, the summer that she got her ship, had annoyed her mightily. It had been a girl, born two months after the *Freyja* first sailed. Erika had known, of course, that it was coming. Her swelling belly and the absence of her monthly blood left no doubt of that. But she'd hoped it would be born dead or die shortly after birth, as so many newborns did. Instead, it was a perfectly healthy infant that was born at sea and howled like a foghorn. So, with no apparent intent of dying on its own and knowing that a *spebarn* would be nothing but a nuisance, Erika had left the squalling little thing with a woman on the west coast of Eire, an old crone whose hut had been spared for that purpose.

Erika didn't know for certain who had been the father of her baby. It could have been any one of the half dozen men she merrily bedded around that time, before she'd met Leif and settled down with him, but that didn't matter now. What mattered was that the *spebarn* was long gone, leaving Erika free to live her dream.

What a year that first one on her longship had been! Ten Viking ships, eight *drekars,* the graceful longships that carried troops, and two *knars,* bulky ships to carry back the plunder, were led by her gallant *far's* gigantic *drekar* ship. They raided and pillaged up and down the coast of Eire, Scotland, and even into northern parts of England, that land whose leaders saw themselves as being above all others. But they had been brought to their knees!

Even though their return home had been less than triumphant—the villagers, led by Erika's silly *mar*, had spurned the raiders', their very own husbands and fathers, return in protest of the killings they'd done—Erika had not been deterred. This was her destiny.

She stood on the deck of her longship thinking about that first expedition when she'd looked up at the huge, square, red-and-white striped sail of her ship, billowing gently in the breeze;

then out at the endless, calm, black, shimmering water; and fi-nally up to the dazzling starlit and moonlit sky. *Could there ever be a more beautiful sight?* She thought not. This was where she belonged. It was where she would always belong. Not in some land-bound longhouse, stoking the fire, fermenting shark meat, churning cow's milk, giving birth every year…. No, that passive life was not for her. She belonged on the ever-changing sea!

With the comfort of the gentle rocking of her ship beneath her feet, Erika padded back to her cubby and lay down again be-side her beloved Leif. Blissfully content, she fell fast asleep.

Erika awoke to the sound of Leif's deep voice shouting orders to the ship's twenty oarsmen to stop rowing. Second-in-command, Leif always did an admirable job of leading the crew.

She looked out to see that they had reached the Isle of Dó-chas off the northwestern coast of Eire, where the Vikings and monks of the Bishop's Monastery had struck up an understand-ing over the years. It wasn't quite a friendship, but was coming to be something akin to such.

The understanding was that the Vikings would provide tanned furs and dried reindeer meat that they brought from home in exchange for the goats cheese, grain, and wine that were the bounty of the monastery farm. It was a fair trade. After all, the monks had nothing else to give, seeing that Erik Bloodtooth, who had acquired his last name because of his necklace made up of his dead opponent's teeth, had long ago pillaged all of the monastery's worldly goods. He'd hauled away gold crosses and chalices, chests full of silver coins, and well-crafted oak furniture. He'd even taken the one small stained glass window from the chapel, but it broke on the trip back home. Now the opening in the peat brick building was covered with nothing more than a simple wood grate.

Still, amidst such original animosity, camaraderie of sorts had evolved, leaving Erika feeling glad they'd reached this shore. She actually liked some of the monks, strange little men though they might be. They kept telling her about their god with nails in his hands, which she found to be impossibly silly, but they were well-intentioned and even listened with acute interest when she told them about some of her gods and goddesses, like *Thor* and *Freyja*.

Today she could see that they must have fallen into some recent good fortune, as the place was bustling with activity. There were strange men about, not monks but craftsmen, working on a new building. A large rectangle of stone walls rose about six feet off the ground, with the current task apparently being the building of scaffolding around the structure so that the work could continue to greater height. While her longship, with its shallow dearth and light weight, was easily pulled ashore, she hopped out to greet her robed acquaintances who waited with waving hands. She had always thought their gestures to be effeminate, but today even more than usual. They seemed a bit frenzied. Excitement, she supposed, at the return of the mighty Vikings.

At the same time, her *far* pulled his *drekar* up next to hers. In his haste, he swept past Erika without noticing her and went straight to the frantically gesturing monks to see what was afoot. She was about to follow him when she noticed that Leif was walking swiftly away from the gathering of people. She couldn't imagine where he was going, so she followed him.

When he trotted across a field of cattle and then ducked behind the monastery barn, her intrigue grew. At first she's thought perhaps he'd simply wanted a private place to urinate, but that could have been done long before this point. As Erika looked around the corner of the stone barn, Leif disappeared through a backdoor that was so short he had to fold his body in half to get through.

Erika went to the door, bent down, and entered.

Right before her eyes was a sight she'd never expected to witness.

Even though he'd only been moments ahead of her, Leif was enwrapped in a lustful embrace with a beautiful young woman. Slashed with beams of light filtering in through the slats of wood that made up the walls, they had an ethereal presence. They stood with their arms around one another, their hands wandering about each other's backsides and lips locked in a deep kiss.

Shocked not only by the sight but also by the realization that it had happened so quickly, Erika knew that the woman must have been there waiting. She and Leif must have had some kind of prior understanding that when the Viking ships were sighted she was to go to the barn and wait for him.

Erika reeled with disbelief. This could not be happening! Her Leif loved her more than he loved life. He'd told her so himself, many times.

The groping couple fell into a bale of hay and began tugging at each other's clothes. It was then that Erika knew what she must do. She would slay them both. So engrossed were they in each other, they hadn't even seen her yet and didn't look like they were about to, so it would be an easy kill. Slowly, she unsheathed her knife…

The sudden wail of the foghorn, a large ram's horn blown into by a Viking sailor appointed to do so in case of emergency, jolted Erika away from her murderous thoughts and she ducked behind a large wood beam. It interrupted Leif's nefarious doings, also, and he jumped up. Grabbing at his clothes to secure them around his body, he ran out of the barn. Erika followed right behind him.

By the time they reached the shore, it was already too late. Erik Bloodtooth lay dead on the pebbly beach, the dark red blood flowing out from around the knife impaled into his heart being swept away with each curling pull of the surf that swept over his lifeless body.

Erika's shrill cry was cast away by the wind as she stood frozen with disbelief, unable to speak or move.

Beside her *far* lay an ugly fat man, also dead from a stab wound. He didn't wear a monk's robe and Erika had never seen him before. Somehow, she managed to stay conscious and sane just enough to overhear the conversation between Leif and the sobbing prior.

"He came last month with the craftsman," the prior said. "But I soon learned his only intent here was to kill Erik the next time he came. *Och!* Erik once killed his brother in a raid. I am so sorry. When we tried to capture the madman to take him away, he disappeared. That's what we were trying to warn Erik about." His voice cracked as he invoked a final appeal to God to have mercy on their souls: "*Go bhfóire Dia orthu!*" Unable to utter another word, the prior put his face into his hands and bawled like a hungry baby.

Leif looked at the prior with what Erika thought to be pity, then looked out to sea for so long a spell it seemed that his thoughts were as deep as the ocean, and eventually brought his eyes back to his beloved dead leader.

"We will bury him at sea tonight," Leif said. He stooped and took hold of Erik's flaccid hands, and carefully pulled the body out of the encroaching grasp of the waves. Slowly, methodically, reverently, he placed Erik's arms across his chest.

"We will build his funeral vessel immediately," he said to the crowd that had gathered, which included the Vikings, the monks, and the craftsmen. "This evening we will send him to where he will live with his gods forever. We will send his burning body out to sea."

"What about your wedding?" the prior asked. "That was to take place this evening, right here where we stand."

"The wedding will take place as planned."

The beautiful woman appeared out of nowhere and came to stand by Leif. He put his arm around her waist, and she looked up at him with sympathy and understanding roiling out of her wide lake-blue eyes.

Overwhelming jealousy, unbearable grief, suffocating confusion——Erika didn't know which was most paralyzing. It was as if she was living a horrifying nightmare, one from which she could not make herself wake up.

With the stealth of a snake just before it strikes, Erika slowly began once again to unsheathe her knife. No matter how much tortured anguish she might feel over her *far's* shocking murder, she could not let this betrayal of her love go unavenged!

"Erika."

Halted by the sound of her name in a haunting voice, she spun around to face the mysterious source. A mist had begun to slither in from the sea and she could not make out who was there. And then he stepped out of the veil of haze.

Erika stared in disbelief.

"*Ja.* Yes. It is me."

Erika whipped her head around to look back at the crowd. There he was, still lying on the ground with his arms majestically crossed over his chest. She looked back in front of her. And here he was, standing tall and healthy as an ox before her.

"*Far!* How are you here?" she asked excitedly, reaching her hand out toward her father.

"You know."

"I know what?"

"You know how I am here. It is the same way that you are here."

Her hand dropped to her side, she stood as still as stone, and then she began to shake her head.

"*Ne,*" she whispered. Then she bellowed, "*Ne! Ne! Ne!* Don't say that!"

"*Ja,* my child, I must. It has been too long that you have been wandering this earth alone, lost and unaware. Now I can take you with me to the next life. We will go together." He stretched his hand out to her. "Come."

Suddenly, as if a leather blindfold that had been strapped over her eyes had been lifted, she saw it all. The barrier of disbelief and sadness fell away, and behind it the scene played out in all of its appalling horror. She had been sailing the *Freyja* for one year to the day when it had happened. Not a brave fight for plunder, not a valiant stand for territory, not even a plucky squirmish with a worthy foe like the Danes, it had been a doltish drowning.

She'd been diving into the ocean all of her life, off of cliffs at the side of the *fjord* at home, off of longships, and, yes, once even off of a homely, sluggish, captured English vessel. So why she inexplicably drowned while playfully swimming with the crew off the coast of Scotland, no one knew. All they knew was that while splashing around she declared, "I bet two gold coins I can find us a sea monster!" She took a deep breath, cast her luminous smile at everyone, and dove under. Pummeling her face downward, her trim bare bottom came up in a graceful arch followed by a splash of her feet, like a miniature version of a great white whale's graceful dive. Then she disappeared.

The seaman, including Leif, laughed at her bragging and watched the spot where she'd vanished, expecting her to surface at any moment. But she did not come.

"Erika!" Leif called out as he frantically dove under.

Every crewmember who was in the water did the same and those who had been on the shore hurriedly joined in.

Leif did not give up the search for three days. Eventually, Erik had to drag him back to the ship and out to sea.

"I drowned," Erika said to her *far*. "I found my sea monster. I thought I could swim a great distance under water and surprise everyone by coming up far away. I was swimming with the arrogant self-assurance of youth and had not been watching for danger. It was too late by the time I saw the long fish that looked like a snake that slithered up and bit me. It took a bite out of the snake on my arm." She ran her fingers over the image. "The moment it struck, I knew I was dead. The tide took my body out to sea, far beyond the reach of anyone searching for me. It was an inglorious and senseless death, a stupid death. But death, all the same.

"*Far*, how could I have forgotten for so long that I am dead?"

"Denial is as deep as the middle of the ocean, as overpowering as an autumn typhoon in the southern seas, and as blinding as an avalanche on a fjord that buries you under a mountain of snow. But now your denial has melted away and you have remembered, so it is time to go."

"But, what about Leif? Oh, *far*, I love him so. I cannot leave him."

"*Ja*, you can and you must. He has a new life now. Don't you want him to be happy? He would have done that for you."

Erika looked back at Leif and his soon-to-be bride. Her heart throbbed with melancholy that she herself would not be the one by his side when he spoke his wedding vows tonight, that she would not be the one to share his bed for years to come, and that she would not be the one to grow old with him.

Her *far* was right. It was time to go. There was nothing left for her here.

Erika took her *far's* huge, rugged hand, pleased that she could feel its strong warmth even though they both were stone cold dead, and walked with him into the mist....

Chapter 15

Jessie Belle's heart ached when she awoke. Her heart felt the pain of overwhelming loss, as if someone had reached into her chest, rustled around, grabbed the core of her being, and squeezed it until it could hardly function. Gloom and fear enveloped her until she couldn't breathe.

A ghost! This dream had been about a Viking haint, a woman who haunted her own longship. She hadn't wanted to give up her craft, her lover, or her life.

Jessie Belle sat up and struggled to gulp in some cool night air. The window to her hotel room was open and fresh mountain air wafted in, as if to save her life. She took more deep breaths.

"I need to get over being traumatized by these dreams," she said aloud to herself. "Apparently they aren't going to go away, so I need to learn to live with them."

"Good observation, dear." Star appeared at her side. Tonight she wore a shiny neon pink and mint green taffeta number with a big gathered circle skirt that looked like it was inspired by a 1960s prom. A small town prom in a smelly gym, with crepe and tissue paper decorations strung across the walls and hanging from the ceiling, and a bad replica of a ballroom globe made out of little squares of mirror glued to a beach ball, circling overhead and letting loose with mirror squares at regular intervals. They'd usually smash onto the floor, but on occasion would strike a geeky kid on the head. Only Star could make an outrageous getup from that schmaltzy era look cute. The rhinestone tiara propped on the top of her beehive hairdo topped it off. "Once you become the real Jessie Belle," she said, "there won't be any need for these visions anymore. But for the time being, they're necessary.

"Now, tell me, what do you think Erika wants you to know about her untimely demise? Why do you think she wanted you—her ancestor who she cares about deeply, by the way—why do you think she wanted you to know about her life and her death?"

Jessie Belle drew her legs up, wrapped her arms around them, and considered the question. "I suppose she wants me to know not to take life for granted. That you never know when it will end, so you need to cherish each moment."

"Correct!" Star said, beaming. "You must live a life that touches your soul, as her life did for her. Even though her beloved sea took her in the end, she wanted no other existence. She felt a connection to it; she loved it. Do you feel connected to your life, Jessie Belle? Do you love your life?"

"Love it? Well, um, I don't know. I mean, I just live it. I haven't had time to think about whether or not I love it."

"Oh, yes, dear, you've had lots of time. But you just fritter your time away. You never take time to think things over, to reflect on how you feel about things. You're always too busy trying to get ahead. Or at least, what you think of as getting ahead. Although, I must say, I've never figured out where it is you think you're going. Has it ever occurred to you that you might have a very narrow point of view about the world? About your life?"

Jessie Belle was stumped. She couldn't think of a word to say.

"That's alright," Star said when silence loomed large. She patted Jessie Belle's hand. "Erika has seen to it that you think about it now."

Jessie Belle pondered that for a minute, while a question took shape in her mind. "Star, these women, the women who made me, as you say, do you go find them and ask them to come to me? Or do they find you? Do they really think I need this much help?"

"Oh, my, the people who made people are always willing to help. Well, the good ones, anyway. It's not like they hang around over your head, watching your every move. They have other things to do, you know! So do I, for that matter. But they drop in to keep a watchful eye and when one of their descended loved ones is in trouble, they like to encourage them. Sometimes they can do it directly. At other times they ask for the aid of an old spirit friend like me, when the person is too, shall I say, dense to take heed of their presence. That would be you."

Jessie Belle ignored the good-natured dig. She said, "So some of my women ancestors came to you, my spirit friend from childhood, and asked for your help?"

"One who you have yet to meet came first. She let the others know you needed them, and they were pleased to share their stories with you. Their stories, after all, are a part of you. The tales of those past lives could help you live a rich, deep life. A life of meaning. But first, you must listen and learn. Do you understand, dear?"

"Yes.

"Wait, though. This story was about Erika. But her mother, her *mor*. Did she really challenge her own husband? A savage Viking named Erik Bloodtooth, no less! Did she really lead a movement to keep him and his gang from coming home in protest of their killings?"

"Yes. Wasn't she amazing? What a gutsy broad!"

"I guess the next time I feel like I'm confronted with a challenge I'll think of her. She'll give me strength."

"Good! Now you think about these things and I'll be back. We're not done yet."

She started to flicker away again, but Jessie Belle said, "One more thing! The get-up." She gestured toward Star's '60s outfit. "You going to a prom or something?" she teased, smiling.

"One can always hope! Actually, I was hoping it would lift your spirits a little and make you smile. And so it did. Toodle-oo!"

She blew a kiss and disappeared, leaving Jessie Belle to ponder the meaning of her life.

"Okey-dokey, Jessie Belle, you stand right there with your back to the railing and Dray can get a shot of you with those magnificent peaks behind you." Joe gave direction as they stood on the deck of the tour boat.

She looked behind her and took in the view. "Magnificent" hardly covered it. The green cliffs vaulting into the air on either side of the fjord were stunning. Each peak, for as far the eye could see, was topped with a glistening cap of snow. She breathed in, letting her lungs revel in the crisp, clean air. Seagulls swooped overhead as they chattered with one another.

"No," Joe said, not unkindly, "you have to look at the camera."

"But looking this way makes more sense," she replied. "It's just so beautiful!"

She hadn't meant to contradict his directions. It was an off-handed remark, stating the obvious. So she was surprised when he agreed.

"You're right. No one in their right mind would be looking at us with this scenery out there. Go ahead, look that way and Dray can catch your profile with the view behind."

She turned toward the railing, spread her hands out onto it on either side of her, and peered down into the water. Its midnight blue color belied its depth, seeming as though it plunged downward as dramatically as the mountains around them plunged upward. Then she scanned the shore, wondering if Erika had ever been right out there somewhere. Perhaps her village had been in one of those lush dales tucked in-between the jagged bluffs, or maybe as a child she'd played on those very cliffs. Or perhaps she'd been right here, sailing her longship, the *Freyja,* down this fjord and out to sea. Jessie Belle would never know for sure, but the thought pleased her.

"Good! Your expression is priceless! It's almost rapture!" Joe noted, indicating a wrap for the shot. "Now let's go talk to the SME."

The SME—subject matter expert—turned out to be two people, an elderly husband and wife team of tour guides who worked on this boat. Waiting in the hold, where the humming engines couldn't be heard, which would make talking for the camera handier, they sat at one of the tables provided for tourists to look out the windows.

After all the introductions and Joe's instructions, the woman began in heavily accented English while Dray filmed her sitting at the table with the backdrop out the window of the majestic view. Jessie Belle sat at her side. The guide explained that this was the Hardangerfjord, one of the largest fjords and the most popular with tourists.

"The fjords were carved out by glaciers throughout many ice ages," she said, "with huge glaciers melting and traveling south. They raked the earth, carrying dirt and rock that was left along the way. That's why geologists love to study it here—it takes them back in time and tells an amazing story of how our land was made."

Her husband, whose English was decidedly better than hers, pointed out the window at the scenery. He continued the saga. "There had once been Nordic settlements up and down these shores, with villages being quite independent of one another. Although the people farmed, the land was not particularly kind to agriculture, so they also developed excellent seafaring skills. Theirs was a lively culture that included farmers, sailors, tradesmen, and skilled laborers. However, in the 700s it was discovered by the first wave of wayward, scavenging Scandinavian sailors that towns up and down the western coast of Europe, up inland rivers that were accessible from the sea, and on the shores of the British Isles were ripe pickings for raiding.

"The independent settlements in Scandinavia started joining together to form large armies of ships, as many as three hundred sailing together at a time. Thus began the take-over of much of Western Europe and the British Isles by the Vikings, who included Danes, Swedes, and Norseman. Sometimes the invasion was complete, with a Viking leader being installed as king in the confiscated land. At other times it was cultural, with languages and beliefs being forever changed by the inculcation of Scandinavian everyday practices. In time, over a period of generations, the invaders settled and assimilated into their surroundings to become farmers, traders, and merchants in the very lands they had once ravaged.

His wife interjected. "Look!" She pointed out the window. "That's the Vorinsfossen Waterfall. Isn't it beautiful?"

Indeed, it was. The conversation paused for some moments while everyone stared in awe at the giant waterfall that seemed to be spilling out of heaven.

Then the man continued, explaining that history tends to portray Vikings as raiders, pillagers, and conquerors. "They were pirates, to be sure," he said, "but so much more! They were settlers and colonists, who brought with them their traditions, including farming techniques, how to organize settlements, language, art, dress, house building, and crafts.

"What most people don't know, when they think of Vikings," he continued, "is that they worked hard but they played hard, too. They sang and danced and played instruments and gambled and had board games. They dressed in brightly colored clothes—bright reds and blues and yellows and greens. They loved jewelry—men and women both wore lots of it. And they favored their tattoos."

Erika's tattoo, which got her killed, popped up in Jessie Belle's mind.

"They were especially interested in establishing new markets for their trade ventures. Many towns in Europe and the British Isles still carry their Nordic names, like anything ending in 'gate.' Ramsgate, Sandgate, and Margate in England are all examples. 'Gate' is an Old Norse word for 'street.'

"And, of course, they were grand sailors, the likes of which no one had seen at that time. We know they sailed to Iceland, Greenland, and Newfoundland, and possibly further down the American shore. They traveled all over Europe, mostly by inland rivers, and across the Mediterranean to the Caspian and Black Seas. They were adventurers more than anything else!"

With her mind constantly wandering back to Erika, Jessie Belle had a hard time concentrating on any more of the lecture. But when they were done, Joe announced it had been a great interview and told her she's asked just the right questions.

The boat tour took up most of the day. The scenery became more and more stunning the further they traveled into the fjord. The coup de grâce was the Folgefonna Glacier at the deepest end. The tour boat docked and waited while passengers took an hour-long hike on the glacier. Joe had prepared Jessie Belle and Dray, so they each wore hiking boots, a jacket, hat, and gloves. They'd also been warned to wear sunglasses, because of the glare from the sun on the white ice and snow of the glacier. The hike was invigorating, even if slippery at times.

Dray filmed endlessly, either live or still shots. Joe was in a heightened state of excitement, directing Dray's shots. "Here! Look at this! Make sure you get this!" he said many times. Dray did as directed, but also wandered around to quell his own artistic desires.

By the time they got back to the tour boat, Joe was thrilled, clearly ecstatic with the day's work. They all were astounded by the haunting beauty of this land and agreed there was an eerie desolateness to it that, because of the lack of distraction from man-made things, made them feel a raw connection to the earth.

This was how Erika must have felt. This was her land. She lived in this grandeur. She sailed these waters. Jessie Belle also felt closer to her ancestor.

When the tour was over, they realized how hungry they were. The tour guides went their way and the three of them stopped at the first place they found, ending up eating cheeseburgers that tasted suspiciously like McDonald's. The connection to nature spell was broken, hurling them back to reality. They had to catch the small plane they'd chartered from Oslo to go back to that city. Early the next morning a couple of hours would be spent at the Viking Ship Museum and then they'd fly to London so that Joe could make his meeting at the CNN London headquarters. Tomorrow night they'd fly to Dublin.

And, thus, the whirlwind trip would continue.

In Oslo, they stayed at a lovely hotel with panoramic views of the city and the hills beyond. Jessie Belle fell into bed expecting a good night's sleep, perhaps enhanced by another dream and visit from Star.

She opened her eyes. Something was amiss in her room. It was dark, or as dark as possible with what she'd learned was "the gloaming," the gray cast over the night because they were so far north the sun only went down for a few hours in the summertime. Even with that, there was something different. She sat up and let her eyes adjust to the darkness. Her cell phone, sitting on the bedside table, told her it was 3:00 a.m.

Nothing. No intruder. Not even Star. Her eyes surveyed the room and fell upon the closed curtains of the window. There were rays of striated, colored light coming through the crack in the center and around the sides. She got up and flung the curtains open.

She thought she'd seen the most fabulous spectacle imaginable at the fjords today, but what glowed before her matched it ooh for aah. The northern lights—she knew they had another more scientific name but couldn't think of it—streamed in flowing rivers of fantastic light across the sky. Jessie Belle had never seen anything like it in her life! Beam after gyrating and pulsating beam, changing colors from green to blue to violet, emanated from the North Pole and danced across the sky. She had to get outdoors to watch it!

Five minutes later she stood in the garden of the hotel, her neck stretched upward to take in nature's show. It was more incredible than anything human beings could ever emulate. Oh, they tried with their laser light shows. But they could never match this: Sheer magic emanating from the earth.

It wasn't five minutes more before other hotel guests started arriving in the garden, everyone focused on the sky. After a few more minutes, Dray showed up at her side with his camera, and then Joe.

Joe said, "The Aurora Borealis!"

They found a bench and sat in virtual silence for a long time. Dray filmed some, but mostly put his camera down and quietly enjoyed the display.

Funny, Jessie Belle thought, *how we've worked so hard, talked so much, and experienced so much over this past week, but sitting here in silence seems to bring us closer together.* She felt that Joe had become a brotherly friend, an enhancement of the casual friendship they already had. In the case of Dray, any claim of friendship was still tenuous. It wasn't a friendship as much as he didn't seem to hate her guts anymore.

But, she assuaged herself, *at least that's something.*

The next morning, tired but still in awe of what they'd had the luck to observe during the night, they headed out for the Viking Ship Museum, the *Vikingskipshuset*. The cab ride was shorter than they'd anticipated, so they arrived early and had to huddle in the entryway for ten minutes before their docent arrived. When he did present himself, they immediately understood that this would be a laze faire ordeal. In khaki pants, a pink polo shirt, and white sneakers, he looked as far removed from a Viking as anyone ever could. However, he was old enough to perhaps have been a Viking, maybe even older. Methuselah came to Jessie Belle's mind. He poked along with a cane but greeted them in a surprisingly hearty voice.

"Good morning, my American friends! Let's do some TV!"

The old codger was sly, Jessie Belle came to think. He enjoyed catching people off guard with his appearance and then wowing them with his knowledge. He taught them that the *drekars*, the Vikings' dragon-headed longships, the troop carriers, had been broad, sleek, flat-bottomed, and fast. That meant they could easily navigate shallow waters like bays and rivers. A marvel of design for that era, each longship held one large, square sail that could be furled when oarsmen were more effective. The sail would come down, the oars would come out, and the ship would play the chameleon of the seas. That was one of the factors that made their raids so successful. The Vikings were the first to use separate cargo vessels, *knarrs*, that were bulkier to carry plunder and trade goods.

This felt more than familiar to Jessie Belle after waking up in a *drekar* in her dream. She'd not seen Erika's life, she'd been in it. Therefore, she felt attached to everything on display at the museum. When they came to the vast room that harbored the ninety-foot-long Oseberg Viking Ship, they all marveled at the craftsmanship.

"Vikings were smart," the docent said in his perfect English, tapping his crinkled forehead. "Their woodworkers used a broad ax rather than a saw to plank oak trees. This allowed them to use iron nails to form the hull. That was the opposite of what shipbuilders in Europe were doing, which was building an inner skeleton first. The end result was a stronger yet more maneuverable vessel.

"This beauty was found preserved in waterlogged clay. It was built around A.D. 890. The Vikings reigned over the seas from about 800 to 1100. When other countries, like Great Britain, figured out better ship designs, the Viking rule was over. But by then they'd settled and acculturated into so many other countries that their influence could never be eliminated."

Jessie Bell longed to touch the beautiful boat with its graceful swirling design and lavish carvings. But, understandably, ropes kept people from getting too close. She closed her eyes for a moment and once again felt Erika laying her hands on the smooth wood on the side of the *Freyja*. Ah, it felt so solid and assuring.

She opened her eyes and wondered if this longboat right here might have been Erika's *Freyja*. Of course, with hundreds, no thousands, of such boats being out there during the three hundred years the Vikings dominated the seas, the odds against this very one being Erika's were decidedly skewed. But one thing Jessie Belle had learned recently was that anything was possible.

Joe called her over to ask the docent a few questions in front of the longship so that Dray could get the shot. When they were done, the docent looked her so intently in the eyes she actually took a step back from him.

"You are a child of the Vikings, are you not?" he inquired.

"Yes, sir. That's why we're here. According to my DNA, this is part of my heritage."

"Pfft! DNA, SchmeeNA. Your red hair gives you away." He touched a strand of her hair. "The first truly red hair came from here." He turned and walked away, and they all shuffled along behind him.

It wasn't long before Joe proclaimed they were done. They hastily bid the docent goodbye and hopped into a taxi. Jessie Belle cocked her head to look back at the museum. There was the old man, a museum in and of himself, standing tall at the front door. He waved at her. She waved back. The taxi sped away.

Chapter 16

Haliakula ran her tongue over her smooth gum, the spot where her two front teeth had once hung. It felt so good! Pleased with the way it had healed after she'd extracted the two decaying little pearls, she mused about her lover's pleasure over the new feeling the last time he'd kissed her. He'd said, "My love, you always surprise me!" She'd grinned at "always," seeing that they'd only been together for two weeks and, although he didn't know it yet, he only had about two more weeks to go. Haliakula didn't like to keep a lover for too long, as the only thing that was "always" was that things became complicated. Oh, she never bedded a taken man, only those grown men who were too young to have yet had a *wahine* or those who were too old to have a living one, so she didn't run into problems with the other women. The problems were always with the men. They wanted to stay!

"'*A'ole*. No," she'd said time and again, "you cannot live with me. I had one *kane*, and I loved him so much that you would not want to try to take his place."

Every man on the island, whether from her village or another, knew that over twenty years ago her *kane,* the father of her five children, sailed off on a carefree fishing trip and did not return. Never mind that he'd been a short, skinny man who'd been much younger than she. They'd loved each other passionately enough to produce a child each year for the time they were together. She pondered the question that often popped into her head: Had her spouse never perished at *kai* at sea, how many children would they have now? She smiled at the thought, an expression that felt different than it had when she'd had a mouth full of teeth. She cackled and ran her tongue over her slick gum once more.

She looked out at the *kai* and thought it couldn't be a more perfect day. But, of course, she thought that just about every day. From her perch on a giant branch of the ancient banyan tree that was so heavy it swooped down from the enormous trunk and out across the ground before rising up again, making a perfect bench in the process, she scanned the scene in front of her. There was the white sand beach, pale blue-green water that turned a deep hue on the horizon, and the light blue sky that also grew richer in color the higher she gazed, with happy white clouds dancing across it.

She cooled herself with a palm-leaf fan and looked down at her big, bare breasts. The dark tan skin that covered them had crinkled over time, just like it had on the rest of her body, after so many years of exposure to the sun. She had become heavier each year, and when she sat, her breasts sagged to the point of resting on her big belly, which was wrapped in the soft tapa cloth she'd made out of crushed coconut shells. The sight of her own form pleased her. It indicated that she'd lived a prosperous life. Her course hair, more gray now than black, streamed over her shoulders and down her back. She pulled on a strand and thought about how fortunate she was to have grown more beautiful with each passing year. Not many women lived such a good, long life.

Her meandering thoughts flitted away until her mind came to rest on nothingness. Her ears found solace in the secret messages the sea gulls called to one another, and her nostrils delighted at the mingling scents of the orchids, eucalyptus, and ginger that grew nearby. Languidly, she let her eyes revel in the scene before her, wandering out to *kai* again.

It was at that moment that she saw it.

It was so far away that it could have been a floating bird, a piece of lost wood, or an innocent speck of nothing. Yet somehow Haliakula knew what it was from the instant her eyes fell upon it.

They had returned.

A gaggle of laughing boys stumbled through the thick foliage behind and onto the beach to her left side, pushing and shoving one another in rugged play.

"Boys!" Haliakula called. They all looked up in surprise. They hadn't seen her there sitting in the shade on the branch of the old banyan tree.

"Yes, grandmother," the tallest boy responded.

"Do your old grandmother a favor and go get Leilani and bring her to me."

"Yes, grandmother!" The whole cluster disappeared back into the greenery, as if an invisible fishing net bound them together.

As she waited, Haliakula felt her heartbeat quicken in anticipation. Her life and the lives of many others were about to change forever.

Before long, Leilani appeared at her side, quiet in her approach, as always. She'd clearly just come from the pool where she loved to frolic under the waterfall. Her luminescent amber skin glistened with moisture and her long black hair shimmered with wetness. Her tapa cloth had hastily been thrown around her waist, covering little and blatantly displaying her immodesty.

"Grandmother, are you alright?" the thirteen-year-old girl asked, sitting down beside the old woman and taking her hand.

"Yes, my love, I am fine. It is you I want to talk about." Haliakula ran her hand down the back of Leilani's hair, enjoying the sensation of touching this grandchild that she loved so much. She had a dozen grandchildren and over the years had discovered that, just like with her own children, there was a special place in her heart for each and every offspring that squirmed its way into the world. No matter how many of them there were, Haliakula's heart always expanded to take in each one and to love it for being the wonderful, unique child that it was. Leilani had been her first grandchild, however, so her spot in Haliakula's heart was front and center.

Leilani looked up at her with patient, respectful, expectant eyes. Set in a perfectly beautiful face, they were oval eyes, sea green rather than brown like everyone else's. They were the eyes of her great grandmother, of Haliakula's own mysterious mother.

"Leilani," Haliakula said softly. "Look." She pointed to the horizon.

Leilani looked, at first uncomprehending, and then stretching her neck when her eyes finally took it in. "Grandmother! What is it?" She squeezed Haliakula's hand in excitement.

"I have a story to tell you, my dear. A rather long story. But we have time, as it will take the big canoe all morning to reach our shores."

"Oh, grandmother! Is it my grandfather who I have never met? Has he finally come back to us?" Leilani stood up and hopped with glee.

"No, no," Haliakula said, surprised at this take on the situation. "He would have come to us long before now, if he had been able to. He has been in the land of the *Akua* for many years. The gods are taking good care of him. I am sure of it!

"This is something else. Something that could change your life, if you wish."

Leilani's eyes widened as she sat back down and leaned in close. "Oh, please tell me, grandmother!" she pleaded, almost breathless in anticipation.

"Do you remember the story of your great-grandmother, of my mother, Kaliniaa?"

"Yes, of course. You have told me many times. She was from another island, one that is far, far away. Not in this *kai*, the Pacific, but an island called Eire in another *kai*, the Atlantic. Is that right?"

"Yes. Very good. You remember it well."

"I do! You said she told you that her island was also very green and beautiful, but that they had different kinds of trees and flowers and it was not as warm each day as it is here. She liked it here better.

"Grandmother!" Leilani exclaimed, light dawning in her mind as she looked out to sea. "Is that a canoe from your mother's island?"

"Yes, I believe that it is. Or an island near hers, another one that would be very much like hers.

"You see, there is a part of the story I have not told you, because it is very hard to understand. My mother always told me that someday another big canoe, a 'ship' she called it in her language, would come. She said that *Kakolika Loma mikanelies*, people she called 'Roman Catholic missionaries,' would want to take me or one of my children or one of my grandchildren, or my children's children's children, if they came after I die. They would want to take someone back to their island with them. It is their way."

"Why? Why do they like to take people away from their homes?"

"Because they believe they have the right to show their masters back at their homeland that they have traveled and worked hard to accomplish their mission."

"What is their mission?"

"To turn us away from our *Akua* and to make us follow their god instead. You see, they believe in only one god and that everyone on earth, all human beings on all of the islands in all of the *kai,* should follow this one god."

"How strange!"

"Yes, I know. But my mother said that, although some of them were evil, many of them were kind people who truly believed they were helping others by leading them to their god."

"What do you think, grandmother?"

"Oh, I think they are crazy! But they are the people of my mother, so we must be kind to them. They might be a little brainsick, but they mean well.

"Let me tell you the rest of the story about my mother. Here her name was Kaliniaa, but when she was a child she was 'Colleen' in Eire. Her parents loved her very much and she loved them, but they died of a terrible disease when she was young. So she went to live with women who believe in this one god, women called 'nuns.' She became a nun. They wore long black robes, like heavy *tapas* over their whole bodies, even over their hair, which made them look like big black birds."

Leilani ran her fingers through her unbound hair and sighed. "Were they not hot in those robes?"

"Yes, very. My mother hated them. But she had to wear them anyway.

"She always had a desire to get out of that place she was in. She dreamed of traveling and seeing new places. So when she was asked to become a *mikanele*, a missionary, to teach other people about their god, she was happy to volunteer to go!

"She got on a big canoe, a ship, with a lot of other people and sailed and sailed and sailed. She threw up every day at first and was miserable. She was sorry she had ever yearned for adventure. But eventually she became used to the rhythm of the *kai* beneath her feet and came to like sailing. They went west from Eire and stopped first at islands they ran into along the way. Then they sailed south and further south until it became very, very cold and she thought she would die. She said that water would become so cold that it would get as hard as teak and their ship could hardly plow through it."

"Grandmother, are you making that up?"

"No, but I think she probably did. She always did like to embellish her stories.

"Anyway, they finally rounded the cold end of the huge island they had been trying to get around, and they went north and west until they came upon us. She said, 'I thought I had died and gone to heaven!' She loved it here that much.

"The crew of the ship took food and rest, and then continued their journey. They asked for one person to go with them, someone they could show their masters back home, and a family from the other side of the island gave them their son. They did not tell the sailors that the son had a very bad temper. Anyway, a man in a long black robe, called a 'priest,' and the woman who would become my mother were left behind to teach our people about their god.

"But the big canoe had only been gone for three days when the priest grabbed his chest, fell to the ground, and died. My mother got down on her knees, said a prayer over his dead body, made an odd gesture around her head and chest, and then stood up and tore off her long black robes. She told me that our people were surprised and pleased to learn that she had long red hair. They thought she looked just like our red-haired goddess of fire and lava and volcanoes, *Peve*. Within a month she had cleaved to my father, and that's where I came from."

"Grandmother, that is a wonderful story!

"But are you telling me that these people on the big canoe might want someone to go back with them and it can be me, if I want?"

"Yes, dear. That's what I am saying. You always have yearned for adventure, just like your great-grandmother. You have her green eyes and I think you have a soul like hers, as well."

"If I go, will I have to wear big black robes? I do not want to go if I have to do that."

"No, only nuns wear those. But you would have to cover up your breasts. These people have a very strange idea that women are not to show their breasts to men."

"Why not? Men love looking at our breasts! Why, women love looking at breasts, too! After all, they are made for feeding babies." Leilani looked down at her own pert, bare bosom.

"I know. I do not understand it but it is their way, so if you go with them, you would have to live by their ways. You would also have to learn their language. And their food, according to my mother, is very dry and dull. So you have a lot to think about if you want to consider going."

"I want to go!"

"Leilani, think about it first. The big canoe will be here for many weeks before they leave again. You have time to think. That is why I wanted to tell you the story and to warn you about the good and bad of going. I knew that if you wanted to go, no one could stop you. But it is important for you to be sure that this is what you really want.

"We would all miss you more than I can imagine. We would all be so pleased if you would choose not to go. But, in the end, it is your choice. Just make sure it is a choice and not a reckless act."

Leilani got up and bent down to kiss her grandmother on the cheek. "I will think about it," she promised. But when the girl looked back out across the water, the speck was closer and no longer a speck. It could be seen that it was a mighty ship with many white sails. The fascination in her green eyes shone like fire spewing out of a *Peve* volcano, and Haliakula feared that her beloved granddaughter was soon to be lost to her forever. But at the same time, that very granddaughter would discover herself. It was a sacrifice that Haliakula would be forced to accept.

When the big canoe with many white sails came close enough for the islanders to swim out to it, Haliakula could see the reactions of those aboard. A lot of men in ragged clothes stood along the side of the ship and ecstatically waved their arms at the naked young women swimming out to greet them. A tall man in long black robes, who must be one of those priests, seemed shocked and held his palms out as if to fend off the greeters. A woman, also in a long black robe that covered her from head to foot, so she must be a nun, stood at his side, frantically moving her lips as she looked down at a black thing in her hands.

Haliakula wondered why those one-god people liked black so much! Did they not know it was hot and depressing?

She scanned the throng of swimmers, trying to pick out Leilani. All of them had young, slim, tan-colored bodies, their rounded bare bottoms bobbing in and out of the gently rolling waves as they glided as gracefully as baby dolphins toward the ship. The long black hair flowing down their backs was the same on every one of them, so it was hard to tell which one might be her granddaughter.

She felt the girl's presence before she looked up to see Leilani silently standing at her side. The young one had carefully secured the tapa cloth around her waist, covering any hint of her body from its center to the middle of her thighs. And around her chest she wore her best ceremonial tapa, the one her grandmother had made for her. Using the tip of a gull's feather and dye made from blackberries, Haliakula had painstakingly decorated the cloth with the pictures her mother had taught her to draw, pictures from her homeland, Eire. There was the cross with equal sides and a circle around it, the swirling spiral, and the dual eel-like creatures that spun around one another. In row upon row, the designs alternated repeatedly to fill the entire surface. Haliakula inhaled deeply upon seeing that Leilani had fastened the tapa cloth in such a way that her pretty breasts were nowhere in sight.

Her granddaughter had made her decision. Or perhaps it had been made before it had even been presented to her. All that was left to do was pray to the *Akua* that Leilani's life in a faraway land would be happy and long, and that above all she would carry the love of her family here with her wherever she may go, while finding even more love in a family of her own.

Haliakula ran her tongue over the smooth patch of gum in her mouth where her front teeth had once resided. She didn't realize that from that day forward every time she thought of Leilani, she would do it again. It would become a habit that would show that she missed her first grandchild, a longing that would never diminish but would not hinder her happiness, either, because she would never allow anything to do that.

Chapter 17

Jessie Belle awoke from her nap on the plane and mused that this was the first time she'd had an ancestor dream that didn't need an ending from Star. It was odd, though, that after being so steeped in Viking visions, she had suddenly dreamt about a Polynesian woman. Haliakula had obviously lived on an island in the Pacific during idyllic times before Europeans ravaged their culture.

The meaning of the dream was the easiest to figure out so far. There were a number of clear messages.

First of all, this roly-poly Polynesian ancestor thought herself beautiful. No hundred belly crunches a day, no twelve-hundred-calorie-a-day starvation diet, no concern about being thin. In fact, a slim body on an elder person connoted a lack of prosperity in her culture. So no doubt Haliakula wanted Jessie Belle to give herself a break on that score. Jessie Belle poked herself in the arm. It was more like a twig than a branch of her body.

Secondly, Haliakula knew how to relax, how to take in the sights and sounds and scents of her fabulous surroundings. Sitting by that stream in Austria had been the first time Jessie Belle had done that since, well, forever. Maybe she needed to start paying more attention to what was going on around her and less to what was going on inside her own head.

Most importantly, Haliakula was happy. Simply happy. Bad things could happen in her life, and—still—she always came back to being loving, light-hearted, and grateful. *But is that really possible in this day and age?* Jessie Belle wondered. Apparently Haliakula thought so or she wouldn't have bothered paying her descendent a visit.

Furthermore, Haliakula had done it all without a permanent man in her life. Once her husband disappeared, she never took another. Jessie Belle mulled that over for a long time. She had never, ever considered life without a husband. That had been her primary goal since she was three years old. She'd been planning her wedding since the day she turned twelve. Her mother had drilled the importance of matrimony into her head every day of her existence: "When you get married you'll have more time for shopping and traveling," or "When you marry a rich man, you can just have your own TV show, seeing that you like being on TV so much."

The Disney fairytale videos she had watched growing up had reinforced the happily-ever-after marriage mentality. The princess *always* ended up marrying the prince. On the seamier side, her mother's favorite television show while Jessie Belle grew up was *Dynasty*. Wedding after wedding on the nighttime soap, interjected by divorces, of course, produced outlandish designer wedding dresses that only the eighties could have appreciated or tolerated.

And then there was Jessie Belle's beloved Dream Bride Barbie Doll—complete with white satin designer gown—who married her dreamboat, Ken, in his tailored black tux. There had also been her favorite movie as a teen, *Titanic*. It came out when she was seventeen and in the throes of juggling multiple crushes on boys. She saw the romantic-disaster movie six times on the big screen and wept each time at the outstretched arms and undying love of Rose and Jack. She felt certain if that nasty old iceberg hadn't come along and ruined everything, the two improbable lovers would have married and lived happily ever after. After Jack managed to get rich, of course.

Yes, the ultimate prize in Jessie Belle Church's world had always been to marry a prominent, rich husband. Sure, she understood that she was ambitious when it came to her career. But marriage was a woman's "real" career. In fact, it surprised her that she was still single. Wasn't she quite a catch herself? But now, with Robert having deserted her, it might be a long while before she'd have that kind of relationship again. Was Haliakula trying to tell her that she could be happy without a man? Jessie Belle couldn't imagine such a thing.

It occurred to her that her mother would be appalled to think that someone like Haliakula, a haggle-toothed, gray-haired, fat, old crone, had been their progenitor. For reasons she couldn't quite reckon, it pleased Jessie Belle to know that her socialite—yes, even snooty—mother was also a descendent of the carefree, nature-loving islander. Her mother was anything but carefree and her idea of communing with nature was to order her yardman to plant some new petunias.

There was one more message in the dream, Jessie Belle suddenly realized. Once again, the science of DNA might be astounding in its discoveries but it still didn't know everything. Who would have guessed that an Irish nun back then would have found her way to a remote island in the Pacific and that her great-granddaughter would find her way to... Jessie Belle didn't know where. She hoped she'd find out. Her curiosity about Leilani had been fanned, and she clamored to know what happened next.

These dreams, at first frightening and stressful, had turned into the best mystery she'd ever known because it was the mystery of her own life. She'd grown to welcome the nights when her sleep would be disturbed by these tales of the ancient women who had made her.

Funny, how I've come to accept these tales as true.

Star's relentless visits had no doubt contributed to that. She hadn't come last night, so Jessie Belle missed the old girl.

Oh well, I'm sure I'll see her again soon.

With that reassuring thought she scampered off the British Air plane that had just landed at Heathrow Airport in London. This time both Dray and Joe were waiting for her outside the ramp. The three of them zigzagged their way through the crowd without trying to talk above the cacophony of voices, screeching warning bleeps of the assistance carts, and other indiscernible noises that echoed through the cavernous terminal.

It wasn't until they stood waiting at the baggage claim carousel that Joe spoke up. "Okay, my little tribe of gypsies, here's the plan. This evening Dray and I meet with the guys at the office to work on some editing. Tomorrow I meet with the marketing guys to put together a final promo. Youse guys can mill around, bored and annoyed and getting on each other's nerves, no doubt, while you wait for me to get done. We catch our plane to Dublin at six tomorrow evening.

"By the way, tomorrow we're putting together a teaser for the big finale, the plantation visit back home with you and your mother." He nodded at Jessie Belle. "But don't worry. I haven't forgotten that we'll need to keep you two separated."

Dray and Joe chuckled but ceased when Jessie Belle shot them a laser glare.

"Okay, well, anyway," Joe said, "the whole thing has been a great success so far. I'm sure our Dublin gig will be no different. Or the interviews back home," he added pointedly. "We're on the home stretch and should be proud of all of our hard work. You've both done a great job."

"You make it easy," Dray said sincerely.

"Oh, Joe, you know I love you," Jessie Belle relented. "Even if you do like to make fun of me."

"I can't help myself! You're such an easy mark! Doncha think?"

This time they all laughed as their luggage showed up and they pulled it off the carousel.

Jessie Belle adored the big, old, black Rolls Royce taxi cab that looked like a 1940s gangster get-away car. Like most cabs in London, it had wonderful, roomy backseats, three-seaters on either side facing each other. The taxi took them from Heathrow Airport to the Ritz London Hotel on Piccadilly Street. It was all so British.

Joe and Dray disappeared as soon as they checked in. So Jessie Belle thought that she'd get settled into her room, then roam around in the shops downstairs and grab a bite of dinner in one of the many cafes or restaurants. Then she supposed she'd dream of another ancestor again, even though she'd fallen asleep on the plane and dreamed then.

But none of that came to pass.

The bed was so enormous and inviting that as soon as she entered her "superior queen" room, Jessie Belle slipped off her shoes and laid down for a feel. The next thing she knew it was four o'clock in the morning. A little disappointed that she hadn't dreamt, she got up, brushed her teeth, and went back to bed for two more hours.

That morning, for the first time since this assignment began, she had no orders and no plans. There was absolutely no place she needed to be. She took advantage of the reprieve and did a lot of nothing, scuffling around her room, ordering room service for breakfast, watching off-kilter British TV shows, and reading the tourist brochures left on the desk.

It was a much needed break from the chaos of travel. This non-stop, never-ending assignment was really taking a physical toll. But that was always true of road assignments. "Road warriors," that's what traveling journalists and their crews called themselves, with good reason. So she savored her R & R away from the battle.

By noon she decided she'd used up her quota of lay-about, ne'r-do-well slovenliness, so she put on a pair of jeans and a tank top and went downstairs in search of lunch.

The moment she stepped out of the elevator, there he was. Dray, looking like a dream come true, stood in the middle of the opulent, old-world lobby, chatting with the concierge. He didn't see her, which gave her an opportunity to gawk at him. Why hadn't she noticed he was this handsome when they'd first met? Oh, sure, she'd thought him good looking in a bohemian sort of way, but why hadn't she noticed *this?*

Suddenly she knew why. Her mind had been so closed in on Robert, she hadn't truly taken Dray in. Or any other man, for that matter. She'd been oblivious to the world around her. It had been like voluntarily locking herself into a cloister so she wouldn't have to face the rest of the world.

Well, Robert, the SOB, was gone and she had unlocked her life. Her mind was *now open!* She mustered up her courage and as soon as the concierge said "Cheerio!" and went away, and she walked up to Dray.

"Hey," she said.

He turned toward her. "Hey," he said.

"I was just thinking of getting some lunch. You hungry?"

"Actually, I just ate."

"Oh. Oh, well, okay then. I'll just go, um, eat."

"Sure. Hey, maybe we could meet up here after and do something."

"Yeah! In about an hour, right here?"

He winked and saluted. "I shall return." Then he turned and walked out the front door.

Jessie Belle had never actually swooned before, but now she knew how Scarlett felt every time she fell in love. The hour droned on into what felt like forever as Jessie Belle attempted to eat a dull lunch of shepherd's pie at a cafe down the street from the hotel. It had sounded good on the menu, but in reality it tasted more like a sheep patty than a pie that a shepherd might have made. Anticipation quelled her appetite anyway.

When the appointed hour finally arrived, she fled back to the lobby of the Ritz.

There he was, standing in the center of the lobby again, looking around. He smiled slightly when he saw her.

"Hi," she said, suddenly feeling shy. It was an emotion that was as foreign to her as Yankee pride.

"Hi," he said.

She looked at him. He looked back at her. She rocked on the balls of her feet. He stuffed his hands into the pockets of his jeans.

"What do you want to do?" he finally asked. "Maybe get a cup of coffee?"

"Sure. That's fine."

"Or is there something else you'd rather do?"

"Like what?"

"I don't know. I don't live here, remember? I don't know what there is to do."

"It is a rather large city. I bet we'll find something if we just walk around."

"Okay."

They walked down the block and into lovely Hyde Park, following the length of the Serpentine, a small lake. They didn't talk much, other than to comment on the verdant vegetation and fragrant flowers.

She mused over her original assessment of Dragan Dlugitch. She'd thought him a barbaric, unkempt, shaggy-haired, creature-man who didn't know any better than to dress in jeans and a tee shirt. *The no-name gorilla.* Now, every time that animal nonchalantly touched her arm or pointed out something of interest, she melted like a two-bit hot fudge sundae on a steamy Georgia day in July. *My, how things change. And how sticky they get.*

On the far side of the park they exited at Sussex Gardens Street, where they window-shopped until coming upon a "Tea Emporium" that promised gourmet coffee. They went inside.

The header of the door was so low it made Dray stoop, as was often the case in buildings constructed hundreds of years ago when people were generally shorter. They stepped out of the sunlight and into a dim space that looked as though the decor hadn't been touched since the Victorian Era. Tin tile ceiling, black-and-white checkerboard marble floor, and scrolly metal tables and chairs spoke of an era gone by. It was spotlessly clean, with a fresh spray of heather and roses in a small vase on each table, and beams of splayed light filtering through the beveled glass windows in the front. Jessie Belle thought it utterly enchanting, but it left her feeling as though she should be wearing a bustier and bustle. Apparently popular with the locals, it was packed. Jessie Belle and Dray spied one unoccupied table in the back and made a beeline for it.

Once they'd each ordered coffee from a goth waitress who looked entirely out of synch with her antique surroundings, there was nothing else to do but talk to each other. Dray didn't seem inclined to strike up a conversation, so Jessie Belle gave it a stab.

"So, Dray, you a Falcons fan?" Most guys liked football, so she figured that was a safe start.

"No," he said. "You?"

"No. Not really." She cleared her throat and looked around. Maybe there was something or someone in the cafe they could talk about.

"The Braves," he said.

"What?" she asked, not understanding.

"The Braves. You know, the baseball team? I like them. My oldest son is a big fan, so he's got me into American baseball."

"Oh! That's nice."

"Do you like baseball?"

For a split second she considered lying. But the truth spilled out. "No, not really. I mean, I've never paid any attention to it, so I guess I don't know if I like it or not."

"Ah, I see." Now it was his turn to clear his throat.

God save the queen! she thought as their coffee arrived. They fussed over fixing up their brews with cream and sugar, then sipped heartily.

"Um-m. Good," she said.

"Yes. Very good."

Then it struck her so clearly she felt like saying "Duh!" and bopping herself on the head. He mentioned his son. His kids: That's what he would undoubtedly feel comfortable talking about.

Half an hour later she gave herself a mental pat on the back. *When you're right, you're right.* After asking if his son played baseball, the flood gates opened and Dray told her about his oldest, Demetri, who was thirteen and loved nothing more than playing baseball. Then there was Andre, ten, who was a brainy computer nerd. Although it seemed that Dray adored the boys, the apple of his eye was the youngest, Lily, who was seven.

"She's all skinny and gawky and hasn't grown into herself yet. I remember when my sister was like that. And then she grew up to be a beautiful woman! Lily will, too, I'm sure of it. But it's impossible to make her believe that when she looks in the mirror and all she sees are awkward angles and glasses and braces and hair that sticks out every-which-way." He gestured to illustrate hair going here and there, and Jessie Belle found herself in a belly laugh. "She's adorable!" Dray insisted, and Jessie Belle realized it was the most animated she'd ever seen him. Gone was the aloof stranger. He'd let down his hair and was enjoying himself with her for the first time.

"My mother and I try not to let her get all caught up in the 'image' thing that has so many American girls strangled around their throats. We want her to feel confident but not—what do you call it?" He snapped his fingers trying to come up with the English words.

"A spoiled brat diva?"

"Oh, no, Jessie Belle," he sat back and put his hand over his heart in mock pain. "Are you never going to let me forget that's what I called you in the beginning?"

"Probably not," she teased. He'd become so happy talking about his children that he was more appealing than ever. His big, smoky gray eyes danced with humor. His tall, strong body electrified with excitement. His melodious, deep voice hypnotized with accented charm. Jessie Belle had an impulse to kiss the appealing line that creased his cheek. Impulse in check, she returned to their conversation.

"I think," she said, "you're saying you don't want her to be conceited, thinking she's the hottest thing alive, but you do want her to understand her own self-worth. Her worth as a woman."

"Yes! That's it. I want her to be confident in her self-worth. I want her to know she can be and do anything she pleases. That's the way my sister was as a woman. I hope my mother and I can instill that in Lily.

"She has a fascination with you. She loves to watch you. You and the other women newscasters. She thinks you're all the smartest, most beautiful women on earth. You're 'like, totally awesome.'"

"We are, aren't we?" She grinned mischievously.

"Well, now, according to my mother you may be all that, but you are too skinny. She said I need to bring you over so she can feed you a proper meal. My mother loves to feed everybody."

Now Jessie Belle laughed out loud. "My mother doesn't think it's possible to be too skinny. Or too rich."

"Ah, she's one of those types?"

"O-o-oh yes." She took the final sip of her coffee to mask her discomfort that the conversation had turned to her bridge-playing, scotch-drinking, highbrow mother.

The waitress appeared and filled up their cups, so they took a few moments to doctor up them up again.

"What about the rest of your family?" Dray eventually asked.

To her horror, tears sprang to Jessie Belle's eyes.

"What is it?" Dray wanted to know, leaning in and putting his hand on hers. "Is something wrong?"

What happened next was as much of a shock to her as it was to him. It was as if an overwrought dam broke and the words came gushing out.

She gave it no forethought. She didn't weigh the consequences. She forgot to control herself in measured words. Instead she spilled her guts and told Dray all about the dreams she'd been having since this trip began. She painstakingly described each ancestor woman, starting with Clacka and ending with Haliakula. She told him there would probably be more.

"So, you see," she concluded, "when you ask about my family, that's a lot of people on my mind right now.

"You probably think I'm crazy. Visions of ancestors and an old spirit friend from my childhood—pretty whacko stuff. That's okay. I suspect I'm Looney tunes, too."

"I don't know what to think, except for one thing." He bent closer, forcing her to look him in the eyes. "You are not crazy. A little stressed, a lot stressed, perhaps. You have had a bad time of things lately, what with that jackass boyfriend and all. But my mom would believe you completely. She's a total believer in the supernatural."

"Wow. That's the polar opposite of my mama. If I ever told her about these wild dreams, she'd send me straight to her psychiatrist.

"What about you, Dray. What do you think?"

"Me? I'm a guy, so what do I know? Except that you are not crazy." He smiled reassuringly and chucked her on the chin.

"You really think Robert is a jackass?" she asked, somewhat mollified.

"Pfft!" He swatted the air. "Like, totally!"

That brought a smile to her lips, but suddenly a man at the next table stood up and declared to his companions that he had to run. At that, both she and Dray clamored for their cell phones to check the time. Dray pulled his out of its belt holder before she could find hers in her purse. He said, "Oh crap! We have to get back or we'll miss the plane!"

He threw money on the table and they trotted back to the CNN building to find Joe standing on the sidewalk frantically looking up and down. When he spied them, he motioned for them to hurry, and they all barreled into the taxicab that would take them to the airport.

Well, gut-spilling time is over. It's back to work. With that thought, Jessie Belle tried not to think about the personal barrier she'd just let down for the first time in her life. She'd shared her deepest, wildest, weirdest, and most honest thoughts with a man.

It scared her stiff.

The rhythmic hum of the jet engines calmed her erratic mind, like a mantra that allows one to not think. *Don't think about what a fool you made of yourself when you got drunk and threw yourself at Dray, undoubtedly making him think you're a scumbag. And don't think about how you spilled your guts to him today, probably making him think you're the scum in the scumbag. Don't think about how hopeless that all seems and how there's not one good reason on earth that the guy would ever be interested in you.* No, she refused to let a couple of dour thoughts ruin her life, so she let the calming hum of the engines sooth her. She dismissed the annoying little ruminations, a skill she'd been mastering since childhood.

This time she sat in a big, cushy leather first class seat by the window on a British Air plane. Joe sat beside her, already nodding off. Dray was across the aisle, on his computer. It wasn't long before her mind meandered into the reality that this trip was over and soon they'd be going home.

Home sweet home. Jessie Belle had started this assignment furious that she'd had to leave the place. Now she dreaded going back. Her mother was so upset with her over "Robert's big dump" that she didn't want to face her.

Besides, she'd sort of become excited about reporting again. Not just sitting in front of a camera and reading off of a teleprompter, which any advanced sixth-grader could do, but actually putting herself out there, meeting new people, being thrust into other cultures, and finding out what's going on in the world. Even when she was a cub reporter, she'd never savored the mission like this. All she'd thought about back then was getting behind that desk in Atlanta. She didn't really pay attention to the impact of what she was covering.

This special "Ancestry Quest" series was different. She had to admit that Harry, her crotchety old boss back home, had been right. Viewers were eating this up. And not just because it was about her. From the tweets and emails they sent, it was clear that viewers saw themselves in these daily reports. They were grasping the fact that their ancestors had made similar journeys and that they had little concept of the lives of the people who had made them. The series was a huge hit, despite the Robert/Bridget/Jessie Belle triangle scandal. That was old news anyway, since yesterday when thirty-three-year-old American rock star Britney Arrows had impulsively married an unknown nineteen-year-old French photographer. For the time being, until the next troubled entertainer did something equally inexplicable and stupid, the waning star took up every available inch and moment of media gossip space. So Jessie Belle's viewers were over the shock that she'd been so summarily dumped in her personal life and replaced by her professional replacement. Now they were tuning in to see the real stories. They were hooked.

The very thought gave Jessie Belle a thrill. This was real journalism. The best she'd ever done. She was at the top of her game, except it wasn't a game. This was real life.

Funny, she thought, *how my life has just fallen to pieces and I'm doing better work than ever. It's as if those women who made me have inspired me to take the shattered pieces of my life and put them back together again in a new formation.*

Suddenly thirsty to learn more about the very project that had inspired this entire assignment, the National Geographic Genographic Project, she took the now tattered report out of her bag and read it once again. She wanted to be ready when she did the final interview with Edwin Sampson, the assistant director of the project, in Dublin tomorrow. Satisfied that she was as prepared as possible, she put the papers away and stared out the window.

Below, the Irish Sea was breathtakingly beautiful. Then, there it was on the horizon, the island that would be her final stepping stone before returning home: Ireland. It was every bit as lush and green as rumored. She'd never had a job here before and had never thought there was any reason to vacation here, so it would be her first time setting foot on Irish soil. For reasons she didn't yet understand, the very thought gave her a thrill.

Chapter 18

Kathleen gazed at Morrough's handsomeness. The strong brow, straight nose, sensuous lips, and square jaw all made for the most comely, masculine face she'd ever laid eyes on. Unfortunately, it was dead.

She didn't know what to feel. He'd been her husband for thirty years, she'd loved him every minute of every day of every one of those years, and yet she was furious at him for dying on her.

She wanted to yell and scream at him, just like she had so many times before.

"How could you forget to milk the cow? The children need to be fed now!"

"Why did you stay at the pub so long? There's work to be done!"

"*How dare you leave me?*" she wanted to shout. "*Here we are, in the prime of our lives; I'm only forty-three and you're only forty-five years old, with a mere three of our nine children left in the house and our final bairn in my belly, and you up and kill yourself! How dare you?*"

"Mrs. O'Sullivan," the old man broke into her tumultuous thoughts. He was one of the hundreds of men and women and children who had ridden or walked from all around County Galway to attend the wake at the O'Sullivan farm. Morrough had been well known and much loved. The old man cleared his throat and said, "I'm so sorry for your loss. It was such a terrible accident. Could have happened to any of us who farm. He was one of the kindest, most friendly men I've ever known. Never met a stranger, that Morrough. Always helping out a neighbor. He helped me once, when I had to rebuild me pig sty. He had me and me wife laughing so hard at his stories. Why, I think even the pigs were laughing! It's so tragic, so tragic." His condolences waned as he hedged away.

Tragic, my arse, Kathleen thought. *It was stupid carelessness! The eejit! Getting in-between that asinine red plow of his—who in hell ever heard of a red plow, anyway—and poor old Jennie, the workhorse. Any farmer worth a penny knows you never do that. Old Jennie spooked and bucked, pulling the plow right into Morrough's gut as he bent over to remove a rock. Killed him on the spot. If he'd just coaxed old Jennie onward and steered the plow around and in front of the rock, he would have been safe. That was all he'd needed to do. But, ná-á! As usual, he acted on impulse. Didn't give a whit for his anam cara, the care of his soul mate, of me. And me without a pot to piss in all these years, being married to a farmer, when I could have married one of those fancy, rich boys in town.*

All because I loved you, Morrough O'Sullivan! You should not have died on me, you feckless fool!

Kathleen began to sob again. Others took that as mourning and left her alone. Little did they know her tears poured forth from full-blown Irish temper.

Mourners stood aside and whispered in pity at how the normally beautiful woman looked haggard today. Her red hair, usually tightly braided and wrapped neatly around her head, had escaped in random spots and hung in disarray. The flawless porcelain skin of her face was now dotted with red blotches from crying. And a widow's required black mourning attire, "widow's weeds," did nothing to enhance her appearance. For as long as anyone could remember, Kathleen had always favored bright colors, so black on her seemed especially stark.

"Mo Mo," Fiona's soft childish voice somehow carried through the din of so many jabbering adults in the cottage. Fiona, Kathleen's six-year-old granddaughter, stood at her side, tugging gently at her black wool skirt. "Would you tell us the story of how you and Po Po met?"

Kathleen dried her eyes with her lace-trimmed white linen handkerchief and looked down to see a number of her granddaughters, from the toddlers to the younger teens, huddled around. They all appeared as though they didn't know what to do with this sobbing version of their usually merry grandmother, whom they affectionately called Mo Mo. She couldn't suppress a smile. They'd heard the love story many times before, but the girls in the family could never seem to get enough of it.

"Of course, me loves," Kathleen said as she sat down in her rocking chair in front of the fireplace. As usual, the girls gathered at her feet, sitting on the colorful braided rag rug that she'd made last year to replace the one that had faded to the point of looking like mud. This scene in front of her, hopeful young faces looking up from the background of the gay floor covering, warmed the cockles of her heart. Her own pre-teen daughter, the same age of her oldest grandchildren, joined them, causing a stab of pain to pierce Kathleen's heart for knowing that her children had lost their father. Not wanting to disappoint any of these dears, she set her anger at Morrough aside in order to tell her tale.

"Well, me loves, as you know, we met at the County Galway Fair, a long, long, time ago...."

As the girls listened raptly to their *seanchai*, storyteller, grandmother's tale, the young boys, at a loss for something to do with their usually entertaining Po Po dead on the table in the middle of the room, sought out their ancient progenitor, their *athair mór,* grandfather who was great-grandfather to some of them and great-great-grandfather to others. He was "older than dirt," he often declared, and he was their Mo Mo Kathleen's father. Her Jewish father.

"*Athair mór,* will you tell us about the shipwreck again?" gangly seven-year-old Tommy O'Sullivan begged.

Aye!" another lad chimed in. "Tell about how it hit the rocks and you had to swim in the cold, stormy sea!"

"And how the fishermen risked their lives to come out in the storm and save you!" a boy said.

"Then you met great-grandmamma and thought she was the most beautiful woman in the world, so you stayed right here and married her," added Sean Levin, a teen who'd just reached puberty and discovered his sexual drive, causing him to suddenly be interested in love stories.

"*Ná,*" Tommy disagreed. "Leave out the mushy stuff. Tell us about the shipwreck!" The lad bashed his knuckles together while making a crashing noise. He looked around for approval, and found it with nods and slaps on the back.

Levi Levin chuckled. "I think you boys know this story better than I do. But, I'll tell it again anyway. Come out here." He gestured for them to join him outdoors. The eldest boy took his elbow opposite the arm that used a cane and helped him hobble outside, where they clustered under the shade of a giant oak tree in the front garden. Levi sat on a stool and his many young male descendants stretched out on the clover-covered ground. The day was mild and clear, with fluffy white clouds slowly drifting overhead. It occurred to Levi that it was a perfect day for working in the field, which was what Morrough should have been doing rather than lying lifeless in his house. He swept that morbid thought aside to tell his tale.

"Well," he began, as had his daughter with the girls, "I was a jeweler in London, England. I was born and raised there, with a wonderful family. A mother and a father and a brother and a sister. I was the baby, so I was rather spoiled." That always got a guffaw and the lads didn't miss their cue. "My father was a jeweler, my grandfather was a jeweler, my great-grandfather was, too, for as far back as anybody knows. Even my brother became one. So, naturally, I learned the trade from my grandfather and father and older brother.

"My family had been in London for as long as anyone could remember. My grandfather said that long before, at the very beginning of the Dark Ages, our ancestors fled from Eastern Europe to escape an unruly tribe of warriors called Visigoths. They didn't like Jews. But they didn't like anybody else, either!"

"Visi-who?" a great-grandson asked.

"Vis-i-goths. They were barbarians in the beginning..."

"With spears that they threw into people?" Tommy asked excitedly.

"I bet blood squirted out all over!" another added, to nods of assent from his fellows.

"Ah, probably," Levi admitted. "So, my ancestors didn't want to have spears thrown into them and have their blood squirt out all over, as you so eloquently put it, so they somehow escaped across the English Channel to settle in England. Every one of you is related to them! You are all related to me and therefore you are related to them, too! You are part Jewish, part Irish, and part who-knows-what-else. What a strong combination!" He pointed emphatically at them one-by-one, making certain not to miss a one.

"So by the time I came along, here was my family, which is your family too, all happy and prosperous in the thriving city of London, England. Then in 1647—if you've learned your numbers you know that was fifty-nine years ago—in 1647 my father and I took a trip, a business trip, where we sailed with many other Jewish businessmen."

"What kind of businessmen?" someone asked, even though they all knew.

"*Oy vey!* Let's see, there were a number of tinkers, opticians, tanners, clothes makers, and weavers. There was another jeweler, a weapons master, a silversmith, a tin merchant, a farrier, and two pharmacists. Everyone had at least one assistant—usually a son, like me, or a nephew—so we had seventy-two of us. Add to that the twenty-seven men on the crew, and we totaled ninety-nine souls on the ship.

"We were to sail out of London, around the south of England, west of Eire here, and up north to Iceland, Norway, and finally Sweden. We had made arrangements to sell our wares in the biggest town in each of those countries. It's very, very cold up there, so not many people ever visit there. Therefore, it was a very important trip, which was made once every five years and was very successful. I had just turned nineteen, which meant it was the first time I was going on this big journey."

"What was the name of your ship?" Tommy asked. Ever the inquisitive one, Levi suspected that someday he'd either be an infamous politician or an outlaw *Taig*. Tommy was only seven years old, so it was hard to tell, but his penchant for speaking up would surely lead him to trouble on either count.

"The ship was named *The Queen's Bounty*. Not many of us liked the real queen, the monarch who ran our country, but we didn't have anything to say about the name of the ship. We didn't own it; you see, we'd merely commissioned it and its crew for this journey.

"Who was the queen?" Levi quizzed the bevy of boys. "Who remembers?"

"Queen Mary II, of the House of Stuart, a Protestant!" the teen proclaimed. "She reigned with her husband, who was her first cousin and therefore their marriage was a sin. William and Mary, they were called."

"Yes, yes," Levi said. "You have a good head for history, Sean. But it wasn't the state of her marriage that made some of us dislike her. It was her disregard for the Parliament, which had written a *Bill of Rights* that limited the powers of the monarchy. You can just imagine what a queen and her king thought of that!

"And, of course, the Irish hated her not only because she forced Protestantism upon the land, but because she ruled the land in the first place."

"Tell about being seasick!" someone demanded. The boys all laughed. They liked that part. They weren't very interested in politics and religion.

"Ah, yes, I did regurgitate over the side of the ship for the first three days."

"What's regur-regurgimate?" a wee one asked.

"Puke!" Tommy offered, and they all squealed with delight.

"Yes," Levi admitted. "I puked the whole first day. Then I got used to the sea. But I still didn't like being on a ship. Sailing is not for me. Wasn't then and has never been since.

"So, we were sailing along just fine, coming up the coast of Eire, when all of a sudden, out of the bowels of the Devil himself, I see these huge, black, rolling clouds to the west, thundering toward us. We looked to the east and there sat calm, green, beautiful Eire. But could we make it to a safe harbor in time? We didn't know!"

"*Ná!*" a small boy bellowed, then clapped his hands over his mouth. Another lad swatted his shoulder.

"Sh-h-h," the swatter said. "Don't ruin the story!"

"We were indeed hit by the storm!"

Levi leaned toward them and lowered his voice. Every boy inched forward, not wanting to miss a word. "The storm turned the sky black in an instant, like the cloak of mourning being thrust over us, and suddenly our ship was being tossed to and fro, to and fro, as if we were nothing more than a defenseless, wee duckling in the stormy sea. The crew had taken down the sails so they wouldn't be destroyed in the howling winds. Enormous waves of water swept over the bow, over and over again! It would not stop! The crew sent us all below deck and then they came down there, too, because there was nothing they could do."

"Was it dark down there?" someone imagined.

"Dark as a grave at midnight!"

The younger boys yelped.

"So there we were in the belly of a big ship that was being tossed about at the will of nature's wrath!"

"Did you puke again?"

"Oh yes." That got giggles. "But so did many of the others. We were all so frightened. Some of us prayed; others said a lot of bad words."

"Like what?" Tommy asked. There were more guffaws.

"Tommy O'Sullivan, you know I won't tell you that. But I will say that it was the most terrifying time of my life. I thought that the grim reaper was going to come snatch my life right then and there in a foreign sea." He made a snatching gesture toward them, causing them to gasp and flinch back out of his grasp. "I thought of my mother and how sad she was going to be for the rest of her life. I thought of my sister and how much she would cry. I thought of my older brother and how much he would miss teasing me. I thought of how much I hated this trip and was so sorry I'd ever left home.

"Then, the next thing I knew, there was the loudest crashing sound I'd ever heard, even louder than the deafening thunder! It was as if a giant sea monster chomped down on our ship and held it in its fangs, slashing its head back and forth, trying to break our poor, helpless ship in two!"

Shouts of horror escaped from his rapt audience. Eyes were like saucers, jaws hung slack, and bodies sat rigid in fear.

Levi continued in his best affrighting voice. "Suddenly great big jagged pieces of wood and huge waves of water bombarded us! The boat had a hole in its side! We all ran up to the deck, even though we knew we might be swept away. Everyone grabbed hold of something that might float, a piece of wood, a barrel, a rail, whatever we could find.

"Before I could think about what to do, I was in the ocean, clinging to a shattered piece of wood. The waves tossed me up to what felt like the soaring top of a mountain and down to what surely was the bottomless pit of Hell, over and over again, up and down, up and down, until I didn't think I could possibly make it. But I wanted to live! So I hung on for dear life!

"After an eternity, the pounding rain let up a little and the thunder wasn't so deafening as the dark clouds started to tumble away. The sea was still chopping, but I wasn't being carried as far up and down on the waves as I had been. I was so exhausted I could hardly focus my eyes, but when I did the full moon shone on the shipwreck. It had landed up against a giant rock that stood like a mythic symbol of saving grace, jutting out of the water near the shore. The front of the ship was lifted up, its tattered end leaning against the enormous stone. Waves still splashed up against it, but there, miracle of miracles, were many of the men, jumping off and swimming toward the nearby shore. Then I saw that others were being rescued by men in small fishing boats!

"At that very moment, someone grabbed me from behind and flung me into their boat! Pulled me up like a flopping fish! I was so weak my arms and legs may as well have been fins for all the good they did me. If they hadn't reeled me in I never would have made it. They saved me! It was the best feeling in the world!"

There were cheers and clapping all around.

"And you know what happened next?

"All of the men on the ship were saved by the brave Irish fishermen from the Aran Islands!" Tommy exclaimed.

"And great-grandmamma was one of the girls who came to nurse the marooned foreigners and you fell in love the moment you saw her," Sean injected.

"And then you decided to stay here forever and ever," another said. "Forty of you never went back to London. You loved us

Irish! The Jews and the Irish got along great because you all hated the Brits." "Your father went back to London, but you stayed and became a jeweler in Galway," Tommy added.

"Aye," Levi said. "I've made thousands of *Claddagh* wedding rings and Celtic crosses over the years. Quite a legacy for a good Jewish boy, isn't it?" He winked and they smiled.

"But the real reason you stayed," Sean said, "was because you met great-grandmamma and thought she was the most beautiful woman in the world. You asked her to marry you after only three days. And she said 'aye' that very day."

"Aye, lads," Levi agreed. "But remember that beauty has to be inside as well as outside. She had both, God rest her soul."

"But she had that long black hair and dark skin because her great-great-grandmother had been from an island far, far away, in the Pacifica Ocean. Remember?" Sean prodded his great-grand-papa.

"I remember well. She was indeed beautiful beyond measure." Levi's eyes misted at the thought. "Remember my old Jewish saying? *Libe is vi puter, s'iz gut mit broyt.* Who remembers what that means?"

One young lad gave it a stab: "Love is like milk. You need to—um—get it from your cow."

Laughter erupted.

"Close," Levi said. "'Love is like butter. It goes well with bread.' Love adds flavor to life."

"I knew this would get mushy at the end!" Tommy groused as he stood up.

"But thanks for the story anyway, *athair mór*," another boy offered. "It was great right up until the lovey-dovey part at the end."

More thank-yous were thrown out from all around as the boys bobbled up, bumping into and shoving each other in the process. One-by-one, they came to Levi for their hug, the family tradition that no one deigned to ignore. Even the most rowdy of them, even Tommy, liked the gesture of affection, although they'd never admit it. Soon they'd all scampered off, except for Sean. The teen pulled over a stool and sat down beside Levi.

"Something on your mind?" Levi asked.

"*Ná, athair mór.* I just want to sit with you a spell."

Levi smiled at the lanky, freckle-faced, red-headed teen, and then let his gaze wander up to the pleasant sky. His life, he mused, had been as good as anyone could ever hope for. He'd been blessed with the love of a wonderful woman. He'd been granted the gift of offspring who gave him more offspring, like Sean here. He'd had work he'd enjoyed and taken pride in. And he'd lived in a beautiful home amongst kind neighbors. Life couldn't get any better than this. He would forever be grateful that God had spared his life that night he'd almost perished on the stormy sea.

In the meantime, Kathleen and the gaggle of girls in front of the fireplace were finishing their story, too.

Kathleen had told them all about how she first laid eyes on Morrough at the County Galway Fair when she was fifteen years old. She'd spied the tall, dark-haired, handsome stranger from afar, and pointed him out to her sister and announced that she would marry him.

And so she did.

Then she embellished the tale with yarns about the good times and the bad, finishing with their twenty-fifth wedding anniversary a few of years earlier, when they'd spent a night alone, their first in many a year, at an inn in Connemara. The girls loved to hear about the romantic stay by the sea with the quiet supper in their room and the long walk along the shore in the moonlight. The younger ones thought it all terribly sweet and innocent, while the older ones knew better than to imagine innocence.

What Kathleen didn't tell her granddaughters was that her father hadn't wanted her to marry Morrough in the first place. In fact, he'd been dead set against it. He thought that the poor farm boy was beneath his cultured, town-bred girl. He'd always pictured her with a solicitor or physician. But a farmer? Never!

Love—or at least lust, as Kathleen immediately became pregnant—won out, and the young couple wed a few short months after they met. Even though the invitation was offered, Morrough had no interest in learning the Levin family jewelry business. It wasn't long before Levi realized that his new son-in-law had little interest in any kind of work at all. So farming would remain his trade, as it rendered him free of working under anyone else's thumb.

No, Kathleen didn't tell her descendant daughters that their progenitor, Morrough, had never been accused by anyone of being a hard worker. He helped neighbors more for an audience for his cockamamie stories than because of wanting to ease their burden. He worked half as long in the field as other farmers but spent twice as much time talking about it in the pub. Morrough was testament to the old Irish saying, "The person of the greatest talk is the person of the least work." Being the center of attention was the breath of life to him. She'd often thought he'd missed his calling. Surely he'd been meant to be a boisterous actor on the stage, receiving daily applause and accolades from his admirers. She even suspected one reason he'd been so happy they'd had so many children was not so that he could give his love but so that he'd get more. Ah, he'd been a loving man, to be sure. It was just that his version of love was a bit self-aggrandizing.

Kathleen had suspected this when she'd first lustily sought his attentions; she'd grown to know it as a fact the longer they'd been married. And yet, she'd loved him. She loved him still, even though his spirit had left his body by now. She supposed he was already regaling angels with his tall tales. The thought made her smile. That was her Morrough.

A picture of him came to mind, in the pub, raising his third or fourth glass of dark ale, shouting out his favorite toast in his booming, mellifluous voice:

May you have food and raiment,
A soft pillow for your head,
May you be forty years in heaven,
Before the Devil knows you're dead!

Indeed, Kathleen thought, *may the Devil never ask you to pay for the sin of leaving your wife like this.* But she felt certain that when the Devil did catch up with him, Morrough would charm his way out of Hell.

The tears began to fall again. With her wallow in self-pity spent, this time they were tears of sorrow. She would miss him terribly. She already ached for his tender touch and soft kiss. She already yearned for one of his outrageous funny bedtime stories that, caused her to giggle herself to sleep. And she already wished he'd never died and that she could fondle his warm, strong body until the end of her days on earth.

Ah, it was not to be. Not now. But someday they would meet again in the Promise Land, and when she was done pummeling him for abandoning her, she would hold him tight in her arms until the end of time. Never would she let him leave her again.

Chapter 19

Jessie Belle opened her eyes to see Star lying on the bed beside her, dressed in full, black regalia.

"Are you in black to mourn Morrough?" she asked.

"Yes," Star admitted, lifting the black veil from over her face. "And because I think it's sexy. You think so?"

Jessie Belle's eyes adjusted to the darkness and she could see that Star's long dress was a provocatively low-cut, lacy affair. To add to the affect, she had diamond dust in her cleavage, on her cheeks, and in her hair. Jessie Belle propped her head up on her hand and looked more closely. "Yes," she concurred. "It's a very sexy look, in a mourning for the dead sort of way."

"Thank you, dear," Star said as she sat up cross-legged and fluffed her skirt. "It isn't often one gets told that when one is, well, you know, invisible to most people.

"What did you think of Kathleen and Levi? She especially wanted you to know about your Jewish heritage."

"They're quite the '*seanchais.*' Shawn-ex-ees." She repeated the word to practice pronouncing it correctly with a Gaelic lilt. "I love that word! Storytellers. I love how in my dreams I hear their languages but I understand it all perfectly well in my language. I'll never forget some of these wonderful words. *Seanchai,*" she said again, delightfully rolling it over on her tongue.

"Hey, did Kathleen have that baby she was carrying when Morrough died?"

"Oh, yes. It was a boy who grew up to be a poet and an artist. You know, he came seven years after the last before him, so he'd been quite a surprise. She'd thought she was done having *bairns.* Then at age forty-three she turns up pregnant, for the tenth time no less. Ah, well, those two always did breed like a couple of rabbits! When her husband up and died on her before the baby was even born, no wonder she was so angry at him. But even though she loved all of her children, that last one turned out to be a great comfort to her in her old age. She lived to be ninety-six!"

"Wow. That was really old back then."

"Yes, very. Oh! There's one more thing Kathleen wants you to remember from her story. Can you guess what it is?"

"Um, let's see. Don't ever bend over to pick up a rock that's between my old workhorse and my red plow?"

"Ha ha. *Ná!* You're more than a wee bit like your ancient grandfather Morrough, don't you think? A little obsessed with wanting attention. Now, that's not necessarily a bad thing, depending on how you use it. She just wants you to remember to use it well."

"I see. Well, I never have had a desire to work too hard at farming, either. So maybe the old boy and I are alike."

They sat in silence for a while as Jessie Belle thought about the convoluted dream. Star sat perfectly still, letting her think.

"Levi's wife," Jessie Belle finally said. "Her ancestor was the Pacific island native girl who left with the missionaries, wasn't she?"

"Yes. Leilani. Your ancestor, too, of course."

"I wondered what ever happened to her. She ended up in Ireland. And her grandmother, the missionary nun, was from there to begin with.

"As for my Jewish heritage, I can hardly believe it! Who would have guessed that Jews lived in western Ireland in the 1600s? I've never really even known any Jews, except a little at places like school or work. They've just always been the people that everyone jokes about."

"Oh no, dear, they're your ancestors. In fact, lots of those people who are doing that joking are actually demeaning themselves. They don't even know it's their heritage, too. For example, when one race or religion displays their bigotry against another, they're just showing their own ignorance because they're really fighting against their own heritage. When Muslims and Christians clash, they're really just fighting their own kin. When one African tribe inflicts genocide upon another tribe, they're killing their own. Everybody has some mixed heritage. No one is what some like to call 'pure.' So do you get the idea by now that most people don't really know where they come from and that we all come from the same beginning anyway? So being prejudiced against any group of people is being prejudiced against yourself."

"Yes, Star. I get it. That message has been made clear. Did I really need it so badly?"

"Oh, my! How can you even ask?" Star tufted the hair on the top of Jessie Belle's head. Jessie Belle sat up, too, to avoid another such admonition of her childishness.

"Okay. I admit," Jessie Belle said, "I was pretty narrow-minded. Believe me, you've broadened my perspective. It'll never go back to its old imprisonment."

"Good! That's what the women who made you wanted. They've been so afraid you'd gaga your life away. They're starting to rest more easily now."

"Star, tell me something. What happens after we die? I mean, are my ancestors just floating around or do they have jobs, like helping me? Or are we just supposed to learn forever and ever, even after we die? That's what a lot of people think, you know."

"Oh, my, no! That belief that the soul lives into eternity is just human beings' fear of finality. Of the real death. It shows they've not thought that through, as with so many other things." She rolled her eyes. "No, the purpose of living is not to be reincarnated and learn more and more in life after life on earth and in life after the human body's demise. My goodness! How boring would that be, if the only reason for existing was to have to work to learn forever? 'Give me liberty or give me death!' Smart man, that Patrick Henry.

"No, the purpose of living is to love. It's that simple. Once you've done all of the loving you can do and reaped all the joy from it possible, either on earth or in the heavens or somewhere else, you choose to die, a real death that extinguishes your soul. It's a choice that's made with great care and with great jubilation, because it means that your existence has been fulfilled. But nothing—nothing—can live forever. Nor should it. You will choose when your time will come to an end. We all do."

Jessie Belle pondered that before saying anything else. "So," she finally said, "my ancestor women who have been telling me their stories in their dreams—their spirits, their souls, are still alive somewhere? They haven't chosen their final death yet?"

"Yes, dear," Star said. "Clacka's spirit has lived a very long time, so she is preparing for her final goodbye. The others aren't as near the end yet, but we all will be someday."

"So when a spirit dies, or when they extinguish their soul, as you say, their stories live on when people like me remember them?"

"Yes! That's the best part! Our souls flicker out but our stories live on forever. It's hard to explain to someone who's used to the limited dimensions of human life, but think of it like a great big storage room for old films. We can go in, pluck out any film, and play it whenever we want. Your ancestors who still exist in spirit decided which ones you should see. They thought a few from long ago would be a good beginning. But, as you've undoubtedly noticed, they're getting more and more recent. The one who started this whole campaign to save your soul has been the catalyst. You haven't met her yet."

"Who is she? When will I see her?"

"All in good time, Jessie Belle. All in good time.

"That's enough for tonight, I think. It's time for you to get some shut-eye."

Star floated up into the air and faded, but came back to whisper into Jessie Belle's ear. "Her name is Giselle. And she loves you with all of her soul."

The spirit blew a diamond-spray kiss and disappeared into the night.

When Jessie Belle awoke the next morning, it took a moment for her to remember where she was. She looked around. This certainly wasn't the Ritz London Hotel, but it was a charming room, which she now recalled was in the Gresham Hotel on O'Connell Street in the heart of Dublin. A slit of dawn's light wended its way between the closed curtains. Jessie Belle jumped out of bed. This was her final day out of the U.S. And her only day in Ireland, the land of Kathleen! Even though Dublin, where she was now, and Galway, Kathleen's hometown, were on opposite sides of the island, this was still the country of her ancestors. She wanted to see as much of it as possible before she had to go. She flung the curtains open to verify that it was indeed daybreak, early enough to take a brisk walk outside before she had to begin work. She threw on her jeans and a tee shirt, and scampered down the stairs to the lobby. At the bellman's desk stood an old man who looked like someone who'd been cast to play a stereotypical Irishman in a movie.

"Good mornin', Miss!" he greeted her, rolling the "r" in genuine Gaelic fashion.

"Good morning, Mr. Patty," she said, reading his name badge.

That brought about a spurt of laughter, after which he said, "My first name is Patty, to be sure."

"Oh, I'm sorry. Patty."

"No need to be sorry, Miss. What can I do for you this lovely mornin'?"

"Where would be a good place to take about an hour-long walk around here at this time of day?"

"Oh, you'll be wantin' to walk around the campus of Trinity College. You'll see the signs when you walk this way." He pointed out the direction. "Then when you come back, take College Street—the name will change until it's Christchurch Place—so you can go by the Christ Church Cathedral. It's open by now, in case you want to go in to pray. It's the oldest church in Ireland and quite a sight to see! Here's a map, so you'll find your way back to us." He handed her a Dublin tourist map and tipped his topper hat.

"Thank you, Patty!" She handed him a five-pound tip and waved as she left the hotel.

"Thank ye, Miss! Top o' the mornin' to ya!" he called out.

The early morning hike was even more invigorating than she'd hoped. Strolling around the ancient college campus made her feel like she'd gone back in time. Perhaps even to Kathleen's time. Then the exquisite cathedral thrust her back even further after reading a sign that explained that the core of the building had been on this very spot for almost one thousand years! People had been drawn to this place to worship for over ten centuries! Maybe that was why she'd felt bidden to come here today.

Dare she go inside? Being a born and bred Southern Baptist, after all, she didn't know if it would be proper. But the call did not ebb, so she walked through the enormous front door, which stood open as if inviting all to enter and escape the world outside. The moment she stepped into the enormous main chapel her fears flowed away, her body released all tension, and her mind enwrapped itself in peace. It was a physical and emotional change that literally shook her.

To reach the pews, she needed to walk past the large stone font of holy water. Now knowing what possessed her to do it, she dipped in her fingers and made the sign of the cross on her forehead, leaving it cool and moist. At a pew in the center of the rows, she kneeled on the low padded bench to pray. But instead of a prayer, her mind only came up with thanks to the Lord for giving her this amazing life. It might be a totally screwed up life but it was an amazing gift all the same. She ended with, "I love You with all my heart and soul."

Renewed and ready to face whatever adventure or misadventure this day might bring, she went back to the hotel to begin her day of work.

"So," Edwin Sampson said, "you've spent the last week tracing your heritage all over the place, following the trail left by your DNA. You started in Africa, went through the Middle East, north through Central Europe, then further north to Scandinavia. Your DNA's predominant markers showed us that Scandinavian ancestry. Knowing that the Scandinavians who were Vikings settled all over the British Isles, we picked this city, Dublin, Ireland, for you to visit because it was established by the Vikings. They named it *Dyflin*, which has turned into the Dublin we know today. This will complete your journey on this side of the pond."

Jessie Belle didn't interrupt to tell him he'd missed side trips to Italy and a Pacific Island. As a scientist, he probably wouldn't cotton to her "dreams." She could just picture it: A CNN international news special report with her saying, "Excuse me, but my spirit friend has been sending me stories of my ancestors, and you've missed a few." *Would that bring the bozo bloggers out of the woodwork or what? Actually,* she decided, *that might be rather fun.*

Back to the matter at hand, Edwin was saying, "So, Jessie Belle, how has this whole experience of an 'Ancestry Quest' been for you? How does it feel to have discovered your ancestors?"

"It's been amazing!" She answered honestly, knowing he had no way of knowing just how amazing it had been. "When this all started I had no idea that I'd become steeped in the cultures of my ancestors' lives. I had no idea how attached I would begin to feel to the people who made me. And I had no idea how much I'd learn about myself."

"What have you learned?"

Briefly, she looked up in thought, then looked back at him and said, "I've learned that I'm the culmination of thousands of lives, some of which were privileged and some of which were deprived. I've learned not to take my life for granted. So many people went through so much so that I could walk this earth—that's a gift to be appreciated every moment of every day."

"That's great, Jessie Belle," Edwin said. "The Genographic Project couldn't ask for any more than that. If we can help people connect to the past so that they can live a more meaningful present and share that insight with future generations, we have fulfilled our mission.

"Thank you so much for including us into your special reports. It's been an honor."

"The pleasure is all mine," Jessie Belle said, grabbing him for a big bear hug. When they parted, they smiled at one another.

"Cut!" Joe said. Dray shut off the camera and put it down.

"Jessie Belle and Edwin!" Joe exclaimed. "That was out of the park. The bigwigs are gonna go ape-shit back at the station. Perfect ending to one of the highest-rated specials they've ever had. Thanks!" He shook Edwin's hand and patted him on the back. Then he grabbed Jessie Belle for a back-pounding brotherly hug. Edwin shook hands with Dray. Joe shook Dray's hand. and Jessie Belle and Dray were left facing each other.

"It's been great working with you," she said. "Thank you for everything."

"Ah, yeah, you, too," he said. He put out his hand, they shook, and then they hugged so awkwardly it was like two turtles trying to embrace.

"Okay! Time to celebrate!" Joe announced, rubbing his hands together in glee. "Beer all around! Except for you, little lady. You're cut off for the rest of your life."

That night in bed she thought about the work, about the project. She'd been so ensconced in her dreams she hadn't given the job her full attention. But it had culminated brilliantly anyway. Today the final taping with Edwin at four-hundred-year-old Trinity College had gone fantastically well. Her walk through the campus that morning had familiarized her with the outdoor areas, but once inside the historic stone buildings she was stunned at the combination of pomp and circumstance, spiritual aura, and sheer marvel of craftsmanship.

Their first segment there had been Jessie Belle and Edwin sitting at a table in the main chamber, the Long Room, of the massive eighteenth-century Old Library building. She suspected their dark oak antique table had been sitting in that same spot since the day it had been brought in brand-spanking new. All of the furniture had that kind of classic, lived-in look. The two-story walls with ornate wood paneling, balconies surrounding the upper gallery, shelf after shelf of valuable books, and golden library lamps with muted light all gave the place an air of times gone by. There were two long rows of plaster busts of stern-looking men down each side of the room. Joe had the librarian collect ancient-looking books on genealogies, which were predominantly piled at the end of the table. Jessie Belle thought the whole setting was the ultimate in scholarly staging. In that segment, Edwin reviewed with the audience what the Genographic Project was all about.

The second segment they taped had been them tracing the entire journey on an old map. That would end up being mostly their voice-overs with the map interjected by the tech guys in Atlanta. Then they took a tour with a history student as their guide. He was a lanky kid in khaki pants and a Trinity College tee shirt, and at first Jessie Belle thought him profoundly under-qualified and under-impressive to be part of this show. But the whipper-snapper proved her wrong by being quick-witted and funny, and by having a voice that could butter bread.

After an enjoyable tour of the campus, he took them back into the Old Library and downstairs to its Treasury, the exhibition area. "And here," he said in his silky smooth voice, "we have the *Book of Kells,*" He pointed out a display case and stepped aside so that Dray could get a good shot of Jessie Belle and Edwin looking down at it. Jessie Belle supposed that at some point in her education she must have learned about the exquisitely hand-written and hand-illustrated Bible before, but didn't remember it. *Drat!* Why hadn't she paid more attention in art history class? The sheer beauty of the book caught her completely off guard.

"It's gorgeous!" she exclaimed.

"Yes," the young guide agreed, "it's considered to be the most elaborate rendition of a Bible in existence. It contains the four Gospels in Latin. It's believed that it was handcrafted at the monastery on the island of Iona, off the west coast of Scotland. It came to Ireland when Vikings raided Iona in the early 800s and monks fled to the Kells monastery here.

Jessie Belle's head spun. Perhaps her own ancestors, Erik Bloodtooth and his daughter Erika, had been those raiders!

"It's ironic that Catholic monks wrote this and I was raised Baptist, being taught that Catholics are practically the anti-Christ," she blurted out without considering political correctness. Oh well, they could always edit it out, so she completed her thought. "But the Catholic monks who did this must have been angels from Heaven itself!"

She ran her fingers over the glass case to emphasize her point. The lavish lettering, brilliant colors, illustrations, and Latin lettering of the book were beyond belief.

"I know," the young guide said. "And my professors always complain that they can't read my hand-writing."

They laughed together and moved on to view three more hand-illustrated books from other monasteries during that same era. They weren't as jaw-dropping as the *Book of Kells*, but were each beautiful in their own way with their own ornamental designs. Edwin asked some intelligent-sounding questions, and the segment concluded without a hitch.

With his part done, the student guide shook hands with everyone and jaunted off as if the whole ordeal hadn't been any more consequential than a cup of coffee with his friends. Jessie Belle envied his nonchalance. That was something she had yet to master.

Then the third segment had been the close, where she and Edwin were back in the Long Room of the Old Library. He'd started the segment by showing her a list of names in an old book. "Trinity College is known for its genealogical records, so we looked up your mother's maiden name, Wallace. Look at this: Here it is in the property survey records, which was something like a census, taken from 1847 to 1864. As you can see, that name showed up 1,401 times, spread across many counties. That's the number of households, not people. The number of people with that name would have been proliferate for that day and age. So it was quite a popular surname."

Jessie Belle bent over the page looking for one county in particular. There it was, Galway. Where her dream about Kathleen had taken place.

"So it is very possible I have Irish heritage, even though I didn't know it," Jessie Belle stated.

"Yes," Edwin agreed. "Very possible."

That's when they'd moved on to finish the segment, which culminated in their spontaneous hug. Funny, but she'd done that without forethought. And when they reviewed the tape after dinner, she realized that her answer to his final question was, of course, an answer about her dreams, not just what she'd learned from the subject matter experts. That's what made it so good.

She rolled over, savoring the comfort of her bed and her last night in Ireland. The men were still down in the pub celebrating. She'd lasted a couple of hours with them, drinking Coke to their Tenants Beer, until she'd decided that her celebration would be sleep.

Chapter 20

A horrible racket sounded at her door. Pulling her pillow over her ears, she hoped whatever it was would shrivel up and die. But no such luck.

"Jessie Belle!" Joe rasped, sounding as if he didn't want to be too loud but failing miserably. "Rise and shine! The plane leaves in one hour. Jessie Belle! Did you hear me?" He pounded again.

She hopped out of bed, opened the door a crack, and peeked around the side. "Yes, Joe. Everyone on this floor heard you. What time is it, anyway?"

"Eight. We have the private jet back, finally! They're locked and loaded and ready to go. Meet you in the lobby in half an hour," he said as he trotted away.

What surprised Jessie Belle the most was that she'd not dreamt or had a visit from Star during the night. Panic struck! What if that was all over now that the trip was over? She didn't know if she could manage on her own.

Foreboding loomed like a storm cloud, one that lingered so low it could dump doom and destruction at any moment. Star had not warned her. No one had told her anything. And yet she felt certain that trouble waited at home.

Most surprising, she seemed to be thinking for herself for the first time in a very long time. Perhaps for the first time ever. Her conclusion to the program, her thoughtful answers to Edwin's questions yesterday, had illustrated a new depth to her thinking. *Is my shallow little old self actually becoming a deep person?* she pondered.

The flight droned on as each of the three of them spread out into an aisle of seats they'd claimed as their own. Joe sat one aisle up and across from Jessie Belle, and Dray sat in the aisle directly across from her.

About an hour into the flight, Joe had Dray record a short informal segment of Jessie Belle telling her thoughts about the trip. It'd been a spontaneous decision on Joe's part, so Jessie Belle felt unprepared, wearing jeans and a tee shirt, and with her hair pulled back into a ponytail and next to no make-up on. When she fussed a little, he told her not to worry about it. "Without a lot of make-up, you look like a cute teenager. It gives you an innocent presence," he insisted. Going with that premise, she instinctively pulled her knees up and wrapped her arms around them as she spoke, giving the segment a naturally casual feel.

"Well," she began, "they want me to talk about my impressions of this trip. I have one impression: It changed my life. I had never before given one iota of thought to the people who came before me, the people who made me, my ancestors. Not beyond a few hundred years. But now that I've visited the homelands of my ancient forebears, now that I've walked the same paths they most likely walked, I feel a connection to them that can never be broken. I have a sense of what they went through so that I could have the privileged life I have today, and I am eternally grateful. I can honestly say I feel love for them." Her audience would never know how true that was because she felt as though she'd come to know some of them so intimately through her dreams.

"So I want to thank the people of the National Geographic Genographic Project, especially assistant director Edwin Sampson, who mapped out my journey, and CNN, including the producer of this special, my boss Harry Hughey who made me do this when I didn't think I wanted to. And thank you to all of the tour guides, professors, and docents who taught us so much along the way. And thank you to the director of these segments, a true road warrior, Joe Hoffman, who's been not only a wonderful director but a good friend as well; and, Dragan Dlugitch, the cameraman whose great work you're viewing at this very moment. Last but not least, thank *you* for your interest in this special series, the 'Ancestry Quest.'

"I hope you've all enjoyed this special as much as I've ended up enjoying doing it. My hope is that, although this was about *my* ancestry, it's inspired you to explore your own. Who knows what you might find? What an exciting adventure!

"But remember, my adventure isn't quite over yet. The grand finale will air on Monday, from my mama's plantation in Social Circle, Georgia. Please join us for a look at the final destination of this long and exhilarating journey.

"See you then! Bye, bye, my friends!" She threw a little kiss into the camera.

"Cut," Joe said, almost in a whisper. Dray stopped rolling and put the camera down. Both men looked at her with what she read as respect. It was a great feeling. "That was terrific!" Joe claimed. "It couldn't have been a more perfect rap to our travels."

After that, the three of them alternately chatted, read, napped, and snacked. They were getting good Wi-Fi connectivity, so Joe and Dray worked on their laptops.

At one point she leaned into the aisle and asked Dray what he was working on, thinking he might be editing segments of their series.

"Oh, I'm just playing around with a story idea."

"What story?" she asked.

"I call it 'Sacred Spaces.' I'd love to get back to producing someday. I used to do documentaries in Romania. This is an idea I have about doing shows about places all over the world that are sacred to people. Saint Brigit's holy well in Ireland, Coptic Christian caves in Egypt, Pueblo Indian kivas in the southwest U.S. That sort of thing. The list has hundreds of places on it, I've been thinking about it for so long."

"Hey!" Joe interjected, sticking his head up over the back of his seat. "That sounds awesome! When you're ready, hire me as your director, eh?"

"It's a deal," Dray promised. "Of course, there are little issues like time and money and the fact I can't travel that much until the kids are grown. But, sure, when that all comes together, you'll be the first I call."

"Jessie Belle can be the host," Joe offered.

Dray studied her for a moment. "Yes, she could be."

"I love the idea," she said. "Count me in. So we're talking what? Ten years down the road?"

"Yes," Dray said. "I'm afraid we all have to keep our day jobs at CNN until then."

They all laughed together and then drifted back to what they'd been doing.

Jessie Belle spent a little time on her iPad. She didn't even bother opening her email. She knew it would be a mess. Thankfully, she had the production assistant Gracie back at the studio to help with that kind of thing.

She was steeped in voting for whether or not an outfit "works" on the *Fashism* website, when Joe said, "Uh, oh. I don't believe it!"

Dray's and her heads both popped up from their tasks. "What?" they said in unison.

"Jessie Belle," Joe said, looking back at her, "I'm not sure you want to hear this. But I know you will, anyway, so here goes.

"Bridget Barker eloped with Mongo Money last night."

Jessie Belle was struck dumb, mute as the Venus de Milo.

"Mongo Money the rock star?" Dray asked, sounding incredulous.

"Could there be any other?" Joe said. "It says here on the 'E!' website that they met when he did a CNN interview last week. It's been a 'whirlwind courtship.' No shit! It also says he's 'one of the richest rock stars of the 21st century' and 'they'll live amongst his seven homes that are scattered around the world.'" He read silently for a moment. "And," he concluded, "she quit CNN."

Both men's heads turned like bobble dolls and gawked at Jessie Belle, gauging her reaction.

A furrow creased her brow. "You, you mean," she stammered, "she left Robert?"

"Apparently she was never really 'with' Robert. Not if she dumped him that easily," Joe noted for the record.

"So... So," she repeated, trying to piece together this incomprehensible puzzle. "Robert dumped me to be with her and she dumped him to be with a rock star. Think there's a chance Mongo will ever dump her? You know, just to keep the cycle going?"

The men grinned like Cheshire cats.

"Well, it does say she's his—wait, let me find it—" Joe said as he scrolled down his screen, "she's his fifth wife. And he's only thirty-five. Oh my god, that leaves a lot of years ahead for more divorces and marriages!"

"I wouldn't trade places with him for all the money in the world," Dray contended.

"Well, seeing that I've already had a lot of divorces, what the hell?" Joe said. "I'd trade places for his money."

"And I'd rather never get married than marry somebody like Mongo Money." Jessie Belle scrunched up her nose in disgust. "All those tattoos and that long greasy hair and that screeching thing he calls 'singing.' Forget the money!"

"That's easy for you to say," Joe said. "You've always had boatloads of it."

"Yes, I have. I'm very lucky," Jessie Belle said, acknowledging her good fortune.

"Yah, well, I bet the head honchos will appreciate you more than ever. You'd never spontaneously run off to get married. You'd never leave them high and dry."

"No, that's just not like me, is it?" Jessie Belle felt a twinge of regret that it was true.

"Jessie Belle," Dray said in a voice gentler than usual, "can we do anything for you?"

"You want a drink or something?" Joe asked. "A real one?"

"No thanks, guys. I appreciate the offers, but I just need to think."

Out of consideration for her wishes, they both turned their attention back to what they'd been doing.

She lowered her seatback, laid her head back, and closed her eyes. Her thoughts and feelings were so jumbled up it was as if her brain was a Mixmaster. Blend, knead, puree, whip, beat. First one speed, then another, only to switch again. She didn't know what to think or feel. She'd loved Robert for a full year. She'd even thought she loved him deeply enough to marry him, to vow to "have and to hold until death do us part." How had she been able to give him up so easily? And why the sudden attraction to Dray? Not that it mattered. He didn't like her all that much anyway. Was Dray just a way to avoid the reality of having been hurt so badly? A band-aid to cover up the real wound? A detour so she wouldn't have to face her life head on?

Question upon question popped into her mind, poked around, and went unanswered. She had no idea what she thought or felt about anything in the world. She didn't even know what was real and what was not. All of the psychological brick walls she'd spent a lifetime building to compartmentalize her beliefs had crumbled. Everything was spilling into everything else. Everything was a blur.

Softly, she wept. When she finally fell into a shallow sleep, it was dreamless and peaceful. For that, at least, she was grateful.

"Jessie Belle."

She opened her eyes to see Dray's face close to hers. Yes, she'd heard correctly. He'd whispered her name.

"Hi." She sat up. The window on the other side of the plane revealed they flew over dark clouds, which meant she'd slept for some time as it had been a bright sunny day last she remembered.

"Hi. I'm sorry to wake you up but we're going to land in a few minutes, and there's something I want to say before we get back. I won't see you for the last shoot, because I'm taking a vacation next week with the kids. We're going camp...."

Suddenly, the plane took a dive to the right. They all gasped and looked at each other in fear. Dray hadn't put the seatbelt on yet since moving across the aisle, so he was jostled around until he grabbed it and snapped it on. The plane corrected itself and flew straight for an instant before jolting to the left. Now, in addition to the normal rumble of the jet engines, out of nowhere thunder crashed outside. Rain pelted the windows as if someone had just turned on a rain machine on a movie set. They hadn't even leveled out yet when they hit an air pocket and felt themselves pummeling straight down toward the earth. Spontaneously, Jessie Belle grabbed Dray's hand and squeezed. Joe threw his arms in the air and said, "Wee." Although his attempt at humor was anemic, Jessie Belle loved him for it.

The co-captain's voice came on over the speaker. "Hang on, folks. We saw this storm and have been attempting to fly around it but have to get through this arm of it to get home. Don't worry, we'll make it. Just hang on tight."

Then the three of them did what passengers so often do in a crisis in the air: they sat stock still in total silence as the sounds of disaster roared around them. They bounced around, they shuttered at the blinding lighting, they held their breath when they hit more air pockets, but they did not speak.

Just as quickly as the storm had hit, it dissipated. Jessie Belle turned toward the window to peek outside, with Dray leaning into her back in order to look, too. The shift in their bodies made her realize they still held hands.

"Oh!" she said, looking back at him and letting go of his hand. "Sorry! Did I squeeze it to death?"

"No." He smiled, still leaning toward her. "I think it will live."

"What's all that?" Joe asked, pointing out the window on his side of the plane.

Both Jessie Belle and Dray looked over to that side, and even from across the aisle could see all kinds of lights and vehicles near the landing strip at the private airport where they'd be touching down, Fulton County Airport, better known as Charlie Brown Field. People often thought it was named after the *Peanuts* character, but there had once been an Atlanta politician by that name. Jessie Belle and Dray unhooked their seatbelts and scurried to that side of the plane to look out.

"They don't look like emergency vehicles," Joe said. "I think they're... news vans? Why in blazes would they be here?"

Before anyone could come up with an answer, the plane glided onto the tarmac as gracefully as a swan landing on a lake. It taxied, making a turn that changed the view of the vehicles to the other side, so Jessie Belle went back to her aisle and looked out. Yes, those were definitely news vans. Even though it was late afternoon, they had their lights on because, although the rain had stopped, the brooding overcast sky made it almost dark as night.

"What the hell?" Joe asked. "Look! There's Fox News, E! Entertainment, and somebody I don't even know. And the *Globe* and *National Enquirer!* Not a real elite group, I gotta say. Eh?"

The storm had left in its wake a gleaming carpet of water that reflected the red and white and blue lights of vehicles and cameras, surrounding them in a surreal setting. That was until she saw the lone vehicle that sat apart from the others. This one was a long, black, stretch Rolls Royce limo that looked all too familiar.

At that moment she realized what was about to happen and didn't know if she should feel as if she were being thrown off a cliff in sacrifice or lifted up onto a thrown in supplication. She settled on feeling nothing.

"What the hell?" Joe repeated but cut it short when the light bulb went on inside his head.

Dray got it, too, and remained speechless.

When the plane parked, the steps were brought up and they disembarked. There he was right at the bottom of the steps. Robert. Impossibly handsome, looking appropriately chagrined, grasping a thick bouquet of pink roses in one hand and holding the other hand out to her.

Jessie Belle knew that non-flight people weren't allowed this close to a plane, but Robert knew everyone and always paid off anyone he didn't know. As usual, the rules didn't apply to him. The journalists and camera operators, held back by a security guard, stood in a cluster about twenty feet away.

Camera lights flashed. Someone hollered a question but was shushed by others who wanted to hear what the two estranged lovers had to say.

Joe and Dray hung back, letting Jessie Belle get off first. When her foot touched the pavement, Robert clasped his outstretched hand over his heart. *Oh, he's good!* she thought. *Very, very good at playing to the media.* He walked up to her and held out the flowers.

To her surprise, she took them.

"Jessie Belle, I know I don't deserve your forgiveness, but I must beg for it," he pled. "These past two weeks have taught me a brutal lesson: that I'm in love with you and no one else. I don't expect, don't even deserve an answer now..." Jessie Belle almost fell over when he got down on one knee, wet tarmac and all, and reached into his pocket and pulled out a red leather ring box. "... but I want to share my life with you. Will you marry me?"

Jessie Belle glared at the fabulous Cartier marquis-cut diamond rock she'd coveted for so long. She looked down into Robert's gorgeous eyes, which were fittingly glazed by impending tears. She looked at the anxious reporters. Then she looked behind her. Joe stood nearby, ready, it seemed, to catch her should she fall or to spirit her away should she want to escape. *What a good friend.*

Dray, however, wasn't there. She looked around. He was gone.

Turning back to Robert, she was aware of all of the paparazzi leaning toward her in rabid anticipation of what she would say. Microphones jabbed in her direction, like hungry wild beasts ready to lunge at their prey.

"You have got to be out of your ever-lovin', snakebit, pixilated, ding-a-ling, lost in la-la-land, lyin', cheatin' mind!" she said, beating him over the head with the roses and then tossing the shattered remains into his face.

Joe stepped up behind her, grabbed her by the elbow, and hustled her into the small terminal so quickly she felt like a little kid being scrambled along by her daddy, her legs trotting twice as fast as his to keep up. Inside, they grabbed their waiting luggage and skedaddled to his Jeep. He drove her to her car, lest someone try to follow, but no one did.

When she got out, Joe rolled down his window and stuck out his head. "You did real good back there, Jessie Belle. I'm proud of you." She nodded without expression and got into her Mercedes Benz, noticing that he waited until she pulled out before he left.

Dray never did appear again. He'd obviously already gone home, done with the assignment and done with her.

Chapter 21

Her Mercedes Benz convertible squealed into the parking garage of her condo building and jerked into her reserved spot. She slammed the door when she got out and went around back to yank her bags out of the trunk. Someone called her name. Looking around, she saw the parking attendant jogging toward her. She'd never bothered to learn his name, but he seemed to be a nice enough fellow, about forty, neat, trim, but poor looking, even in his required uniform of navy pants and navy shirt, with "Buckhead Arms" embroidered in gold across his left breast pocket.

"Here, Miss Church. Let me do that." He took control of the bags and they headed toward the elevator. "Um, Miss Church, Roger just called. He said there's someone waiting for you there." They stepped inside the elevator, he punched the lobby button, the doors closed, and the motor started to whirl. Roger was the concierge who reigned over the lobby, and controlled all comings and goings in his domain. "Listen," the attendant went on as they rode up, "Roger has instructed all of us to keep the media away from you, unless you tell us otherwise." He leaned in conspiratorially. "We all know what just happened at the Charlie Brown airport." He leaned back and shrugged. "Anyway, that means it's not a reporter. Our major domo feels it's important that you talk to this person and I don't think he'd lead you astray." He nodded at her reassuringly. "So he's asked that you stop in the lobby to speak to him before going up to your place."

The elevator stopped and the doors opened to reveal Roger, dressed as nattily as usual in a navy blue suit, who was obviously waiting for them. Jessie Belle remembered that he had a bank of security camera monitors at his desk, so he'd seen her coming.

"Welcome home, Miss Church," he said, taking her bags from the attendant, who saluted and punched the button to return to his bailiwick in the basement. "Let me have these sent to your condo. I believe you know that someone is waiting here to speak with you."

On the way up to the lobby she'd pondered who it might be. Robert's limo couldn't have made it here ahead of her. She'd driven like a bat out of hell and that limo just didn't have that kind of flying flexibility. It couldn't be her mama. She couldn't have missed noticing her mama's bright yellow Cadillac land yacht in visitor parking. And it certainly wouldn't be her brother. They'd barely spoken since she was about five, when she realized he was a bully and that she didn't really like him all that much.

So she was totally bowled over when she turned around and saw who it was.

"Ms. Church, I'm so sorry to intrude like this but it's imperative that we have a word in private. I didn't want to make you come to the office after having just returned from your long trip, so I took the liberty of coming here. I hope you don't mind."

Seeing the family lawyer in her own condo building was unnerving. Lawrence Davidson had never so much as suggested having a personal conversation with her in her entire lifetime, the length of time she'd known him. As the founding partner of one of Atlanta's most elite law firms, as a friend of her late daddy's, and as the conservator of her daddy's estate, he'd always dealt with her mother and her brother. Jeff—Jefferson Davis Church, to be exact—had been named the executor of the estate in her daddy's will and took on that responsibility when the man died ten years ago. This was something that had always flummoxed Jessie Belle, who wondered why her mama hadn't been named executor. In any case, Mr. Davidson had never talked directly to Jessie Belle and his presence alarmed her.

"Has something happened to my mama?" she asked.

"No, no. She's fine—physically, at least. I was afraid that was what you'd think the moment you saw me. No, that's not it. May we speak in private?"

"Certainly. Let's go up to my place."

Without comment, they got into the elevator. The ride up was tense as a rollercoaster ride at Six Flags, except stone still.

Once inside her condo, she squired him into the living room that looked like a *Southern Living* model room, where they sat on the overstuffed chintz-covered armchairs. They had barely sat down when the doorbell rang.

Jessie Belle answered to receive her bags from the bellman, tipped him quickly, and returned to her guest.

"Now," she said as she returned to her seat, "what is this mystery all about?"

"Ms. Church…"

She interrupted him. "You've known me all my life. Please call me Jessie Belle. May I call you Lawrence?"

"Certainly. Jessie Belle," he said pointedly, nodding, "I'm not one for skirting an issue, so this is it: Your brother has lost the family fortune. It's gone. All of it. Including your inheritance. As executor of your trust fund, he's managed to drain even that dry. I'm so sorry to have to bring you this horrible news but I thought it the right thing to do to let you know before it might make the news. Let me reassure you, however, that my firm is doing everything in its power to keep that from happening.

"I'll do my best to answer any questions you might have."

He was so fastidiously groomed, with perfectly coifed healthy gray hair and dressed in a black suit with a white shirt and red silk tie, it made Jessie Belle notice the incongruence of the sweat sprouting on his upper lip. *It looks as out of place as a prize fighter wearing an ascot in the ring,* she thought. She could see that this indeed was as difficult as a boxing match for Lawrence Davidson.

"Lawrence, would you like a drink?"

"Why, yes, I believe I would."

"Let's go into the kitchen."

In the kitchen, she poured him a stiff Glenrothes 1985 on the rocks. It was an exclusive imported scotch whiskey that she'd kept on hand for Robert. It gave her pleasure now to give it away. Maybe she'd perform a ceremony later and dump the remainder of it down the toilet. She'd surely never drink it, so she poured herself a glass of white zinfandel. They sat on stools around the marble-topped island.

"My first question is," Jessie Belle said after she'd taken a swig of courage, "are you sure it's all gone? I mean, it was boatloads of money. Millions and millions and millions of dollars."

He took a big gulp of his scotch, closed his eyes in obvious pleasure at the smooth taste of the aged liquid gliding down his throat, and then opened his eyes to look directly at her. "Unfortunately, yes, I'm sure. The family accountant and I have been in touch for some time. The fact that the funds were dwindling was not news to me, but I was shocked at how quickly the last of it went. Jeffrey demolished your 45 million-dollar trust fund in two weeks. I know you've been receiving half a million dollars a year to live on and that you'd planned your life knowing that amount, and much more, would always be there. This must be a terrible shock to you. I'm so sorry."

Jessie Belle didn't know why she didn't feel more shocked. She was unhappy about this, to be sure, but nothing shocked her anymore.

The lawyer went on. "The very fact that Jeffrey resorted to dipping into your trust fund is absolutely appalling to me. Your father left that money to you. It was yours! I never, ever expected that your brother would stoop that low or I would have warned you earlier. I'm afraid I gravely underestimated the depth of Jeffrey's irresponsibility."

"How did he lose it all?"

"A number of ways. Bad investments: a beach resort on some remote island in the Pacific that never caught on, an Internet company that went belly-up, real estate deals that hit the skids with the recession. I think he was trying to be another Robert Brentz, but a brilliant businessman like that he is not. There was even an affair with an actress that cost millions to hush up and other such things. But mostly it was his gambling. He's lost a fortune in Las Vegas. He's confessed to losing as much as a million a night at the baccarat table at Caesar's Palace." He took another chug of his drink, clearly miserable at having to deliver this wretched news. Jessie Belle refilled his glass. The toilet ceremony might not be necessary after all.

"I see," she said. "Have you told Mama? She still has her family money, right? So she'll be okay?"

"Oh, her inheritance has been gone for years. And she's known for a long time there was a problem with your father's fortune. But you know your mother; she doesn't like to think about unpleasant things, so I could never get her to focus on the reality that Jeffrey was driving the whole family into a sink hole."

"True. Reality is not Mama's forte." *Or mine, until recently.*

"In deference to your father's legacy, I tried to get the firm to save the plantation by purchasing it and putting it into trust for you and your brother. But the partners wouldn't agree to that. So now the proposal I've put on the table is for us to buy it and let your mother live there until her death. Hopefully, that's a long time off. But at that time, it would belong to the firm. I'm sorry to say, that's the most I've been able to do. It looks like the partners may agree to that. I can't do anything about what else has been lost."

"Of course not. I can't thank you enough for trying to save my mama's home. Why, if she lost it, she might have to come live with me! So I thank you from the bottom of my heart." She managed a wan smile.

His face remained grave. It was at that moment that Jessie Belle realized that Lawrence Davidson, the stiff, upper-crust, no-nonsense lawyer-man, had a crush on her mama. Why else would he be trying so hard to save her plantation home for her?

He finished his scotch and she escorted him to the door, all the while reassuring him that she would be okay. She reminded him that this three-million-dollar condo was paid for; her car, the $140,000 Mercedes Benz convertible, was also paid for; and her only other major bills were her seven credit cards, which she paid off each month.

Standing at the door, he said, "I have worried about you, Jessie Belle. This is going to be an enormous change in lifestyle for you. You'll have to live on your salary. Thank goodness you have your career. You're very good at it, by the way."

"Thank you. I only make $125,000 a year, but there are lots of people who'd give anything for that kind of money." *Like Dray,* she thought, *supporting an entire family on a cameraman's salary.* "Don't you worry, I can do it. I'll just have to stop shopping."

He nodded, handed her his business card, and said, "Call me if you ever need me. I will always do whatever I can."

"Why, thank you, Lawrence. You are a true gentleman."

A slight glow flickered from his eyes, revealing that was the best compliment she ever could have paid him.

He walked away and she closed the door.

"Star! Star!" Jessie Belle rasped as she roamed from room to room, hoping her muse would appear. "Where are you?"

Georgia on My Mind interrupted her thoughts. She pulled her cell phone out of her pocket and looked at caller ID.

"Argh!" she groaned but punched it on knowing she couldn't hold off this conversation forever. "Hi, Mama."

For twenty minutes her mama, sounding chipper as a retriever puppy with a new toy instead of a socialite whose favorite plaything, her bank account, had just been taken away, blathered on and on about what a sensation Robert had been on TV a half hour earlier. She claimed Jessie Belle had been clever for playing it the way she did. "That cute little hissy fit was perfect! And hitting him with the flowers...." She lost her voice with tittering.

Jessie Belle wanted to inform her there was no "hissy fit" plan, only what she'd felt like doing. But she knew better than to try to interrupt her mama's flow of thought. And this was a veritable tsunami.

Jessie Belle hadn't seen Robert on TV, so had no idea why he'd been such a "sensation."

When she could finally get a word in edgewise, she attempted to approach the money issue. "Mama, I've talked to Lawrence Davidson. He told me we're broke. Jeff has lost all of our money."

"Oh! He's such a nice man, that Mr. Davidson. I really must invite him out for Sunday dinner sometime soon."

"Mama, we're broke. Aren't you worried?"

"Now don't you get mad at your brother. He does the best he can."

"Unfortunately, his best ain't worth diddly squat."

"My, what a potty mouth you've acquired lately! Your language leaves a lot to be desired, Miss Church."

"Mama, pay attention to the real problem here. We don't have 'more money than God' anymore. We don't have any money. At least I have my job, the one you've always wanted me to give up. But how in hell are you going to live?"

"There you go again with that unladylike language! My oh my, you always have been such a worrywart! Never-you-mind about all that. You need to concentrate on Robert. He's right there in your net! All you have to do now is slowly reel him in with your feminine wiles, careful that he doesn't wiggle off that hook."

Jessie Belle blocked out the inanity while her mama blathered on about Robert and wiles and wiggling. Totally exasperated, Jessie Belle gave up. Maisy Church never had and apparently never would admit there was any world other than her imaginary one where everyone and everything revolved around her own desires and demands.

When the one-sided phone conversation came to a blessed end, Jessie Belle plopped down on her plump sofa and clicked on the 42-inch flat screen television that was recessed into the wall above the fireplace mantel. Sure enough, there he was, looking dapper as all get out, even though fading rose petals hung from his hair and peppered his Armani suit.

"You saw it all, folks," Robert said into the camera. "She refused my marriage proposal. She even beat me over the head with the roses I gave her! Isn't she something? What man couldn't love that gumption, that bravery, that sense of righteousness? She has every right to be furious with me; I don't blame her! I was a fool. That's why I intend to get down on bended knee again and again until Jessie Belle Church agrees to marry me!"

Furious at his arrogance, Jessie Belle marched into her kitchen, picked up the bottle of Glenrothes 1985, and stormed back into the living room ready to smash Robert's precious booze bottle into his oversized face on the TV screen. She hefted it back, then froze. *I can't destroy my TV! I'm broke. I can't afford to buy a new one.*

Defeated, she let her arm fall, went into the bathroom, flushed what little was left down the toilet, and dropped the empty bottle into the trashcan. Wiping her hands together to conclude the ritual, she decided to go take a nice, long nap.

Jet lag had kicked in and she was just too pooped to participate in anger over love or money or family. She didn't know who to be angriest at, anyway. Her daddy for giving her nincompoop brother control of the family purse strings? Robert for cheating on her? Her brother for being such an irresponsible piss-ant? Her mother for living her faux proper Southern belle life in a bottle? Or herself for letting any of this happen to her? For one thing, why hadn't she fought to take control of her own money years ago? It felt like she'd just been charged with a slew of crimes she didn't commit, and she needed to make a break for it. Aware that "like mother like daughter" might still be truer than she cared to admit, she crawled into bed and made her getaway by falling fast asleep.

The feathery kiss to her forehead awoke her.

"Hello, dear," Star said.

Jessie Belle looked up at her friend and felt such warmth, such love, that she knew she could never express it in words.

Star smiled as if reading her mind.

"I'm at a crossroads, Star. I need to decide which way to go."

Star gently stroked her hair. "Yes, Jessie Belle. Whichever path you take, it will be the life that you choose. No one else can take the credit or the blame. It's up to you now."

Jessie Belle looked deeply into the spirit's bright ethereal eyes. They told her that their time together would soon come to an end, and that it was time for Jessie Belle to take the gift of friendship Star had given her and put it to good use in her life.

She wondered about Giselle, the ancestor that Star had told her during her last visit was yet to come.

"She'll come when you are ready for her," Star whispered.

Then she was gone.

Noon! She couldn't believe the clock on her nightstand insisted she'd slept for sixteen hours. That was either major exhaustion or major avoidance. Probably both, she decided.

Padding into the bathroom to clean up, she couldn't help but wonder what doom and gloom this day would bring. It was Saturday. Maybe God would give her a break in preparation for the blessed day tomorrow.

Once dressed, she decided that the answer to all of her problems, at least for the moment, would be a Starbucks venti café mocha with whipped cream. Yes! That was it! Surely Starbucks would someday save the world by encouraging people to occupy themselves with drinking coffee rather than fighting each other.

She went down in the elevator and when the doors opened at the lobby she was bombarded with the smell of roses, dozens and dozens of pink roses in crystal vases scattered around the room.

Roger hustled up to her. "Good morning, Miss Church. These," he said, sweeping his arm around to indicate the flowers, "have been coming every hour on the hour since six o'clock this morning. They are for you, of course, from Mr. Brentz. I didn't have them sent up, as I assumed you were tired from your journey and didn't want to be awakened. Shall I have them sent up now?"

Jessie Belle gnawed at her lower lip, considering this. Then she considered Roger. He did a great job of taking care of his residents but always looked like a rod was stuck up his you-know-what. Maybe mid-thirties, slightly paunchy, with nondescript looks, this flower thing clearly had him flustered.

"Roger," she said, "is there still that assisted living place down the street? You know, the place for old—elder—people?"

"Why, yes, there is. The Peachtree Ridge assisted living facility."

"Call them and see if any of their residents would like some flowers. If they do, keep sending whatever comes here. If they run out of space there, send them to the children's ward at the hospital. After that, send them anyplace you can think of. I don't want them and don't have plans to beat anybody over the head with them today, so find something else to do with them."

"Yes, Miss Church," he said, without a smile at her self-deprecating remark.

Oh, Roger, she thought as she exited the building, someday you need to try to loosen up and pull that stick out of your derrière.

Not long after, she was smiling. Her hot, delicious, creamy Starbuck's café mocha calmed her nerves, gave her pleasure, and made her feel at peace with the world. How could she possibly do battle with anyone today after drinking the nectar of the gods? Her day would be nothing but quiet solitude, a day just for her.

Chapter 22

Ah, what a difference a day makes, Jessie Belle caught herself thinking the next day.

Keeping her Saturday peaceful had been a challenge, what with her mama calling every hour and Robert every couple of hours. She'd looked at caller ID for a while, then turned her phone off, pretending it was broken. Then Roger the doorman called to tell her Mr. Brentz was in the lobby and wanted to come up. She asked Roger if there were any roses left and when he said yes, that one newly-delivered dozen hadn't been taken to the assisted living facility yet, she suggested that he use them to beat Mr. Brentz over the head.

"Oh, Miss Church, I'm sorry, but I cannot do that," he'd said, stoically.

"Roger, I'm kidding. Don't worry about it. Just tell Mr. Brentz I do not want to see him."

Barring those interruptions, she'd spent a blissful Saturday sans TV, reading the magazines that had come in the mail and piled up while she was gone, putzing around in her kitchen, napping on her comfy couch, snacking on popcorn and Coke, taking a long bubble bath, and doing her best not to think.

But now it was Sunday, and reality had barreled in like a raging bull. It was the day of the last shoot for the CNN special genographic series, shot at her mama's plantation.

The bull, in the form of her attractive petite mother, attacked the moment Jessie Belle arrived. Maisy Church flew out of her house, clomped down the wide veranda steps, and stomped up to the car before her daughter could even get out.

"Where have you been? I tried to call all day yesterday! I was worried sick about you! What's got into you? We have to get ready for this taping! And Robert called me a dozen times yesterday. He couldn't get a hold of you, either. Listen to me, girl, playing hard to get is good, but you have to do it just right. You can't be too hard. Remember, give him some line, reel him in a little, let out a little more line.... Goodness gracious! By now you should know how it goes. You're thirty years old! You don't have forever to be finding new rich boyfriends. You don't want to lose this one!"

Jessie Belle calmly got out of her car with the door shoving her mama back a little in the process. Mama had come up close to the open window in order to deliver her diatribe.

"I'm sorry, Mama," Jessie Belle lied. "Yesterday I was so exhausted from the trip I slept all day. But I'm good to go now."

Not mollified one bit, Mama scurried Jessie Belle into the house to help her choose which outfit to wear. Joe and the cameraman would be there soon, so they had little time to lose.

Her mama oozed charm for the camera. Jessie Belle couldn't deny that. Viewers would lap it up. Joe had her sitting in one of the white wicker rocking chairs on her expansive white porch with its traditional pale blue bead board ceiling made to mimic the sky on a pretty summer day and ceiling fans that lazily circled in unhurried Southern style. Maisy had finally settled on her pastel pink and green flowered chiffon sundress, which made her look like a beautiful, albeit mature, Southern belle. Her white hair had been coiffed to perfection and whatever touchup work her plastic surgeon had done had been tactful and tasteful. Her makeup was so flawless it could have been applied by a Hollywood studio make-up artist. The raging bull had become a sweet, purring kitten.

Jessie Belle was seated in another white wicker rocking chair beside her mother and was wearing a pale pink sundress. Her mama had chosen her own outfit to make sure they "complimented" each other, just like she'd been doing all of her daughter's life.

Two crystal glasses filled with iced tea and garnished with lemon wedges sat on the table between them, the perfect prop. It was so good, though, that Jessie Belle gobbled half of hers down, causing Joe to ask that it be refilled.

That task went to Ida, Maisy's African American housekeeper. Ida had been there all of Jessie Belle's life. The tall, statuesque woman with broad features, velvety dark brown skin, and mass of black hair that had become painted with streaks of white in recent years, was like a second mama. Except that she was the antithesis of mama number one. Jessie Belle loved Ida and loved her fresh brewed iced tea. It was all she could do to keep from chugging it all down again, which would ruin its intent as a prop.

The scene set to his satisfaction, Joe said, "Action," just like in the movies, and Jessie Belle asked her first question of her mama.

"Why," Maisy drawled into the camera in response to the query about what she thought of the discovery of their Scandinavian ancestry, "when you told me your DNA says our heritage includes people from northern Europe, I was so delightfully surprised!" Jessie Belle knew that was a bold-faced lie, but her mama was very convincing. Maisy Church was not one bit proud of their pillaging, pirating, raping, murdering Viking ancestors. As far as she was concerned, Scandinavians were to the British what Yankees were to Southerners. The political correctness was for the cameras only. "You see," Maisy continued, "my mother, grandmothers, and great-grandmothers are all from right here in the wonderful peach state of Georgia. Of course, there is British lineage in the family from way back. But, northern European, why, no, I'd never heard of that."

Jessie Belle wondered how many viewers would catch the fact that she hadn't even said "Scandinavian," let alone "Viking." And that she'd managed to dilute the "northern" connection considerably.

Jessie Belle just couldn't resist. "What do you think about our ancestors having been Vikings who raided and raped and murdered?" she asked.

"Oh my!" Maisy's hand flew to her chest and her head cocked in mock surprise. "I doubt that every Northern European person did any such thing, so who knows?"

Thinking of the dream she'd had about Erika and how Erika's mother had not agreed with her family's Viking pursuits, Jessie Belle had no retort. She was a little shocked at her mama's accidental astuteness.

"How about if we talk a bit about the history of this family plantation while we take a walk around to show our viewers where the long travels of our ancestors ended, at least as of today," Jessie Belle suggested, just as Joe had instructed her to do.

"Of course, dear," Maisy said sweetly. They left the porch and walked around the yard, inspecting the colorful flower gardens and giant old live oak trees. It was a perfect picture of serenity and brought back memories for Jessie Belle of how much she'd loved playing here when she was a child. Even though she now came out almost every Sunday afternoon for dinner, taking the easy forty-minute drive from her Buckhead section of Atlanta straight east out Interstate 20 to Social Circle, she seldom thought anymore about her happy childhood days here. Since middle school, it seemed, her mind had been filled with boys and shopping and hairstyles and fans and how much press she could generate.

But today the recollections of that carefree time gone by—
or at least as carefree as possible with Maisy for a mother—came
flooding back. Ida letting her climb that tree right there whenever her mother was at bridge club, and then timing it just right to
get her inside and cleaned up before her mama came home. Her
daddy having the yard man put up a rope swing with a flat wood
board seat, hanging from that treasured tree, and then pushing
her himself while she chirped with glee, "Higher, daddy! Higher!" And sitting on a tree stump in the cool shade under the front
porch on hot summer days, playing with her beloved cat Buster
and pretending he was her audience while she sang songs and
told stories. She poked way back into her memory, trying to clear
the cobwebs. What had those stories been about?

Here I sit upon a stump.
Don't I cut a figure?
If the boys don't like me now,
they will when I get bigger.

Her daddy had taught her that one. She also recalled lectur-
ing Buster on the importance of sitting up straight and keeping
your elbows off the table while eating a meal. Buster had not
seemed to be impressed. And… what else had she told Buster
about?

While she and her mama were being filmed walking the
flagstone path through the exuberant backyard flower garden,
the memory came back like a slowly rising tide. Bits and pieces
came, and then one telling wave flowed over her and the memory
became complete.

It had been the day after her ninth birthday. With her usual elaborate birthday celebration done and gone, Jessie Belle
found herself playing hopscotch alone on the backyard flagstone
path when she saw Ida come out of the greenhouse and head
out across the pasture. Even though the greenhouse was some
distance away, out back by the old stables, there was no mistaking that stately gait, even from behind, as she pecked her way

through the pasture. That field had once grown cotton but in modern times had been turned over to cattle to keep the land fertile for who-knew-what potential future use.

Ida, as Jessie Belle had seen her do before, carried a gardening bucket with the handle of a trowel sticking out of the top. She wore her well-worn leather gardening gloves, even though it was hot enough to fry an egg on the sidewalk. Jessie Belle didn't bother running to catch up and asking if she could go with her. She'd tried that a few times and the woman had always told her to run along back to the house. So this time Jessie Belle crept up close enough to follow but far enough behind to avoid being caught. They went through the pasture. Ida swatted the butt a friendly cow to shoo it out of the way, and Jessie Belle followed Ida's lead in skirting a cow patty.

On the other side of the expansive pasture stood a stand of trees that Jessie Belle had never ventured into before, even though she'd roamed a lot of the plantation land. Ida disappeared into the trees.

Carefully, Jessie Belle followed until the path through the woods suddenly stopped short at an old wooden fence that enclosed a large cleared, albeit overgrown, area that had a bunch of rocks strewn around. The child ducked down and peeked between two rails of the fence to watch the grown-up.

Ida set down her bucket, took off her gloves and cast them onto the ground, got down on bended knee, bowed her head, and started saying a prayer. "Dear Lord, bless these poor souls whose names are not so much as recorded on their graves. Bless them for the nameless lives they were forced to live. I know you would never cheat them in death as they were cheated in life, and that you will bless them with your love in eternity...."

Jessie Belle was confused. What was this place? Graves? Certainly it wasn't a cemetery. The Church family cemetery was on the other side of the plantation. Unlike this place, it was well tended by yard workers and had beautifully scrolled and scripted headstones. Then the realization hit the nine-year-old girl. This was the old slave cemetery. They didn't have headstones. Just a plain rock to mark each grave. No one even knew the names of the people who were buried here.

Jessie Belle carefully worked her way through the tangled foliage that had overtaken the fence until she reached the battered gate that hung on one rusted hinge. Thin as a rail herself, she slipped through without having to open it any further, quietly went to Ida, and kneeled down beside her. Ida, not surprised, finished her prayer with a gentle "Amen." The child whispered "Amen" and put her small, soft, white hand into the large, calloused, black hand. They knelt in silence until the woman said, "Come on, child. We have work to do."

"What are we going to do?" Jessie Belle asked as she jumped up and helped her elder stand up.

"It's daffodil time!" Ida said, her smile broad as could be. "These slaves had nothing of their own, except a handful of unused daffodil bulbs that they planted. Those bulbs grew, year after year, until they had hundreds of daffodil bulbs planted on this burial ground and around their cabins. That meadow out yonder," she said, pointing further into the woods to a place that couldn't be seen from here, "is where their cabins stood. Those are long gone but in about a week those bright yellow daffodils will push themselves up out of their captivity and bloom with life. They represent the slaves, the human beings, who lived and died working this land. Their names may be forgotten, but those daffodils make certain we remember they were here!" Even in her jubilation at the thought of remembrance, she wiped away a melancholy tear.

"What can I do?" Jessie Belle wanted to know.

"See all those little green spuds peaking up through the old fallen leaves and twigs? We need to clear everything away from each one of them so they get as much sun as possible. These old trees have grown so much in the last hundred and fifty years, the ground here doesn't get as much sun as it used to. So we help the new blooms get the light they need. Then we'll clear debris away from the stones."

Jessie Belle looked up at the giant trees that surrounded the cemetery. One had grown through the split-rail fence and truly split it in the process. A couple more had jumped the fence altogether and grew inside the clearing. They were wonderful trees, casting shade on the graves as if sheltering them from any possible danger. Then she studied the ground around her feet. Sure enough, there were inch-long sprouts coming up everywhere. And there were more rocks than she'd seen at first, with many buried beneath the natural rubble of the woods.

They went to work, with the student following her teacher's example. By the time they lifted their heads from their tasks, the sun shone in low, prismed beams of light through the trunks of the trees.

"We need to get back to the house and get you cleaned up 'fore your mama gets home."

"Yes, m'am."

They held hands all the way back to the house.

The recollection faded as Jessie Belle eased out of her reverie. They were still in the back flower garden, with her mama describing in agonizing detail each flower and fern. Joe would never be able to use all this footage, Jessie Belle realized, but had this new cameraman keep shooting just to be polite to her mother. She needed to harness control of this interview.

"Mama," she said when her mother finally took a breath, "why don't we go back to the front porch and finish our tea."

Never one to linger outdoors beyond the porch to begin with, Maisy heartily agreed.

They finished the interview from their rocking chairs, sipping their tea with their pinkies in the air. Jessie Belle would introduce the segment herself on-air tomorrow, when she finally got back to her newsdesk. She would also wrap up the entire series. That promised to be a good spot and she looked forward to it.

The minute Joe said, "Cut!" Maisy called Ida to put a shot of scotch into her tea. She offered some to Joe and the cameraman, but they declined. Jessie Belle missed Dray, who had seemed to know what to capture for a story like this. The new guy seemed lost. She understood that Dray had promised to take his kids camping and that he could not break that promise, but it was too bad he had to miss this final shoot after investing so much work in the series.

The men were saying their goodbyes when Jessie Belle had a spur-of-the-moment idea.

"Listen, Joe, there's a slave cemetery on the property, out in the woods. It's not too hard to get to from here. It's one of those 'sacred spaces' we talked about once. How about getting some shots back there? Then I could talk a little bit about it in my story tomorrow. After all, it is part of the family history."

Maisy objected. "Why do you always want to bring up such unpleasant things, Jessie Belle?" she said, the sugar in her voice hardening as if it'd been boiled into rock candy. "And don't forget, we have our usual Sunday dinner in a little while. We've missed the last two. I'm anxious to sit down and talk to my daughter. I missed you so much while you were gone."

No one responded to Maisy. Instead, Joe said, "I love it! Let's go! Which way is it?"

With Ida as their guide, everyone except Maisy hiked through the pasture and into the woods. Although she was more than twenty years older than she'd been the first time Jessie Belle had followed her out here, Ida was still spry as a spring chicken. The rest of them had to huff and puff to keep up. When they came upon the cemetery, it was clear that the older woman had continued to keep it up all these years.

Transfixed, Joe had the cameraman take a number of shots while the two women stood side-by-side and watched.

Then Joe said, "Ida, would you let Jessie Belle interview you, right here, right now? You could tell us about how and why you've been taking care of this place. Eh?"

The story about forgotten, nameless graves and daffodils that bloomed in remembrance each spring was a story that Jessie Belle felt certain their viewers would never forget.

They did the interview and at the end Jessie Belle said, "When I was a carefree child running around this land playing," she gestured to indicate the cow pasture, "I never realized that my bare feet were touching upon the same earth that other bare feet had trot before me——the feet of the slaves who worked so hard. Today I have learned to feel that connection. Thank you for bringing us here, Ida. Because of you, people whose names have been lost to us have not been forgotten in spirit."

"And because of you," Ida said, "others will finally see and acknowledge that these people, these human beings, existed. Finally, they will be remembered."

They closed the interview with tears in their eyes and a big hug. Joe was thrilled with the piece.

When they got back to the house, the men offered their thank-yous and goodbyes and left, and the women went into the house.

"More of my special tea!" her mama declared.

"Coming right up," Ida said.

"Let's go into the sitting room while we wait for our dinner guest," Maisy said to Jessie Belle, gesturing toward the sunny room off the kitchen. They walked into the space that blasted its inhabitants with big, bright, bold flower patterns on every available piece of furniture and accessory. Ever since her mama had it redecorated three years ago, this room had looked to Jessie Belle like a cartoon flower shop gone awry. She always expected the flowers to jump up and start doing a jig, and sing in tinny little caricature voices.

As they sat down, Jessie Belle said, "What guest, Mama? I thought it would probably be just the two of us today."

"Oh, it's a surprise!"

Ida brought in a tray of iced tea in a pitcher, with two fresh glasses of ice and, having given up all pretense, the bottle of Johnny Walker Scotch in the middle of the tray. As she set it down on the coffee table she said, "Some 'surprise.' Hmph!" She gave Jessie Belle a long, knowing look.

At that moment Jessie Belle noticed the bouquet of pink roses on the side table and jumped when the doorbell rang.

"No!" she wailed. "No! Mama, you wouldn't!"

"I told her not to," Ida noted for the record.

Chapter 23

In the end, she supposed she'd always known how the scene would eventually play out. It took Robert one week to talk Jessie Belle into becoming his wedded wife.

On the Sunday evening her mother had invited him to dinner, Jessie Belle had stormed out of her mama's house, leaving a trail of dust in her wake as she sped out of the gravel driveway.

On Monday she returned to work early in the morning, even though her show wasn't until the afternoon, to prepare the script for the final "Ancestry Quest" segment. As soon as the show aired, viewer feedback started pouring in and the consensus was that it was Jessie Belle's best work ever. Her boss, Harry, was elated. Harry also told her that Robert Brentz had called and asked if he could perform a surprise on-air marriage proposal. Harry thought the idea preposterous and denied the request. Robert, not accustomed to being denied anything, had not been too pleased. He was, however, polite, Harry said.

Tuesday meant back to work as usual, only to hear someone else's news story that Robert Brentz had sent a dozen pink roses to every woman in the Peachtree Battle assisted living home, seeing that they hadn't received any like the residents of Peachtree Ridge down the road from them. It was a cute human interest story, with an elderly woman being interviewed and cooing about how Robert Brentz was the kindest man on earth and that she didn't see why "that woman" wouldn't forgive him and take him back.

By Wednesday Jessie Belle found herself wondering how Dray's camping trip with the kids was going, only to shake it off and turn her mind back to work. There had been so much viewer feedback on her network blog about the ancestor story that Harry wanted her to do a follow-up segment on Friday. He called it "Ancestry Quest Q & A." Usually Jessie Belle let the production assistant, Gracie, handle that kind of thing, reading viewer posts and selecting the best ones to reply to, but Jessie Belle's interest remained keen and she wanted to cull through the blog with Gracie. Her only contacts with Robert on Wednesday were a brief phone message and a short tweet from him, both entreating her to have a casual dinner with him on Saturday night at the Buckhead Diner. She ignored the messages.

On Thursday she was surprised at the list of guests Harry had put together for her show, as it included Yemen's Consulate General, Mr. Tuma, the man who'd put the wheel in motion in the first place, the great big, squeaking, grinding gear that thrust Jessie Belle to the hinterlands and ultimately changed her life. It was her on-air rudeness to him that had impelled the bigwigs upstairs to send her on the genographic story assignment. She'd hated his guts in the beginning but now she looked at him through new eyes.

She was supposed to interview him regarding Yemen's international policy, but decided that a little ad lib was called for at the beginning of the interview.

"Mr. Tuma," she began, "thank you for coming here today. I'm told that I was a tad rude to you the last time you were here and I want to apologize. I didn't mean to cut you short." That last part was a bold-faced lie, but she hadn't totally lost her mind and forgotten how to make things look good for an audience. "I'm glad you're back."

The sliver of a moment of silence it took him to respond communicated to her that he got the unspoken message.

"Oh, Ms. Church, that is perfectly fine," he also lied, but in mutual understanding. "I don't even know how you newscasters do the job that you do when so much is going on all at once. You're talking to people like me and news is being flashed on a monitor and someone is talking into the little thing in your ear. I understand completely. No offense taken."

Then it struck her that he'd said "newz-casters," "zo," and "offenze." He didn't have trouble with all of his esses, but some of them. Where had she heard that same pronunciation before? She thought back... Sean Connery, the actor! Some years ago when she first suspected he got false teeth. While asking Mr. Tuma a question about international policy, she watched his big, broad, white teeth. Not veneers, as she'd thought last time—false! He hadn't purposely mispronounced her name; he couldn't help it sometimes. It was when he'd called her "Jezzie Belle" that she's become offended and cut him off in that first interview. That had caused him to complain to her superiors, they had kicked her halfway around the world, and her life would never be the same. All because she'd jumped to a conclusion about a man who had false teeth!

His long answer to her present question was politically correct, but she wasn't even paying much attention. In the first interview, she'd also assumed he was chauvinistic, not just because of his culture but because of the way she thought he treated her. Now she had a burning desire to know about the women in his life. The lives of women had become extremely important to her in the last few weeks, seeing that so many dead ones had chosen to pay her visits.

When he finished answering her question about politics, she said, "Mr. Tuma, I just had a thought about your wife. I've met her a few times at social gatherings, as you know, like the Habitat for Humanity event last year. She's such a gracious, beautiful woman, by the way, but I'm interesting in knowing what life is like for her here. This is a country and a culture she was not raised in. Does she like it here?"

The Consulate General smiled so broadly that his ears looked ready to pop off. "Ah, she is beautiful, isn't she? My Sarah. Beautiful on the inside and the outside."

Jessie Belle blinked hard. That's just what Levi, her Jewish ancestor, had said about his Irish wife. Star had talked about it, too. Was this man related to Levi, also? Did he know Star? Had that spirit rascal sent him for an interview in the first place? She doubted Star could conjure that up but suspected she would have if she could have.

Mr. Tuma continued, "You would have to ask Sarah for a complete answer to your question. In fact, she'd probably be a much more interesting interview than I am. She's an amazing woman! But she tells me that she loves living here in Atlanta. She likes the weather, the schools for our children and grandchildren, and the easy drive to Florida beaches. Yes, we're very happy here."

The floor producer was screaming into Jessie Belle's earpiece to get back to the topic of international policy.

"How many children and grandchildren do you have?" she asked.

He smiled again. This was a topic he clearly relished. "I have five children, all grown now, of course, and eleven grandchildren. You always hear that being a grandparent is the best thing in the world, and it is! No responsibility, lots of fun, and love, love, love. It's great."

Love, love, love. Maybe he was Star's long-lost brother.

Seeing that the screaming in her ear had not relented, she made a stab at pulling the interview back on track. "Do your children and grandchildren understand your work in international relations, or are they like most kids and don't care about politics?"

This made him laugh out loud. "My children understand my work now that they are adults, but they didn't care when they were young. Many years ago when my son was in kindergarten, he told his classmates I was in poppy-ticks. The teacher asked him what that meant and he said he didn't know for sure, but he thought it was some kind of game.

"Actually, he wasn't too far off.

"As for my grandchildren, they only think of me as their old grandpa who tussles with them in the grass and plays soccer with them and takes them to interesting places, like Disneyworld. Foreign policy to them is eating a safari corn dog at Animal Kingdom."

Jessie Belle chuckled along with him while her earpiece almost blasted out of her head.

"I am a blessed man to have such a family," he reflected in afterthought.

"And," Jessie Belle said, "those grandchildren are lucky to have a grandpa who does all of those fun things with them.

"Well, Mr. Tuma, our time is up for today," she said, finally responding to the voice in her head, "but I do hope you'll come back again. It's been a pleasure to get to know you a little better and to look at the human side of politics." She was proud of herself for pulling that connection together on the spur of the moment. Whenever she did that she thought of it as marrying a turtle and a hippopotamus. Outwardly the two are different, but they have much in common like sitting in water, sunbathing, sauntering, and foraging for food. Find the common threads and almost anything could be tied together.

"Before I leave," Mr. Tuma said, "I want to tell you that I watched every one of your 'Ancestry Quest' episodes. They were wonderful, Jessie Belle! A reminder to us all to respect those who came before us and gave us the lives we have today."

Ignoring the loud, impatient sigh coming from her earpiece, she said, "Thank you, Mr. Tuma. It means a lot to me that a family man like you enjoyed that series. We'll see you again soon."

They shook hands and the politician said, "My pleasure."

The floor producer cut to a late ad and Gracie materialized to escort Mr. Tuma away. He gave a quick wave and was gone.

He didn't seem one bit chauvinistic. I was wrong about him, as I was about so many other things.

"Jessie Belle!" The floor producer, a new man she hadn't worked with before, stampeded out of his booth and interrupted her thoughts. "Please, pay attention to my directions. Our sponsor will not be happy their spot aired late. And Mr. Tuma was supposed to be your political interview. You turned him into the personal interest story. In half an hour your personal interest interview, that little old lady who saved a baby from a fire, is coming up. What do you intend to do with her? Ask her about her politics?" He withdrew to his little glass room before she could so much as respond.

Actually, she thought that was a good idea, but decided to be a good girl for the rest of the day. Who knew where she might get sent next if the head honchos didn't like her attitude? Antarctica? She hated the cold.

Before leaving the studio that afternoon she received a hand-delivered note from Robert, a formal invitation brought by currier, inviting her again to the informal dinner on Saturday night. She threw it in the trashcan on her way out of the building.

By the next day, Thursday, she was so buried in work in preparation for Friday's follow-up show that she didn't give Robert one moment of thought. Not until she got home that night and saw his limo outside her elegant marble condo building. When he saw her Mercedes pull into the garage, he got out and trod to the garage entrance. His vehicle couldn't get past the security gate, so he just stood there calling her name. She thought him somewhat pathetic and scurried into the elevator, punching the button frantically until the door closed.

Friday's show went spectacularly. Later she thought maybe it was the celebration of the culmination of the weeks of work or the letdown of having completed a goal and not knowing what might be next, but for one reason or another when Robert phoned she talked to him for a minute.

He called again Saturday morning and she finally said yes to his invitation. It was that evening when, although the press had been sidetracked recently by other salacious antics of the rich and famous, one independent photographer caught the moment at the Buckhead Diner when Jessie Belle relented and finally accepted the honker of a diamond engagement ring. That lone photo played on page one or two of every tabloid in the country.

She also supposed that one reason she hadn't been more outraged and panicked, although she certainly was angry, that her brother lost all of the family money had been because deep down she'd known she'd take care of things by marrying money. Robert's money.

But this time around things would be different. She insisted on it. She had been happy being Robert's lucky chosen one in the past, but now she demanded that he treat her as an equal. She didn't just want his name and fortune; she wanted his respect and loyalty. And his love.

"I won't be a trophy wife, Robert," she said the moment he brought up marriage again, which was as soon as they sat down at their table at the Buckhead Diner. "I won't be the elusive 'prize' you covet and then forget once it's won. I also want to keep my job; I love my work. That means I'll have to travel sometimes and when I do I refuse to have to be worrying about whether or not my husband is faithful to me. You cheated on me once; I have to know you won't do it again."

He took her hand, looked into her eyes, and said, "You will never have to worry about that again. I promise that, Jessie Belle. Believe me, I learned my lesson.

"You're right. I didn't see your career as being all that important. I was acting like a spoiled brat, thinking you should have stayed here to be with me. It was the most asinine thing I've ever done in my life and I won't ever do it again.

"I understand now that your career is as important to you as mine is to me. I know that trust is the foundation of a good marriage. And most of all, I'm certain that I don't ever want to lose you. I love you, Jessie Belle!"

Good answers. She couldn't deny that he delivered all of the right responses to her concerns.

But she wasn't done yet. "There's one more thing, Robert: money. I know that men with money like yours want a prenuptial agreement. That's okay with me." She didn't miss the glint of relief in his eyes. "But I want to negotiate the terms. If we ever divorce—and I mean *ever*, even within fifteen minutes of the 'I do's'—I want a $50 million settlement. That's chump change to you, but it's a replacement for the inheritance my idiot brother lost when he lost the rest of the family fortune. I assume you've heard about that by now."

He didn't flinch, letting her know that he'd heard about it through the proverbial grapevine.

"Furthermore," she continued, "I want you to purchase my mama's plantation and sign an agreement to let her live there for the rest of her life. Upon her death, the plantation will go to me, not my brother.

"As for that low-down scumbag, I want you to promise me that you will never lift a finger to help him out. Let him fend for himself for a change. He might actually have to get a real job. It'll do him good."

He stared at her for a few moments then burst into laughter. "When, my love, did you become such an astute business-woman?"

"When you screwed Bridget Barker."

His smile disintegrated like sugar on acid. "Fair enough," he said seriously.

"Oh, there's one more thing! On my trip I learned that the word 'virgin' originally meant renewal, not never having had sex. In olden times, women became virgins, renewed, every year. I want to feel renewed for our wedding. I don't want to have sex again until our wedding night. I want to be a 'virgin.'"

He smiled. "What a charming tradition, Jessie Belle. I guess that means we need to get married sooner rather than later. I'd been thinking of having our wedding within a month anyway. How about an intimate affair, maybe a couple hundred people, at your church in a couple of weeks?"

In response to the look of shock on her face, he said, "Don't worry. I've already looked into everything. It can be done. I even called Vera. She'll have an assistant here to measure you for a gown as soon as you give the word. And, of course, I'll pay for everything."

She mulled that over. The Vera Wang wedding gown would finally be hers.

"Okay," she said, "if you agree to my conditions. You've heard my offer. Take it or leave it."

"Ms. Church, I accept your offer. Now, will you accept mine?"

That was when he raised her left hand to his lips, kissed her knuckles, slipped the ring on her finger, and kissed her hand again. It was that photograph, Robert Brentz kissing Jessie Belle Church's bejeweled hand, taken by someone purposefully passing by their table with a clandestine camera, which circled the globe.

Chapter 24

Where in blazes was Star when she needed her? She'd felt so strong while sitting there in the Buckhead Diner with Robert, planning her life away. Her ancestors, the women in her dreams, and Star, her spirit friend, had given her that strength. If the women who made her could endure the tragedies and triumphs of their lives, she certainly could endure her own. And marrying Robert seemed like the best way to do that.

Wasn't it?

Jessie Belle lay in bed, eyes wide open, mulling over her future. She stretched her left arm up, spread her fingers, and looked at her engagement ring. Even in the dark, the rock was so humungous it sparkled in the wisp of moonlight that trickled through the window.

She looked at the clock on the nightstand. Two o'clock in the morning. Geez! She needed some sleep. But now that she was alone in the dark of night, bleeding doubts riddled her muddled thoughts. She needed to bounce her thoughts off of Star, like she'd done so many times before. And where was that Giselle, the final ancestor who was supposed to tell her story? Maybe that would help.

Once again, she ran through the parade of women who had appeared in her dreams. There was the ancient African, Clacka, who measured her happiness solely by the closeness of her loved ones and had been profoundly content with her life. Karum, the Egyptian girl, sold by her own father into slavery and raped by her Arab husband, found life so foreboding that she chose to end it by hurling herself off a cliff. But at the last instant she had cared enough for her baby to leave it in the arms of a maternalistic woman. Then there was Julia, the Venezian vintner who lived a privileged and joyful, albeit unconventional, life with her lover with whom she had children. Brunhild had endured abuse and devastating hardship with her Celtic husband until her prince in shining armor, in the form of a barbarian, saved her daughter and her so that they could live happily ever after. Erika, the bodacious Viking, had been dead as a doornail and didn't even know it. Erika's mother had protested her Viking family's pirating ways but had been ignored. Not exactly the motherly type herself, Erika had left her bastard baby in the care of a crone she didn't even know. Then there was Haliakula, a fat, toothless, straggly-haired Polynesian who reveled in her docile life and doted on her offspring. And Kathleen, the Irish widow left to head her family of ten children and countless grandchildren.

As her mind revisited the story of each woman, an idea dawned on Jessie Belle. A mere glint at first, it quickly intensified to become an obsessive desire. She would do a special series about women. Specifically, she wanted to research and report about how the women of her ancestry trail would have been treated according to the cultures of their times. She also wanted to learn more about their beliefs, their gods or goddesses, or their lack of beliefs in anything at all. Of course, she had insights from her dreams. But she felt an urgent need to know more and to help other women learn about the cultures of the women who made them, too.

The purpose would be to highlight those same issues for women today and to help mold beliefs that would assist them. For example, there was still an underground slave trade in the world, where girls were sold and sexually abused, even slaughtered, as though their lives held no value whatsoever. Just like Karum. Jessie Belle wanted to fight that practice. Why, even in Atlanta it was reported that 5,000 children, girls and boys, were sold each year, most to be sex slaves. Also, domestic abuse against women still ran rampant in many cultures, including in the good old U. S. of A. Brunhild certainly knew a thing or two about that. Jessie Belle wanted to continue public awareness and show women how to get help. And women all over the world objected to war but their voices were drowned out by the sounds of battle. Erika's mother would have been able to add her voice to that cause. Jessie Belle also wondered if widows with families were helped as much as they needed to be. Kathleen would have been able to provide insight into that. She needed to find out.

The story could culminate with an investigation of the lives of the slaves, especially the female slaves, who had lived on her own family land, the Church Plantation. There might be records somewhere; she'd heard about diaries and receipts of sale of human goods. She ached to know more. Were those women tormented by the sale of their children, as was common practice? Did they believe in the Christian God? Or had they clung to their African roots? Why had she never wondered about them before?

All of these issues were thousands of years old. So why were they still "issues?" Why had human beings not learned better?

Her "Ancestry Quest" had raised more questions than it had provided answers.

They were good questions that would take the input of a lot of good subject matter experts to attempt to address. In fact, there were so many things to talk about, it would take a number of special series, as the time allotted on her show for this kind of thing was so short. This really called for a History or Discover Channel series, but that wasn't going to happen now, so Jessie Belle would content herself with doing what she could in a short time. Ideas zoomed in and out of her head, furiously vying for attention. She considered getting up to start writing things down but decided to harbor her inspirations internally for now. But she couldn't wait to get to work on it later today during daylight hours! It would be a great series! She'd call it "Women's Worlds" or "Women's Worth" or "The Women Who Made Us" or some such thing. She'd have to run the idea by Harry, praying he'd like it.

She looked at the clock again. 3:30 a.m. She'd spent an hour and a half thinking about other women. But at the moment that didn't help her as a woman.

Wishing Star were here to help, she recalled that during her last visit Star had reminded her it was time to think for herself.

Not yet, Star. After this marriage mess gets sorted out. Then, I promise. But not now!

Thre was no answer. So she tried to cipher it for herself.

Am I out of my gourd? Is this what I really want?

Was she in denial, off in la-la land somewhere? Was she as bad as her mama when it came to facing the truth? She shuddered at the thought. Or was this the truth, the fact that she was thirty years old, had lost her inheritance, and was darned lucky that one of the richest and most famous business tycoons in the country wanted to marry her? Even if it didn't work out, she'd be set for life. So what was her problem?

What was it someone had said about denial in one of her dreams? Her mind flipped through its dream memories once again and came up with it. It had been Erika's father, the Viking Erik Bloodtooth, of all people, who said, "Denial is as deep as the middle of the ocean...."

He'd been telling his daughter that it was time to move out of her denial and cross over into life after death. But what about Jessie Belle?

She wondered if she, too, was in her own kind of denial. Was this leap she was about to take the most practical thing to do or was it just another step backwards? Was she entering into

a revitalizing new life or facing a kind of emotional death? She
didn't know.

"Star! Where are you?"

Star did not appear to brighten the dark of this night.

"So, you see," Jessie Belle said, aware that her voice had taken
on an almost pleading tone as she wrapped up her pitch to Harry, "this could be a terrific follow-up to the 'Ancestry Quest.' It
would appeal more to women than men—yes, that's true—but
it would also appeal to arm-chair historians, archaeologists, and
anthropologists. And teachers. And feminists of both sexes, journalists, other writers, social do-gooders, and lots of other people,
too." She knew her list had run out of steam at the end, but she
did the best she could.

Harry sat on his desk, swinging his feet like a little kid, his
arms folded across his barrel chest, looking at her over the rim
of his glasses which were, as usual, perched half-way down his
bulbous nose. He didn't say anything.

Jessie Belle, standing in the middle of his office, took a deep
breath, clasped her hands in front of her, and stood stone still,
looking at him hopefully.

He looked back, his jaw working itself back and forth.

Finally, he spoke. "That's the best idea you've ever had, kid.
I like it. In fact, it's one of the best ideas anyone around here
has had in quite some time. Your work on the 'Ancestry Quest'
assignment was outstanding. This promises to be just as good.
And because it was your idea, you'll be assistant producer. You're
turning into a real news pro.

"Let's do it!" He shoved himself off the desk and strode to
her to shake her hand.

Stunned, she shook heartily. She'd hoped for approval for
the program but hadn't expected the added praise.

"Thank you, sir," she said, beaming. "Thank you so much!"

"Now I know we can't start right away," he said, walking back to his desk to look at his calendar, "not with your wedding coming up in two weeks and then you having a week off for your honeymoon. So when you get back from that we'll lay out a program schedule." .

Her first thought was that she would be willing to skip the honeymoon on Robert's private Caribbean island to get to work on this. But she shucked the ludicrous notion. Who in their right mind would ever do that?

"That'll work out fine," she said.

"By the way, how are the wedding plans coming along? It's all been so fast."

"Oh, everything is fine, I guess. Mama took care of the invitations and Robert is doing everything else. Well, actually, he's paying other people to do everything else, of course. He's having a Vera Wang assistant flown in from New York on his private jet this weekend to fit my dress." She snapped her mouth closed, realizing this was more information than any crusty old dude wanted.

"Good. That's good, I suppose.

"Listen, I know I said some unkind things about Robert when I found out about—you know—that Bridget thing. I'm not going to apologize for my honest opinion, but I do want you to know that I'll keep my trap shut from now on. It's your life, Jessie Belle, and you have a right to live it as you please."

"I appreciate that, Harry. Thank you."

She left his office pondering what it was that she pleased.

Vera Wang's assistant was an efficient, funny, quirky young woman whom Jessie Belle immediately liked. When the bride-to-be put on the dress the assistant had brought, the one Jessie Belle picked out of the army of dresses on Vera's website, it slipped over her head and slithered down her body to fit like a glove.

Jessie Belle stood in her dressing room staring at herself in the full-length mirror. The assistant, who'd zipped the dress up the back and then stooped to fluff out the bottom of the skirt, took one look, plopped down on the floor to lean back on her hands, and exclaimed, "That's rad! I've never seen a dress fit so perfectly right off the sewing machine. You look gorgeous!"

"Thank you." Mesmerized by the sheer beauty of the garment, Jessie Belle felt prettier than ever before in her life. For years she'd dreamt of a bright white Vera Wang princess gown with a stiff beaded and sequined strapless top that would leverage her cleavage, a bustier that would cinch her waist down to the size of a stick, and layer upon layer of sparkling lacy toile for a big puffy skirt.

This dress was nothing like that. It had shocked her as she perused the website that the flamboyant style she'd once yearned for no longer appealed to her. What caught her eye instead was this more relaxed, strapless, ivory chiffon gown with a plain silk band around the waist and a full skirt made of layers of fabric folded back on itself. The website described it as an "asymmetrically draped bias tiered origami skirt." It was natural and flowing, like a waterfall. There wasn't a gaudy bead or flamboyant sequin in sight. It didn't even have a showy train. And for a Vera Wang gown it was a bargain at only fifty thousand dollars, about a third of what Jessie Belle had always expected to pay. Yet it was just right.

"Maybe the fact that it fits so well right from the get-go is a good omen for your marriage," the assistant suggested as she secured the lengthy plain organza veil into Jessie Belle's hair.

"Yeah, maybe," the bride-to-be said as she twirled around holding each side of the veil to watch it flutter through the air.

The dress not needing any alterations meant the assistant got to fly home that same day, which pleased her. She left saying, in her thick New York accent, "No offense, Jessie Belle, but Atlanta seems a little kooky to me, what with all those polite people at the airport calling me 'ma'am.' I prefer good old New Yorkers who say, 'Yo, you!'"

They laughed and hugged goodbye.

Even in the relentless chaos of keeping up with last-minute wedding plans while she continued to do her daily job, Jessie Belle's mind wandered back to the "Ancestry Quest." As worn out as she'd become from their travels, she missed the excitement of the journey. And she missed Joe and Dray. Joe had already been sent out on another assignment. She assumed Dray was back to work on the morning shift, his camping trip with his three kids over by now. How was he doing? Was he glad to be rid of her?

But then she'd think about that plane ride home when he'd come to sit by her at the end. He'd told her he wouldn't be at the last shoot because he was going on vacation with his family. It was at that moment the airplane went haywire in tumultuous air. Had Dray been ready to tell her, or better yet ask her, something else? Was it possible he'd intended to ask her out on a date? Of course, if that had been his plan, he'd had no way of carrying it out, not with Robert and the media fiasco right there. And not with her consequent engagement.

It occurred to her that her new women's series and Dray's idea for a series about "Sacred Spaces" would complement each other. Now that they'd overcome their initial loathing of each other, they would be able to work amicably together.

Ah, well, it didn't matter now. Dray was water over the dam. Her spectacular wedding to Robert would take place in twenty-four short hours.

The flutter of a kiss on her forehead, light as the wings of a butterfly, caused Jessie Belle to stir in her sleep. In the mist of muted awareness, she knew that Star was with her still. Blissfully content, feeling safe and loved, she settled back into deep slumber.

Chapter 25

Giselle kneeled on the thick burgundy-and-green-and-gold Persian carpet, hunched over her *gris-gris*. Frantically rolling the Voodoo sticks between her palms, she chanted her fervent spell.

"Save the girl, save the girl, save the girl!

Curse all those who would deign to harm her!

Death to those who would touch one curl!"

She repeated the familiar missive over and over, faster and faster, her voice gnarled with loathing for those upon whom she cast the spell, with "death" sounding more like the spitting hiss of a copperhead snake than the spoken word of an auburn-haired woman. Lost in her world of the dead, she believed with all of her tormented soul that the unliving would wend their magic by reaching out across the planes of existence to save the child from the same fate she had suffered. Her rolling of the enchanted sticks became frenzied. The wood became so hot against her skin that it felt as if it was about to burst into flames when she suddenly stopped. After nine repetitions of the spell—in reverence to her lucky number—her slender fingers burst open wide to let the sticks tumble onto the *gris-gris*, her collection of protective holy items. Tonight it consisted of a red candle, a bundle of ashen twigs from the fire of a roasted pig, crushed chicken bones in an alabaster bowl, a green glass bottle of holy water from the font of

St. Louis Cathedral, and three Voodoo dolls. Pins poked out of the small straw figurines, securing a piece of parchment paper to each. One said "Mother," another "her bastard husband," and the third "her Satan son."

Giselle's sensuous lips slackened and fell still, her doe-shaped eyes closed in what looked like a drunken stupor, and her pretty head fell upon her chest to dangle like a tethered buoy cast over the side of a boat.

The flickering light of the ninety-nine candles scattered about her decadent bedroom made her perspiring amber skin glisten and caught the dazzling auburn highlights in her abundant dark hair, causing the reddish strands to appear to perform a merry jig in the night light. Burning incense, strewn about in bowls, emitted the strong odor of jasmine. Numerous wood and metal crucifixes, some encrusted with gems, laid on the floor in a circle around her and her *gris-gris* altar, a protective barrier from evil spirits who might try to invade her urgent, sacred ritual. Adding to the mystique were the long bolts of pink and red and orange gauze that draped the four tall intricately carved posts of her enormous mahogany bed behind her, which itself was covered with a sumptuous fur spread. The ethereal enchantment that she'd cultivated in her bedroom consumed Giselle.

Lost in the stupor of her trance, she thrust her head heavenward, opened her eyes, and gazed at the candles shining in the crystal chandelier that hung from the high, sky-blue ceiling. Her eyes glistening with manic emotion as she prayed to God, Allah, Jesus Christ, the Virgin Mary, the saints, the angels, and especially the spirits of her dead ancestors, whoever they might be, it was the practice in her religion to cover all possibilities.

"Please let the girl be safe, please let the girl be safe, please let the girl be safe," she pleaded, her hands clasped together at her heaving bosom in a gesture of desperate supplication. "I beseech you who have come before me to help me protect this child from the *bête noire!*"

The soft rap on the door startled her.

A deep breath caught in the back of her throat and her eyes widened as she tried to shake herself awake from her reverie.

"Who is it?" she rasped.

"It's me."

The voice was so small that had she not intuitively known who it was, she never would have gone to the door. But she knew immediately that it was her, the girl for whom she begged the mysterious powers of the otherworld to keep safe and sound from the bad people. She quickly arose, yanked up the skirts of her black lace dressing gown to peck her way around the crosses on the floor, removed the broom she's laid across the doorway to keep out wicked witches, and thrust open the door.

"Come in, sweetheart!" Giselle tried to look and sound like a normal woman, pushing her wayward hair behind her ears and taking care to level her voice. "Why are you up so late, my child? Could you not sleep?"

The girl came in. Giselle quickly closed the door and then knelt down so that Deidre could fall into her embrace. She stroked the girl's long, curly blond hair, inhaling its musty scent.

"Ma Ma," Deidre whispered, the maternal endearment touching Giselle's heart every time her daughter uttered it, as they were so seldom allowed to behave like mother and child.

She'd put the girl to bed on her cot in the pantry off the kitchen, as usual, just an hour earlier, so she was quite surprised to see her now. Deidre had taken a great risk by visiting her mother's boudoir, as Madame vehemently prohibited it. No one was to know that the esteemed lady-of-the-night Giselle; the consort who made the most perverted fantasies of politicians, businessmen, plantation owners, soldiers, sailors, preachers, priests, and Yankee visitors come true; had a child.

That had been part of the bargain eight years ago when MiMi Champlain, madam of the infamous *Painted Lady* bordello of New Orleans, had taken in the young, destitute, unwed mother and her infant. Normally, she would have told the housekeeper to give the beggar a piece of bread and send her on her way. But when Madame MiMi glanced up from the *Picayune* newspaper that she read at her kitchen table and saw Giselle standing hopefully at her backdoor, her cunning business-oriented mind immediately ascertained that she could make many a pretty penny off of the homeless young mother. The exotic beauty of the fourteen-year-old, who was clearly a Creole quadroon of mixed blood, was truly astonishing! So the madam had agreed to take them in, with stipulations. They would both work for their keep, the teenager in a bedroom and the baby, the moment she was old enough to stand, in the kitchen. And once she was old enough, the child could entertain men as well.

"Ma Ma," Deidre said, choking back sobs in an effort to speak. She pushed herself away from her mother's clutch in order to look at her. What Giselle saw in her daughter's beautiful blue eyes was sheer terror.

"*Mon Dieu!* What is it, darling?" Giselle asked, horrified.

"I just heard Madame MiMi talking to a man. I couldn't sleep. The house is so noisy tonight!" Indeed, the piano player's bluesy trill of the ivory keys seemed to produce an especially raucous echo this evening. A melancholy tune wafted up from the gambling parlor on the first floor and filtered through the walls, even though Giselle's large boudoir sat on the third floor. "I snuck into the study," Deidre continued, "through the back door, the one covered by the heavy velvet curtain, so no one would see me."

"Deidre! You must never go in there at night! You know you must stay away from those men!"

"I know, I know. But I wanted a piece of that taffy Madame keeps in the candy jar. Just one piece!" She began to cry uncontrollably.

"Sh-sh, *ma amour*," Giselle soothed while her ire riled up within her, like a mama bear ready to claw to death anyone who harmed her cub. "What has frightened you so?"

"Madame didn't see me, so when I realized she was in there with a man, I stayed hidden behind the curtain. She told him, 'You may purchase the girl on her ninth birthday one week from today. Come back that night, bring the money, and she will be yours, Master Williams.'"

Giselle's heart skipped a beat. So he had found her at last. And this was his revenge.

"Ma Ma!" Deidre continued woefully. "She had to be talking about me! My ninth birthday is one week from today and I am the only girl here!" She fell into her mother's arms and wept.

Giselle comforted her child, saying, "*Ma amour*, I will never let that happen! Don't worry, your Ma Ma will take care of this misunderstanding." But she did not weep with her child. Allowing the force of her anger to settle into her bones, which did nothing but strengthen her resolve, she instead made a solemn vow to herself. It was a promise that would change the course of her existence forever. Her life as she knew it was over so that the life of her daughter could begin anew.

"Tammy, will you watch over Deidre while I go out?" Giselle asked the kindly housekeeper. Giselle had just entered the kitchen and the smell of bread baking made her stomach lurch with sudden hunger.

"Just a moment, dear," Tammy said as she concentrated on her task. With a thick towel in her hand, she pulled a pan of fresh croissants out of the brick oven that was built into the side of the enormous kitchen fireplace. She placed the pan on the work table in the center of the room and, without asking, gingerly picked out a croissant and plopped it onto a plate. She shoved it across the table to Giselle.

"*Merci beaucoup!*" Giselle exclaimed as she ripped the steaming little piece of rolled bread apart so it would cool faster. Always amazed at Tammy's skill in the kitchen, she watched as her friend now shoved a pan of unbaked baguettes into the oven.

When Giselle and Deidre first arrived at the *Painted Lady* almost nine years earlier, it had been ebullient Tammy whom Madame MiMi shouldered with the responsibility of teaching the young mother about *savoir vivre*, proper etiquette, and other necessities of the trade, like *haute couture* and *cuisine*. And, of course, the more lascivious tricks of the trade as well. Tammy had done such a good job that Madame soon billed her new talent as "Madame MiMi's ingénue niece, Mademoiselle Giselle." Giselle immediately garnered a huge following, much of which remained in her favor to this day. Now, as the premier calling card of the household, Giselle enjoyed certain privileges, like one night off a week. That night allowed her to practice her holy Voodoo religion, sometimes in the solitude of her room, like last night, and sometimes at a gathering of the famous Voodoo master Queen Marie out by the cemetery at the river's edge. If Madame knew of Giselle's religious beliefs, she ignored that knowledge. As long as her "niece" continued to lie on her back and open her legs, the madam didn't care what went on in the whore's head.

Madame MiMi also never asked about Giselle's past or how she came to be a young mother begging at the door of a bordello. Giselle knew that the madam must have suspected from the very beginning that her brown eyed, auburn haired, amber skinned charge was a mixed blood run-away slave. But the businesswoman didn't care about the sordid past. Her attention focused only on the sultry present and how much money one might make in it.

Tammy did know of Giselle's past and of her Voodoo practices and could be trusted to keep her silence. She'd been a profitable prostitute in the beginning but as the advancing years added more and more flesh to her frame and after she had demonstrated an uncanny ability to take care of this huge house and its residents, Madame gave her the position of head housekeeper and cook.

Tammy wiped her hands on her apron and responded to Giselle's question about watching over Deidre today. "Why, of course, darlin'. Don't I always watch over our little love?" She smiled at Giselle.

"Yes, and God knows how much I appreciate it." Giselle talked between taking bites of her delicious croissant. "But she had a hard time sleeping last night, so I let her stay with me. Neither of us slept much, so she's tired today."

"God's blood! Madame would have a conniption fit if she knew that! But she won't be hearing it from me, that I can swear. I'll take special care of our little one today, don't you fret."

Deidre came into the kitchen with the bucket of water she'd fetched from the well out back. She did indeed look exhausted, her usually curly hair hanging limply about her shoulders and her eyes ringed with dark circles.

"Where are you going, Ma… Giselle?" the girl asked, almost forgetting herself as she took the cast iron bucket and hung it on a hook in the fireplace, allowing it to dangle over the flames for heating. She straightened herself, swiped her sweaty forehead with her sleeve, and looked at her mother.

Tammy pushed a croissant over to Deidre and pointed at it as if to say, "Eat!"

Deidre immediately started chomping on the twirly bread.

Giselle swallowed hard on her last bite and then let loose with her lie. "I'm going to the mayor's office to renew my license. Then I plan to stop at a couple of dress boutiques. I'll be back this afternoon before Madame gets up at three o'clock." She grabbed her closed parasol, waved, and hustled out the backdoor before they might remember that a New Orleans prostitute was required to renew her license once a year and she'd done so only seven months earlier.

As a legal "consort," Giselle enjoyed many freedoms in the city. Furthermore, Madame didn't care what her girls did during the day as long as it didn't interfere with their performances at night. Giselle had her thick hair caught up in ornate Spanish combs, with a chirpy straw bonnet with flowers on it to top off the hairdo. Her slender body was attired in a pretty French morning dress of pink and white checked silk. It was a glorious summer morning, the brilliant blue sky scattered with wispy striated white clouds. She opened her parasol, which matched her dress, in protection against the sun as she walked down the cobbled streets of the French Quarter, admiring, as usual, the beauty of her chosen hometown. The block-long buildings with their brightly painted facades and lacy ironwork on the overhanging balconies, with an array of colorful flowers like fuchsia bougainvillea and blue hydrangea trailing down from planter boxes, always thrilled Giselle.

She passed her beloved St. Louis Cathedral, officially the Cathedral-Basilica of Saint Louis King of France, which sat upon the site that had been designated for a place of Catholic worship in 1721. After a primitive initial structure and a more elaborate one that burned to ground in 1788, this magnificent cathedral was built and had come to be the focal point of the city in its sixty-three-year existence. Giselle loved the history of the place and all of the haints who dwelt there, many of whom were buried right beneath the stone floor. Her heart felt heavy with remorse that she would never again have the leisure of praying within those old walls and of mingling with those spirits.

She turned toward the street; waited for an elegant, black, enclosed carriage to pass; and nodded politely to the gentleman who gaped from the carriage window in unabashed admiration. She crossed the street and went through the iron gate that allowed her entrance into Jackson Square, which overlooked the Mississippi River at the heart of the city. She passed the revered statue of Andrew Jackson astride his bucking horse, the man having been honored with the enormous bronze statue for winning the conclusive battle of the War of 1812, the Battle of New Orleans, thereby saving New Orleans and indeed all of the United States' Louisiana Purchase from being stolen by the British. Giselle followed the flagstone path around the statue and on through the lush formal gardens, all the while reflecting on how this park, like the cathedral, felt like home.

Home. The place where she'd grown up had been anything but.

Willow Way, fifty miles up the Mississippi River near Baton Rouge, was one of the largest plantations in Louisiana. Its owner was a wealthy French Creole by birth, having made his own fortune by planting sugarcane in the marshlands alongside the Mississippi River. He'd made that fortune and more. By acquiring more land in Texas and planting cotton out there, he'd managed to amass more money than most men ever dreamt of.

It was during his two-year-long stay in Texas to set up his holdings there that Giselle came into the world. Unfortunately, her mother was the man's wife, sequestered away on remote Willow Way plantation in Louisiana and far away from her husband at the time she became pregnant. Indeed, she hadn't seen her spouse in over a year at the time that she conceived.

Never mind that her husband enjoyed numerous dalliances with high-born and low-down women during their marriage, whether with or away from his wife. Never mind that he paid large sums to two prominent families in exchange for ruining their daughters by impregnating them and then abandoning them while they were with child. Never mind that he'd spewed his seed into countless slave women by means of rape and then counted none of their children as his responsibility. He saw those offspring as nothing more than free field hands.

He'd turned out to be an ice-cold man, interested only in his own promotion and pleasure, rather than the dashing gentleman Giselle's mother thought she'd married. As a sixteen-year-old, the pretty Irish girl, just off a ship from her homeland, had been dazzled by the charming young planter. However, after they married and she bore him a son, she was horrified by the realization that although he held his male heir in high esteem, she and all other females were nothing more than mere possessions to him. She held no more status than the hundreds of slaves in his plantations' sugarcane and cotton fields.

He'd married her, she'd finally reckoned, because she was young and pretty and hale and hearty, all of which would bode well for childbearing. All he wanted was a bauble on his arm for public display and a conduit for an heir in his private domain.

Giselle's mother had once told her this story in a desperate bid to try to make her understand why she could not be acknowledged as her daughter, why she must be hidden amongst the slaves. At first believing herself to be motherless, Giselle worked with the household slaves when she was little. It wasn't until she was nine, about Deidre's age, a foreboding age as it turned out, that she'd overheard two women slaves talking about how the "poor, little, light-skinned girl" was the secret daughter of the master's wife. One of them bemoaned the fact that "the child ain't black or white and ain't ne'er gonna find a home, bless her lonesome little tetched soul."

It was then that Giselle confronted the master's wife. She waited, of course, until the master was out patrolling his fields for the day, then boldly asked the pretty foreign woman, who still had a bit of Irish brogue, if the rumor was true. Expecting to be told that the gossip was absurd and that she could rest assured her slave mother had died in childbirth, Giselle had been dumbfounded when the woman instead burst into tears and told her the woeful tale.

She'd lamented about how her husband had been so furious when he'd come home and found her pregnant, he'd tried to beat the baby out of her womb by repeatedly kicking her in the belly. "But you were strong, Giselle!" her mother had said. "So strong!

You refused to give up your hold on life! Thank God you were born while he was away or I truly believe he would have killed us both right then and there." She went on to explain to Giselle that immediately after her birth she'd been handed over to a household slave, who took care of the infant as best she could. Indeed, it was even she who called the child Giselle, a name she'd overheard from French travelers who'd once visited the plantation.

Giselle's mother had confessed, "So you see, I told him I had a miscarriage. It was his pride that wouldn't let him admit to anyone that I'd cheated on him. Besides, by not telling he could entertain himself with torturing me for the rest of my life. He's a vile, evil man, Giselle. You have no idea." She'd let tears flow unabated down her beautiful face while frantically twisting her handkerchief in her hand. Giselle had always thought it odd that she didn't wipe her tears. It was as if she'd lost awareness of her physical being. "If I'd claimed you and tarnished his reputation," her mother had gone on, "and publicly injured his pride, he would have killed us both! His powerful friends would have stood by him. We would be dead! What good would that do? At least this way we live and breathe!"

They were empty words to Giselle's ears. She walked out of the room and never spoke directly to her mother again. No excuse could soften her heart toward the woman. Not then and certainly not now that she was a mother herself.

The memory faded, however, and her heart melted when she turned a corner in the path of Jackson Square and came upon the bench where the old Negro man sat.

"*Bonjo*, Pa Pa," she said in greeting, sliding down beside him. She closed her parasol, set it down, looked around, and upon seeing no one, leaned over to kiss his dark brown, lined cheek. He'd once explained to her that his skin was a bit lighter than some blacks' because, although he had mostly African heritage, his grandmother had been a Choctaw Indian. He must have been extraordinarily handsome in his youth, she'd often speculated, what with those big eyes and high cheekbones. It did her good to see him smile at her now, his thick lips arching up so grandly that they caused happy little lines to radiate out all over his aged face.

"*Bonjo, ma cher.*" *Ma cher,* my love. How she reveled in it when he called her that French Creole term of endearment! His deep voice soothed her ears.

She would miss him so.

They'd been meeting on this very bench once a week for a year, ever since he'd managed to get a note delivered to her through Tammy, to let her know that her own father lived in New Orleans and wanted to meet her. At first confused, as she'd never had any idea whatsoever who her father might be, other than he'd probably been a Negro, she'd met him that first time with trepidation. It had only taken minutes for her fears to evaporate as his concern for her emanated out from the very core of his being and encased her in love.

Even though he was now a freedman, once having been a slave on Willow Way and other plantations, they took care when appearing together in public. It wasn't acceptable for a Creole woman to cavort with a Negro man, even if she was a mulatto lady of the night, unless it had to do with her doling out menial work. So the few times they'd been seen by someone Giselle knew, she'd introduced him as the handyman who'd taken care of her family home while she was growing up.

No one else knew of their real connection. He'd insisted on that, for her safety and Deidre's, as a Negro's life was precarious, even when "free." He'd met Deidre on several occasions, Giselle using the old family handyman ruse with the child, and he knew that the girl had such fair skin, blond hair, and blue eyes that no one would ever guess that the little girl had a Negro grandfather. That would make her life easier, so he wanted it to stay that way.

"*Konmen to yé?*" Giselle asked how he was doing, taking his big hand in hers. He was nearly eighty years old but still strong and tall, his gray hair full and his brown eyes clear.

He squeezed her hand. *"C'est bon, mèsi.* As long as they let me play that piano and sing in that saloon, I'll always be alright." She adored how he said "pie-an-oh" and "sah-loon." His language was a unique mix of plantation slave Creole, which had strong African, Haitian, French, and Spanish influences, and New Orleans lingo. The slave dialect was the same one that Giselle had come with to New Orleans, until Madame MiMi had it coached out of her. But she slipped back into it easily enough when around her father.

Early on he'd told her about being a slave at Willow Way, the plantation her mother's husband owned, where Giselle had grown up. She knew the story of how he and every male slave of an age to be virile enough to impregnate her mother had been savagely beaten and then sold. He'd gone to a plantation that subsequently went bankrupt, so he was set free. His natural talent for music landed him on Bourbon Street in New Orleans, and his freedom had allowed him to make discreet inquiries into the whereabouts of his daughter. After putting a number of puzzle pieces together and seeing Madame MiMi's advertisement for her "niece," he'd taken a chance and contacted Giselle.

"I'm glad we're together today," Giselle said, "because I'll be going away soon. This will be our last meeting." His eyes clouded with grief, but he remained silent as he watched her closely. "You know I've been saving my money so I can take Deidre to go live up north. I've always known that I have to get out of this business. I have to get her away from it." She cast her eyes down in shame.

"Ma cher, look at me." She lifted her head to grant him his request. "I've ne'er asked you how you came to do what you do or how you came to have a child. I've got no right, ne'er bein' a real daddy to you. And you've ne'er asked many questions of me. But I want you to know I felt so helpless all those years! Knowin' I had a child out there somewhere and not knowin' how you faired. It damn near killed me.

"You know I was married and had five chil'ren a'fore you was born. That bastard master of ours, your mama's husband, sold all those youngins. My wife and I ne'er knowed where they went. It tore us up inside! Then after my wife died and yer mama and me…" He paused, considering how to continue. "After you was born and I was sold so I couldn't even lay my eyes on you to see if you was alright, it added one more child to my worries. I was workin' the fields and I'd spend all day thinkin' 'bout all my chil'ren. My hands were pickin' cotton but my mind was a million miles away. It was my very own flesh and blood that I couldn't even talk to or feed or look at! I wanted to die at first. If it wasn't for music, I think I would've withered up and kicked the bucket a long time ago." He paused, looking at the sky. When he looked back, his eyes held hers.

"Here's what I want you to know," he said. "I loved my wife and all of our chil'ren. When she died and with our youngins already gone, my grief was unbearable! Yer mama was jes as lonely as I was. I worked in the stables then and she used to come in to ride every day. We came together out of deep, devastating sorrow. God forgive us, but we ended up with deep affection for one another, too." He shook his head. "We knowed it was wrong. We knowed it was forbidden. We knowed we might be killed for it. We knowed we was goin' to Hell. And we didn't care. That's how lonely we was. We had a bond that grew into love.

"So I want you to always remember that you was conceived in love, Giselle.

"And you was the one thing that kept me goin'. You was the one ray of hope in my life. Perhaps you, I prayed, was livin' a happy life. When I realized it was you who was workin' as a prostitute—forgive my boldness, Giselle, but that's what you are—my heart broke. I wanted to help you if I could.

"What I'm sayin' is, maybe if you tell me what's wrong, maybe if I knew how you ended up in a bordello, I'd understand.

Maybe I could help. For once, let me be the daddy you never had."

Giselle's heart swelled with love for this man. She wished with all of her being that she could tell him the whole story and what was about to transpire as a result, but he'd been broken up so many times in his life, she couldn't shatter his hope even more. If all worked out as she planned, he'd never know what really happened. He'd know just enough truth that he'd never suspect the lie and that thread of truth would help mend his heart.

"I can't wait two more years until I have enough money! I'm giving Deidre up for adoption now," she blurted out. "Tammy has a sister back in her hometown in Georgia. You remember me telling you about Tammy? She's a white woman. These people are white and they own forestland and have a lumber mill. They've always wanted children and can't have any. Tammy swears they're good people and will take good care of Deidre. She'll grow up away from prostitutes and filthy-minded men. She'll be in trees, no less! In the forest, Pa Pa! Can you imagine that? I want her to have a better life than I do, so I have to let her go." She began to cry softly and took a lace handkerchief from her pocket to dab at her eyes.

Her father sat still, deep in thought. Finally he said, "I think you've made a very brave, very wise, very difficult decision. I admire you for it. At least you'll know where she is. There's a lot to be said for that.

"Now, what about you? What will you do?"

She couldn't let him know that her fate was sealed.

"I'm going away," she said, "probably up north. Saving hasn't been as easy as I'd expected, not with Madame MiMi taking a bigger and bigger cut all the time. But with just myself to look after, I should be able to survive. Maybe I can find a job as a maid or something. I don't know. Maybe I'll go out west and become a cowgirl!"

They chuckled at the image that conjured up and the doom lifted enough that Giselle felt as if she could finally breathe again.

"Pa Pa, will you always remember that *ma l'aime toi?*"

His eyes bore into her soul and ripped it to shreds in their sorrow.

"*Oui,*" he said, choking back tears, "if you promise to always remember how much *mo l'aime toi.* Love is the only thing in this world that matters, *ma cher.* No matter what's goin' on in our lives, nothin' can diminish the love we hold for one another in our hearts."

Propriety be damned, she thought as she reached out and hugged him to her chest. He grabbed hold with all his might and Giselle thought she might die from the regret that she had to let go.

The sorrow of their parting hung like an albatross around Giselle's neck as she entered Queen Marie's cottage. The Voodoo oracle looked up from where she sat at her table reading the Bible. She took one look at her favored follower and with the aura of many colors radiating out of Giselle's body, Queen Marie knew that catastrophe and good fortune were about to butt heads in this young woman's life.

"*Bonjour,*" Giselle said softly.

"*Bonjour,* Giselle."

Without another word, Queen Marie unwrapped her large glossy gray snake, Zombie, from around the back of her neck and her arms, and coiled it into the tall basket at her side. She placed the lid on the basket.

"Come." She motioned to Giselle to sit in the chair across from her.

Giselle sat in the purple velvet high-back chair, instantly feeling comfort in its embrace. This room always put her at ease, so much so that she'd patterned her own boudoir after it with similar hues and fabrics and accessories. A cacophony of colors splayed about the room, candles glistened everywhere, and crucifixes protected every nook and cranny.

"The time has come," Giselle said, looking intently at the queen. "All of my suspicions and fears, all of the events that you predicted, they have all come to be.

"Last night Deidre overheard Madame arranging for her sale next week. To Mr. Williams."

Queen Marie's eyes widened, not in surprise but in comprehension. They'd been talking about this for a long time. The day of reckoning had finally come.

She stood, motioning for Giselle to follow her. A tall, imposing Creole woman, she wore a voluminous black dress with a bright green Oriental silk shawl that was delicately embroidered with creamy pearls and pink beads. Pearl earrings decorated her earlobes, while her pink silk headdress, looking like a folded and tied cloth sculpture, towered atop her head. She wore a gold crucifix on a chain about her neck.

Leading Giselle to a hallway, she took her through the roomy kitchen and into the greenhouse at the back of the house. Giselle had been in this room before for the gathering of notions for her minor spells. This time was more odious. Queen Marie wound her way through potted plants and tables full of mysterious curios and concoctions, arriving at a large cabinet that stood against the back wall. Somberly, she took a key out of her pocket and unlocked the cabinet door. Reaching inside, she removed a little white linen bag and laid it in the palm of Giselle's hand. It was so small that Giselle was incredulous that it could do what it was purported to do.

"I prepared this for you yesterday," the queen said. "I knew you would be coming."

Giselle stared at the small bundle. "I know what this *ouanga* will do," she said, "but I don't know what's in it."

Queen Marie smiled. "Does it matter? Ah, if you must know, it's the ground up root of the figure maudit tree. It only grows in Africa and must be smuggled through the West Indies. I combine it with ground up bones and one drop of holy water. Do not fear. It will take care of your problem."

Giselle's throat tightened as they left the greenhouse and returned to the parlor. *Am I really going to do this? Oui.* She had no doubt. Not anymore.

She took a wad of money out of her pocket and laid it on the table. "Queen Marie, have you ever done this before?" she asked.

The regal woman did not hesitate. "*Oui.* Twice. As you know, Voodoo is not about hurting people; it's about helping people. But there are those who allow themselves to be so wrought with evil that they cannot be helped. They have lost the right to walk this earth with the living. I have helped murder two men who sexually abused children. All such monsters should die, but only those two have come to my attention in a way in which I could participate in doling out their just due. Now this. If I am lucky, there will be more in the future." She released her beatific smile and Giselle felt total peace with her decision.

The two women kissed on the lips and Giselle left.

She'd not been in this house before, but having been a house slave girl for all of her young life, thereby excelling at slipping in and out of rooms without being seen or heard, she had no trouble getting into the kitchen of the Williams townhouse. Like all wealthy plantation owners, her mother's husband had a home in the city, something that had never occurred to Giselle when she was a fourteen-year-old runaway. Fifty miles down the river, she and her baby stowed away in the front of a kind Choctaw Indian's canoe for the journey, had seemed like a world away to the teen. It had only been in recent years that she'd realized that he had a home here, and that he and his son stayed here often. If one of them had visited the *Painted Lady* last night to do business with the madam, then surely they were staying here at this time.

Eerily, though, she'd felt their sinister presence in the city before she'd known of it for certain. The hair would sometimes stand up on the nape of her neck and she'd whirl around to see if someone was spying on her. At times she'd become fearful of allowing Deidre to go to market. And, most of all, she'd had a knot in her stomach that told her to beware. Queen Marie lectured all of her followers about the importance of paying attention to their gut feelings, as the gut often knew what was going on before the closed mind could open its doors enough to see.

Giselle's gut told her that her wretched stepfather and stepbrother had known where she was for a long time and that, in revenge for her having been born, they would do the one thing that would hurt her the most. They were going to buy her daughter and ravage the child, just as they'd raped her all of her life until she ran away with her baby. Hers and her half-brother's baby. She'd never let the fact that such a despicable person had fathered her child get in the way of her love for that child. Deidre was her daughter, as far as she was concerned, not his. The child would never be his.

When she'd first harbored her suspicions, Giselle had gone to Queen Marie for guidance. After hours of meditation, praying, and casting spells, she believed this was the only course left. Nothing less could cast out such evil.

What else could she do? Go to the sheriff? She was a runaway slave. He'd just give her and her daughter back to their "owners," the two men she despised more than the Devil himself. She couldn't run away with Deidre. How would they live? Prostitution was all she knew; if she did that somewhere else, she'd end up just the same as here. There was Tammy's sister in Georgia, who might take in a child but to ask her to harbor a run-away slave prostitute was too much. So in the end the decision had been no decision at all. It had been the only thing to do.

It had been easy to find the address of the Williams townhouse in the county records in the courthouse. And easier still to stand in their back hallway, peering into their unoccupied kitchen. She slipped through that room, noticing that someone had peeled an apple and left the knife and peelings unattended on the table. She went through the kitchen and into the butler's pantry that connected to the dining room. Even though she'd never been here before, this was a common design for these places, so she'd expected this small room to be here. And, as hoped, there sat a bottle of port, just as one had always been open and handy at the plantation. Next to it, to her delight, stood a flask of whiskey. Two in one. This was turning out to be easier than she thought.

Then, hidden behind the whiskey, she saw the tip of another bottle, this one tall and slender. In disbelief, she pushed the flask aside and glared at the bottle of expensive French merlot. Next to it sat a bottle of laudanum, medicine used to numb a person's worried mind. So, *she* was here, also.

Quickly, she withdrew the small cloth sack from her pocket. As she hurriedly untied its string closure, she considered what to do with the contents. It was formulated to be divided into two. Should she split it three ways?

No, that may not work at all. She pulled the cork out of the port, poured in half of the potion, replaced the cork, and shook the bottle to mix it up. Then she opened the flask and dumped in the rest of the deadly poison. She closed it and shook it, too. Slipping the empty sack back into her pocket, she turned to go.

She'd taken but three steps into the kitchen when a voice from behind frightened her so violently she tripped and had to catch herself by grabbing onto the edge of the table.

"Well, well, well! What have we here?"

She turned to face her nemesis. Refusing to reveal her fear, she said, "Hello, Charles."

Her half-brother strode toward her, a catty smirk on his face. Deidre looked so like him, with blond curly hair and blue eyes, that Giselle shuttered at the unwelcome comparison.

Frozen in place, she watched as he stopped about three feet away and put his hands on his hips. "To what do we owe the honor of this visit?" he mocked, cocking his head to one side.

Giselle turned to run, only to slam into the potbelly of her stepfather. He grabbed her upper arm but she twisted away. Now she stood between the two louts, her chest heaving in an effort to take in air.

"How fortunate that you've stopped by," her stepfather said snidely. He looked like a man who ate and drank too much, with any semblance of his youthful handsomeness long ago demolished. "We've been meaning to pay you a proper call," he said, his voice more gravely since she's last seen him. "We want to inform you that in six days that little bastard daughter of yours will be ours. You could be, too, if we wanted to go to the sheriff. But we've decided we don't want you. Only her. That way you can roll around in that big bed of yours, whoring your life away, all the while thinking about how we're doing the same thing to your precious little girl."

"What?" The growl from the doorway was so primitive that Giselle turned to see its source, while the preying men's eyes darted in that direction, too. "You are going to do *what*?"

Giselle's mother was a total stranger to her. It had been less than nine years, but the woman looked twenty-five years older. Her once strawberry blond hair had dulled and thinned, and stuck out in all directions from her head like a spider web; her body had sunken to the point of being little more than a skeleton; and her eyes reflected no light, as if she were a zombie. She glared at Giselle, at first not knowing her, then a flicker of a memory shown behind those dull orbs and she seemed to recognize her offspring.

"This is none of your concern, bitch!" Giselle's stepfather bellowed. "Go back to your room!"

"It's Gis…" She choked on her words and reached out toward her daughter.

"Mother!" Charles spat. "Get out of here!"

Then something unbelievable happened. Both men drew their watchful eyes completely away from their hated intruder, Giselle, and glared at the pathetic figure standing in the doorway. Without conscious thought, Giselle grabbed the knife off the table, thrust it into her half-brother's middle, and yanked it out.

The look of shock on Charles's face as blood spurted from his abdomen both appalled and delighted his murderess. Instinctively knowing she couldn't waste one second, she spun around on the balls of her feet and forged the knife deep into her stepfather's chest. He'd been so stunned by the deadly stabbing of his precious son that he hadn't even raised his hands in defense. The arrogant jackass had assumed she wouldn't have the grit to slay him, too.

The men fell to the floor in tandem, as if the dramatic moment had been rehearsed for a play. Blood oozed from their muscular bodies, rendering them as weak and helpless as the dying animals they were.

Giselle stood there immobile, the blood of her life-long adversaries having soiled her clothes, the knife poised in her hand. She looked at her mother.

Clearly crazy, the expressionless woman methodically stepped over the now dead body of her husband, faced her daughter, unbuttoned the bodice of her own dress, took her child's wrist in both of her hands, and guided the gory knife to her exposed throat. In one swift, shockingly strong thrust, she forced Giselle's hand to plunge the knife into her body.

Giselle dropped the knife to the floor in disbelief! Her mother fell beside the deadly weapon, a sickening smile upon her lips.

Giselle fled from the house of horror.

Nine years later at her execution, Giselle still didn't recall what had happened after she'd committed the three murders. It had been Tammy who found her half an hour after she'd returned to the *Painted Lady*, sitting in a trance on her bed. Her soiled morning dress lay crumbled on the floor, dried blood causing it to stand up in furrows of mocking display. Giselle still wore her fancy white petticoat, but even it was splattered on the top of the bodice and on the hem with dark red blood. It had been the deadly smell of decaying blood that had assaulted Tammy when she first entered the room, the visual impact of the scene striking her a split second later.

Try as she might, Tammy couldn't shake Giselle out of her comatose state. Other women of the house came in to help but to no avail. Within the hour Tammy had known what she must do. Post haste, she gathered her hidden savings, packed a few clothes, and scurried down the street to the outdoor vegetable market, where Deidre was shopping for supper fixings. Gently taking the child by the arm, she hustled her into a rental carriage and bade the driver to deliver them to the train station.

Within two days they were in her hometown in Georgia, never to return.

In the meantime, the moment that Madame MiMi looked into Giselle's boudoir to see what the commotion was all about, she called the sheriff. Deciding that Giselle had made all the money she was ever going to make, all she wanted now was to get the murderess out of her house with as little hubbub and notoriety as possible. As another of her nieces was a favorite of the sheriff's, she got her wish.

The identity of the run-away slave who'd slain the Williams family was never recorded nor publicized. Giselle, who had no real legal rights—she was a slave, a woman, an unwed mother, a harlot, and a quadroon Creole—was thrown into prison without a trial and given a death sentence. She languished there, not even allowed visits from her devoted friend who'd surreptitiously learned of her whereabouts, Queen Marie. The War Between the States raged and ended but made nary a dent in Giselle's life other than to render the sheriff too busy to take much notice of his prisoners. The prostitute had no idea that her former home, the famous *Painted Lady* whorehouse, enjoyed more success during the war than ever before, what with the influx of Yankee soldiers, sailors, politicians, and carpetbaggers once the city had been taken.

Years passed, political turmoil reigned, and eventually some forgot why the insane woman in Cell #3 was there in the first place. Even her name was seldom used, the guards referring to her as "the one with bats in her belfry in cell number three." When a young, ambitious new sheriff took the helm, however, it was decreed that her death sentence would finally be carried out, nine years after the crime had been committed.

On the way to her execution, which would be a hanging followed by a single shot to the heart if death by dangling by the neck became too prolonged, Giselle had no idea that she looked much like her mother had at the end of her life. Crazed, blank eyed, bone thin, and unkempt, no one would ever have guessed she'd once been the voluptuous, popular, exotic "ingénue Mademoiselle Giselle."

Out of her dank cell for the first time in so many years, Giselle roused enough to realize that she was being taken somewhere. When she was guided out of the horse cart and up to the wooden platform, her dementia lifted like a bridal veil, and she had her first cogent thought since the killings. *I am going to die now.* She was escorted up the stairs and positioned under a thick, knotted rope. Someone behind her placed a black cloth bag over her head. *How odd,* she thought, *that they don't want me to see the sky as I die.*

Then suddenly, in a miraculous flash of radiant sanity, a memory came back to her in vivid display, the glorious summer day when she'd been sitting on a bench in a park with a Negro man. The sky had been so blue! She'd worn a pretty dress and bonnet, and carried a parasol. The man had been her father.

The rope was placed about her neck, chafing her skin.

Her father's deep, melodic voice resonated in her ears as he said once more, "Love is the only thing in this world that matters, *ma cher*. No matter what's goin' on in our lives, nothin' can diminish the love we hold for one another in our hearts."

When the floor went out from under her feet and the rope yanked her neck to the point of strangulation, another memory flooded her thoughts. She had a daughter, Deidre. This had all been for Deidre.

Giselle's last thought as the shot pierced her heart was that it had all been worth it if her child lived in love.

Chapter 26

Jessie Belle sat up in bed and drew her knees up so as to wrap her arms around them, and rested her chin atop them. No longer frightened by her dreams, she felt instead an overwhelming melancholy. She didn't doubt the validity of Giselle's story. More importantly she didn't feel at all shocked at the genetic connection. She simply felt sad.

Acutely aware that, based upon what Star had been hinting, this was most likely her last such dream at this point in her life, she also felt an emptiness that the stories were over. She'd miss the discovery of more ancestor women who she could learn from.

So what had this dream, oddly timed on the eve of her wedding, been all about? Well, she now knew her recent heritage included an African American man. She'd come full circle, having started in Africa.

But the past also included savage slavery, spousal abuse, and prostitution, not to mention the incest, murder, and dementia. Even Scarlett O'Hara couldn't top that!

This, Jessie Belle knew, was her real heritage. Not the fairy tale story her mother had spun over the years. She had no doubt that her mama believed that fluff, though, and always would. There would be no satisfaction in ever telling her about these dreams in order to try to change her mind. "Change" was not in

Maisy Church's vocabulary. Jessie Belle decided never to waste her time trying to change that.

However, regardless of the tenor of Giselle's saga, a message of love had once again, as in all of Jessie Belle's other dreams, been the essence of the tale.

Star faded in and sat by her side. There was no quirky costume on this night, only a solemn spirit woman in a flowing, diaphanous blue garment.

"Was she happy, Star? Deidre," Jessie Belle inquired.

"Yes. That's what Giselle wanted you to know. That no matter how troubled your life may be, there's always a way out. There's always hope. There was for Deidre.

"She was so happy with her new parents in Georgia. Having her Aunt Tammy by her side was good, too. She finally got to be a normal kid. And a year later the couple, who had tried for years to have a baby, had a boy! They were thrilled! They loved both of those children. And Deidre and her little brother adored each other for the rest of their lives.

"The memory of the *Painted Lady* faded, although she always remembered her exotically beautiful birth mother. Tammy helped her understand that her Ma Ma had to give her up so she'd have a better life. She grew up to marry a nice small-town grocery store owner and they had two children. They were happy together until their dying days.

"Finally, Giselle's spirit was able to rest in peace.

"After Deidre's adopted parents died, she and her brother inherited the lumber business. It was the next generation that started the furniture manufacturing business and made the first of the big-time money. The women in the family didn't start getting hoity-toity, like your mother, until then. It's that line, of course, that leads straight down to you."

"My mama would just die if she knew she was descended from a woman who'd been part Negro, and a slave, and a prostitute, and who had a child of incest. And was a demented murderer. Think I should tell her?" Jessie Belle curled her lips mischievously.

"Now that's a scene I'd like to see!"

"Actually, I've already decided it won't do any good. She'll never change her mind about anything."

"I suspect you're right."

"Star, have you ever tried to get through to her?"

"I used to but gave up years ago. She blocked me out in every way imaginable, especially with booze once she grew up. People who don't want to be helped can't very well be helped."

"So I must have wanted to be helped in some way I didn't even realize. All I know is that I was so confused. Now many things have been cleared up but I'm still confused about marrying Robert. Is it the right thing for me to do?"

"Only you can decide that, dear. Remember, as I've said before, it isn't always a matter of right and wrong as much as what you do with the choices you make. There are many ways to live a good life. You have to ask yourself what will make you happy. Unless you're truly happy, you can't be of much good to anyone else. All you do otherwise is contribute to their misery. The world has enough of that. It needs loving human beings who can help lift people up, and the way to do that is to love and lift you up first."

Jessie Belle contemplated that thought for so long she almost forgot that Star was at her side. She suddenly looked up and said, "Oh! I'm so glad you're here tonight. I've needed to think this through, and you've helped me see that I need to stop doubting myself and just do it! I'm getting married tomorrow! Isn't it wonderful? Think of all the good things I can accomplish by being the wife of such a wealthy man!" She threw her arms around Star, causing the spirit's spectral form to falter and flicker for a moment.

"Oh, my, well, huh," Star stammered as Jessie Belle let go and clasped her hands together in delight like a child. "You're sure that's what you want to do?" Star asked.

"Yes! My mind is made up. Thank you so much, Star. Thank you for everything."

"Well, now, you have, let's see, about twelve hours to think it over. Don't make any rash decisions. And for sure, don't let the fact that it's all planned make you feel pressured."

"I don't feel pressured. I want to do it!"

"You do? Um, isn't that, uh, nice." Star's voice trailed off as her image began to fade.

"Star, I love you," Jessie Belle said as she fell back onto her pillow.

"I love you, too, dear. I love you, too," Star said as she disappeared.

Jessie Belle stood at the back of the one-hundred-year-old Victorian-styled Social Circle Baptist Church, her treasured place of worship. She'd envisioned this enchanting moment countless times and it was finally here. Her dream had come true.

Chamber music from the quartet that sat in the balcony floated down to suffuse the space with joy. Pachelbel's *Canon in D* soothed any flicker of nervousness she felt.

The scent of roses permeated the air, with dazzling pink and cream sprays of the flowers tied up with big creamy satin bows attached to the end of each oakwood pew all the way down the center aisle. The accompanying greenery on each one trailed down to the floor. Three enormous matching flower arrangements adorned the altar.

The old church's beamed ceiling angled up to a tall gable overhead and the oak wood floor lay polished to a bright sheen. New, plushy ivory carpet ran the length of the center aisle. Original antique windows in a multitude of vibrant colors lined each side wall. A huge wooden cross hung above the altar.

Jessie Belle had loved this place, her sacred space, all of her life. She loved it even more now.

Packed to the rafters with two hundred guests, the church felt welcoming and cozy. Those who Robert and she cared about the most were here.

Her maid of honor, Gracie the production assistant, stood stiffly in front of her and turned to offer a reassuring nod. Gracie looked better than Jessie Belle had ever seen her, decked out in a pink designer gown and done up with professional makeup. Her hair coiled prettily on top of her head. She carried a bouquet of pink roses. And, most surprisingly, she looked slightly happy. Jessie Belle had never seen her look happy. Gracie turned back toward the front of the church, squared her shoulders, and started her cadenced walk down the aisle.

After a few measured moments, Jessie Belle followed by herself. She'd refused her mother's command that she let her brother Jeff walk her down the aisle. No way! Not only did she harbor no respect whatsoever for the slug, but this was the one thing in her life that she wanted to do on her own.

The origami skirt of her ivory-colored chiffon gown swished sensuously around her legs, her bare shoulders felt downright sexy, and her long veil, which flowed from underneath her hair that was gathered with roses, made her feel like a majestic medieval maiden. She felt more magnificently feminine than ever before in her life.

This was even though her mama had fought her tooth and nail over this "plain Jane" dress. "It doesn't even have any beading!" her pouty parent had railed. "How can you get married without beading?" She'd become even more enraged when Jessie Belle politely refused the diamond necklace she'd worn at her own wedding. "No diamonds, either? Crimony, Jessie Belle! What's wrong with you? You'll look as unalluring as a nun!"

Jessie Belle stubbornly replied, "I'll look like me."

Her mama cruelly retorted, "That's the problem!"

At this moment, Jessie Belle didn't care what her mama thought. She was completely content with the simple pearl earrings, bouquet of cream-colored roses, and engagement ring that served as her only accessories.

As she walked slowly down the aisle, perusing the guests who had turned to witness her entrance, she saw that Robert's side held a number of people she didn't know. Seeing that she'd met his few family members and closest friends, she supposed some of these were business associates he thought would feel slighted if not invited to the big event. *Ever the business man*, she thought. *It's why he's so successful.*

She turned her head to see that on her side stood Mr. Tuma, the Consulate General of Yemen. She'd invited him and his wife, expecting they wouldn't come, as they didn't really know her that well. But there they were. Jessie Belle tipped her head in recognition, very glad to see them. They both smiled in return.

She looked at Robert's side again. Designer dresses. Tailored suits. Expensive jewelry. Top-notch plastic surgery.

Suddenly she caught a glimpse of someone who made her gasp. Surely she'd been mistaken. She looked again. There! Right in the middle of all of those social climbers stood the bare-chested African Clacka! Her black skin glistened and her kinky hair stuck out in a riotously wild halo. When she smiled her teeth gleamed until her entire face lit up. And then a man in a black suit leaned forward and Jessie Belle lost sight of her ancestor.

She slowed her pace even more. Her heart skipped a beat in excitement as she wondered who else might be here!

Looking on her side this time, there was an entire row of her mama's bridge club, and the few shriveled up old fossil husbands who were still alive and kicking. Aha! This time it was her ancient Egyptian ancestor Karum, appearing warm and friendly. It was the antithesis of the misery she'd displayed during her time on earth as the reluctant child slave-bride. Donned in a lovely papaya-colored linen shawl over a lemon yellow linen robe, colors that complimented her olive skin, with her thick black hair flowing freely down her back, she looked like the carefree young girl she should have been but never had a chance to be. Her smile thrilled Jessie Belle, who smiled back. But Jessie Belle's mama's bridge friend who stepped in front of the vision thought that the bride was smiling at her, so the old dame waved back gaily.

Continuing haltingly down the aisle, she saw her boss Harry with his wife. Looking away, he suppressed a yawn. When he looked back and saw that the bride was staring right at him, he grimaced, shrugged, and grinned apologetically.

And then, right behind Harry's wife stood the Venezian vintner Julia! She was dressed in a sea-blue silk toga with a fabulous pearl-strewn broach securing it on one pale shoulder. Her golden hair caught the light to frame her exquisitely chiseled face. The affection that passed between Jessie Belle and Julia bespoke a connection that needed no words. Julia became lost in the crowd and Jessie Belle's brother, his trophy wife—looking a little tarnished since the loss of their fortune—and their two bratty sons filled the view.

Jessie Belle looked down at the floor to avoid her brother and at the next aisle saw a buttery soft leather shoe with decorative brass grommets that stuck out slightly into the aisle. She glanced up to find the Austrian brewer Brunhild looking at her kindly. Clean, healthily robust, her once-ruddy skin pleasingly pink, dressed in a nice frock, and with a fancy bejeweled gold Celtic torc about her neck, she winked at Jessie Belle. The bride giggled at the chirpiness of the once dour, abused woman. A stranger took Brunhild's place, so Jessie Belle turned her attention to the other side.

There stood Joe, her director friend who was finally home from his latest assignment. Jessie Belle was so glad to see him and equally tickled to see Erika the Viking step out from behind his far side. Scantily clad in her usual strips of leather and fur, exposing lots of white skin, her thick coppery braids hanging down each side of her chest, ornate gold jewelry adorning her ears and throat and wrists, and her snake tattoo intact on her upper arm as if it had never been bitten, she cast her descendant a fierce look that demanded attention. She seemed to be ordering Jessie Belle to stay alert. For what Jessie Belle wasn't sure. Then Joe shifted his position and Erika disappeared.

In the second row, behind old family friends, including the staid family lawyer Lawrence Davidson who'd informed her that she was broke, Jessie Belle thought she saw…. She stretched her neck to see better. Yes! Haliakula's large bare breasts dangled, her best tapa cloth encircled her roly-poly waist, her tan skin shone, and her frizzy gray hair hung loose with a big purple orchid tucked behind one ear. Haliakula nodded and let loose with her toothless smile. Jessie Belle nodded. Then the lighthearted Polynesian vanished behind the staid lawyer.

Turning her head again, Jessie Belle wasn't even surprised by now to see Kathleen, the red-haired Irishwoman, in a bright red dress with a low-cut bodice, cinched waist, and voluminous skirt. Apparently done with her widow's weeds, she also wore a wide-brimmed straw hat with a red and white plaid band. The two women looked at one another until Ida, her mama's beloved housekeeper, stepped in the way.

Finally, in the front row, there stood Giselle, whose existence in Louisiana had included slavery, abuse, incest, motherhood, prostitution, murder, and execution. Yet on this day she stood tall and proud as a queen! It was Giselle in her prime, her amber-toned skin and dark auburn hair enhancing the exotic beauty of her mulatto features. She wore a light green morning dress with matching bonnet and parasol. Looking pretty as a picture and perfectly sane, she flashed a coquettish grin. Jessie Belle grinned back until her mother took Giselle's place. The transition jolted Jessie Belle, causing an involuntary flinch.

When her walk down the aisle came to an abrupt end and the music concluded with a crescendo, she suddenly remembered why she was here. She focused on the preacher in his religious regalia. She needed to pull herself out of her reverie. She needed to quell her visions. She needed to face reality. She was here to marry Robert.

There he was, standing right beside her: Robert Brentz, one of the most eligible and richest bachelors in the country. Women far and wide had fought over him. And she'd won. More handsome than ever, if that was even possible, he wore a black Armani tuxedo that complimented his silvery hair. His piercing blue eyes looked down at her with pure love. He'd finally made a decision to commit to her and she knew she should be eternally grateful.

They held each other's gaze as the preacher said his piece, "Dearly beloved, we are gathered here…" Eventually the preacher asked her to give her bouquet to the maid of honor so that she and Robert could hold hands while saying their vows.

She turned to hand over her flowers, and lo and behold, Star leaned forward from behind Gracie. In a pink dress identical to the maid of honor's, Star gave a little wave accompanied by a sheepish grin. Distracted by these antics, Jessie Belle momentarily forgot herself and almost queried out loud, "What are you doing here?"

Then the oddest thing happened. Jessie Belle's stomach growled. *Gr-r-r-r!* She realized she was starved! She'd been so busy the past couple of days getting ready for this wedding, she'd hardly eaten a bite. She remembered Dray saying his mother wanted to feed her. That errant thought made clear her elusive true desire.

She knew what she wanted.

Cramming her bouquet into Gracie's hands, she turned back toward her intended. Robert let out a sigh of relief, having been confused by her hesitation while her back was turned to him.

"I'm sorry, Robert," Jessie Belle announced in a loud, clear voice. "I can't marry you." She yanked off her fabulous marquis-cut diamond Cartier engagement ring and stuck it into his palm.

"You're a good man. Well, sort of. Give this ring to someone who will love you. Unfortunately, that isn't me."

As she turned toward the congregation, she heard gasps and protests from all corners, intermingled with a large thump as someone, probably Mama, fell to the floor in a dead faint. Jessie Belle hoisted up her skirt, turned left, turned right, then realized she didn't know which way to go.

Magically, Joe appeared at her side, grabbed her by the elbow, and said, "This way!" He shuttled her into the hallway beside the altar and out a side door. Within moments they were in his battered-up Chevy truck, her long veil billowing out the window as they sped away.

Back at the church, guests chattered like gossiping teenage girls, Mama moaned like a dying banshee, Gracie let loose with a gigantic smile, Robert stomped down the aisle and out the front entrance, paparazzi out front bumped into each other like stooges as they tried to figure out what they'd just missed, and Harry guffawed like someone who'd just witnessed the funniest show on earth. And Star, although unseen, did a merry jig right there in front of the altar.

"Where are we going?" Jessie Belle asked weakly.

Joe hadn't pressed her to talk, figuring she was in shock over what she'd done. This was the first thing she'd said in the thirty minutes they'd been zooming down I-20 toward the city.

"The one place you want to be."

"How do you know where I want to be?"

He glanced her way, shook his head, and said, "How can you ask? Youse guys oozed attraction for one another the whole time we were on assignment."

Stunned, she stared at him for a moment. "We did? I mean, I thought we oozed mutual loathing or something. At least at first. Then I sort of changed my mind. But that didn't matter because he still hates me." She clamped her mouth shut, realizing she was jabbering with no idea where she was going with this.

"Believe me, he doesn't hate you. He might not even know it yet, but he doesn't."

He turned into the Midtown section of Atlanta and drove for ten more minutes before reaching a mature neighborhood with well-kept old homes, giant live oak trees, and blooming azalea bushes galore. It was stunning. After a few turns, he pulled up in front of a pretty brick-and-shingle Queen Anne style house.

"Here you go," he said.

"Are you sure this is where he lives?"

"Yes, I'm sure. We've become friends. Our kids play together."

"Maybe he isn't home."

"His Jeep is in the driveway."

"Oh, Joe, I can't! I mean, what if he won't talk to me?

He reached across and shoved her door open. "He'll talk to you."

"Thank you so much, Joe. You're such a good friend."

"Yah, hey, I know. Unfortunately, every woman in my life says that."

Jessie Belle hugged him. "Okay," she said, turning toward the house. "I can do this." She started to get out but stopped. "Wait! I can't go in there like this!" she said as if just noticing that she wore a voluminous wedding dress.

"Yes you can. Now go." He shooed her away.

"This is ridiculous!" she objected as she gathered her skirt and got out. She dropped the skirt and stood there for a moment staring at the charming home with its lush, well-kept yard. It was all too picture perfect. She turned to get back into the truck.

The Chevy truck, however, was already coasting away. Joe threw her a wave, then gunned it.

Her gallant rescuer was gone.

She was going to have to save herself.

Chapter 27

"Daddy! There's a bride at the door!"

The little girl took one look, shouted her announcement, and slammed the door in Jessie Belle's face.

"The bride" considered using the opportunity to bolt.

Before she could run, however, the door opened again.

Of course she remembered that Dray was handsome, but now he looked absolutely drop-dead gorgeous. In safari shorts, an aqua blue tee shirt, sandals, and mussed up hair, he made her heart flip flop with desire. Even with his jaw hanging open.

Finally finding his voice, he rasped, "Jessie Belle."

"Hi," she said with a ridiculous little wave.

Four sets of enormous oval eyes glared at her as if she were an absolute freak. Well, Jessie Belle realized, she was. After all, it wasn't every day that a bride showed up on your doorstep.

There was thirteen-year-old Demetri who, being a typical hormonal pubescent boy, unabashedly looked her up and down as if to calculate her worth as a girl. He wore his Morningside Middle School baseball tee shirt, and seeing that his grandmother didn't allow him to wear it at the table, had his Atlanta Braves baseball cap hooked over the back of his chair. He had what Jessie Belle remembered as a "butch" haircut, but she supposed kids called it something else these days.

Ten-year-old Andre had a more analytical gaze. Jessie Belle feared he saw her as a specimen for a science experience, appearing as if he wanted to dissect her to see what made her breathe. He wore a rather serious plaid shirt and sported spiky short hair.

Then there was seven-year-old Lily. Ah, Lily. Dray hadn't been kidding when he claimed she was going through a gawky stage. Her thick, red-framed glasses accentuated her stare and made her look like a small Mr. Magoo. When she'd commented on Jessie Belle's pretty dress and veil, the faux bride had taken off the expensive designer veil and pinned it into the little girl's wayward brown hair. That had garnered a huge buck-toothed smile. But now that they all sat around the dining room table, even though Lily clearly loved her new veil and fingered its edges non-stop, her smile had morphed into a curious gape.

The fourth set of curious eyes belonged to Rocket, the dog, who glared at her as if considering pouncing at any moment. Jessie Belle had no idea what kind of dog he was, other than the kind who didn't like strangers. He'd barked furiously when she first entered the house. Dray had insisted he was usually better mannered and speculated that the big white gown had thrown him for a loop. The kids obviously loved the little brown-and-black-and-white beast and he loved them back. Rocket calmed down only after Demetri said, "Cool it, Rock." Still, the mutt sat vigil at the intruder's side.

Dray sat silently, still in a state of disbelief, keeping a watchful eye on this ragtag group at his table.

"Okay!" Dray's mom declared. "I found a nice apron for you, Jessie Belle, and here's our lunch." Lillian Dlugitch entered the dining room carrying a big bowl, carefully holding it with hot pads, and with a brightly printed apron draped over her forearm. She set the bowl in the middle of the table and went to Jessie Belle. "Here, dear, put this on." She handed over the apron. "We wouldn't want you to get a spot of goulash on that nice dress." Jessie Belle obeyed by putting the apron strings over her head and leaning forward to tie the back at the waist, all the while wondering what goulash was.

"We already had lunch," Demetri protested.

"Yeah, two hours ago," Andre added.

"That's okay," Lily offered. "We can have more."

"That's right," Lillian said as she sat down at the head of the table. "We have a guest who hasn't had lunch yet, so we can have a little more to keep her company. Besides, goulash is always better reheated." Jessie Belle would be eternally grateful to the woman for her nonchalance, even though having a hungry runaway bride show up announced at her door had to have been a total shock. It seemed this woman had been taken by surprise many a time in her life and this odd incident didn't ruffle her feathers one bit.

Demetri held his plate out to Dray but Lillian motioned for him to put it down. "Remember, guests always come first," she said.

"Oh, yeah, I forgot," Demetri mumbled. "Sorry."

Jessie Belle did, however, get the message that it was a ritual for Dray to fill the plates, so she handed hers over. "Thank you!" she said when the heaping thing came back to her. This goulash stuff, elbow macaroni in some kind of reddish meat sauce, smelled delicious! Her stomach growled again and she couldn't wait to dig in.

One-by-one the kids and Lillian handed Dray their plates, which he filled modestly, as they'd already eaten. But when it came to his, he piled it on. Apparently having an unexpected guest made him ravenous.

The ensuing conversation delighted Jessie Belle. She liked Dray's mom immensely. Not at all the stereotypical old-fashioned Eastern European hausfrau in a housedress and babushka that Jessie Belle had envisioned, Lillian was instead a tall, slim, attractive, middle-aged woman. Not having planned on an uninvited visitor in a fifty-thousand-dollar designer bridal gown, she was casually dressed in running shorts and a tee shirt, with her dark, grey-tinged hair pulled back into a ponytail. She ran, as Jessie Belle learned from the table conversation, five to ten miles a day in training for her ninth marathon. The talk flowed from Lillian's running to Demetri's baseball aspirations to Andre's plan to become a NASA nuclear physicist. When Jessie Belle asked Lily what she wanted to be when she grew up, the waif shyly said, "I want to tell the news on TV, just like you." Jessie Belle didn't know if she'd ever received such a meaningful compliment in her entire life. It made her feel honored.

Goulash, as she discovered, was awesome. She had seconds, something she never allowed herself to do. When finished, Lillian insisted that the kids help her clean up while Jessie Belle and Dray go into the living room to talk. Lillian said, "You two must have a lot to discuss. Go ahead and have a nice chat."

Jessie Belle attempted to stand up, only to discover that Rocket had nestled into the overflowing skirt of her gown. Apparently she'd finally passed some kind of secret dog test and the guard in the dog had gone down, as he snoozed on the delicate, white fabric.

Lillian and Dray both reacted when they saw the situation. "Oh, no! Rocket!" Lillian yelped. "Rocket! Get off!" Dray ordered. Lillian fluttered her hands at the dog, who lazily opened his eyes, yawned, got up, and sauntered away, as if he couldn't imagine what all the fuss was about.

Finally able to stand all the way up, Jessie Belle reassured Lillian it was okay. She and Dray went into the living room. This was a lovely old home with original hardwood floors, crafted molding, fireplaces, high ceilings, and doorways that stood broad and tall. It felt like a real home.

"I love your family," Jessie Belle said once settled into the cushy couch. "Lily is such a little doll."

Dray beamed. "They're my life. I love them more than I can ever express. When I was younger I'd hear people talk about their kids that way and I just didn't get it. Now I get it."

"I think I'm starting to understand, too, Dray. I can understand why they mean so much to you." She looked away from him in thought. *Where does all of this leave me?*

"Jessie Belle," he said. He sounded serious but suddenly burst into laughter. "I'm sorry, you just look so funny in that apron! You do realize, don't you, that it's totally bizarre that you're sitting in my living room in your Vera Wang wedding gown with my mom's Wal-Mart apron on over it? The tabloids would have a field day with this!"

"True," she agreed, patting her apron, "but it'll only be a day or two before the paparazzi forget all about Robert Brentz's runaway-bride. Some other more famous idiot will do something even more bizarre, so I'll be off the hook.

"Speaking of which, I've put you on the hook here. I know that. You don't have to feel obligated in any way. You were so nice to let me in, especially when I started blathering about your mom feeding me. I really was hungry!"

"That was all? That's the only reason you're here?"

They sat side-by-side but about a foot apart. Now he put his arm up on the back of the couch behind her and leaned toward her.

She leaned in, too.

"Well, I have been going crazy about something," she said. "On the plane ride back, just before we hit turbulence and the whole Robert debacle," she said, rolling her eyes, "you started to ask me something. What was it?"

"You won't believe me."

"What? Tell me!"

"I wanted to invite you over for a goulash supper."

"You did not!"

He raised his hand in a pledge. "I swear."

"No kidding. And here we are. Invitation accepted."

"So what comes next, Jessie Belle?"

"I don't know. I haven't had time to think about it. I didn't exactly plan ahead for coming here," she noted, motioning to her dress.

He grinned. "I'd give anything to have been—how do you say it? A flea on the wall."

"A fly."

"Yes! A fly on the wall. I'm sure you left some really pissed off people in that church."

"Oh, yeah. But not Harry. He was having the time of his life."

They laughed together, leaning closer and closer....

Out of the corner of her eye Jessie Belle saw Lily peeking around the wide doorway. She pulled away from Dray and cocked her head toward the child.

"Lily, honey," Dray said, "come on in. My, you look lovely in your veil."

The little girl stiffly sashayed toward them, holding her arms out at her sides in an imitation of a model's walk down a fashion show runway. Rocket followed behind, nipping at the trailing veil.

When Lily reached them, Dray grabbed her and plopped her onto the couch between Jessie Belle and himself, and proceeded to tickle her like crazy. Lily giggled uproariously and Jessie Belle couldn't help but join in. Rocket hopped up to get in on the fun. When Lily and Dray turned to gang up on Jessie Belle, the almost-bride couldn't remember the last time in her life she'd laughed so hard. She'd always thought this tickling thing was stupid, but she was actually having fun. Rocket even licked her face.

After everyone calmed down, Lily softly placed her hand into Jessie Belle's. Jessie Belle gently took hold.

Lillian and the boys joined them with trays of brownies and iced tea. "Not quite the wedding cake you thought you'd be having today," Lillian teased, "but I do make good brownies, if I say so myself."

"I say so, too!" Lily said, helping herself to a big piece.

Jessie Belle sat back and watched this happy family. They'd redefined happy for her because in this house it had nothing to do with stature and money. She wondered if she'd ever fit it. Could she ever be happy living like this, with children and a modest, albeit comfy and inviting, home? Would she be satisfied with an income like Dray's that, even combined with hers, was far below what she used to?

Ah, she decided, if we do end up together and if we want more money, we'll just have to make it ourselves. Somehow that thought felt liberating. They wouldn't be beholden to relatives or banks or an inheritance. They wouldn't be dependent on anyone or anything but themselves. The shackles of oppressive tradition would be unlocked and cast off. She reveled in the new feeling of freedom.

An hour later when she felt as if she'd interrupted enough of the Dlugitch family's day with her unexpected visit, Jessie Belle announced that she was tired and needed to get home. Lillian found her a chambray shirt to put over her wedding gown and a ball cap to cover her hair, in case photographers were waiting outside her condo building. Demetri said his goodbye while tossing a baseball into a mitt, Andre eyed her skeptically while reciting a polite farewell, and Rocket, upon realizing that something was happening at the door, ran over wagging his tail so ecstatically it was impossible for Jessie Belle to resist giving him a good scratch behind his ear. He leaned into her hand until he tumbled sideways onto the floor. For her farewell Lily took Jessie Belle's hand once again and, looking up with those big Mr. Magoo eyes, asked her to please come visit them again. Jessie Belle promised she would and hugged the little girl. Jessie Belle and

Lillian also hugged. Then Jessie Belle was in Dray's Jeep and on her way home.

"This has been the afternoon that changed my life," Jessie Belle said as they tooled down the street. "In more ways than one."

She hadn't known that there was one more way to come.

Dray made love to her in ways she'd never imagined. It wasn't just his great physique, thrilling technique, or impassioned desire. Wonderful as that was, she'd had all that before. No, this was something more. This was that elusive thing called intimacy that she had never truly known.

I expected to have great sex on my wedding night, she mused, *but I didn't know it wouldn't be with the groom.*

After their second round of love-making, she threw on a tee shirt and he donned his boxers, and they padded into the kitchen seeking sustenance. Sitting on the stools at the kitchen island, their legs entwined underneath, neither spoke as they drank Cokes in glass bottles. After greedily chugging most of his, Dray turned his attention toward the window over the sink and gazed outside at the golden late afternoon light.

"What is it, Dray? Are you sorry you've done this?"

When he lowered his eyes back to hers, she melted under the intensity of those steely gray pools.

"Never. I will never be sorry for this," he said. "No matter where it does or does not lead.

"You know, I spent our whole trip doing everything in my power to deny my attraction to you." His voice took on a thoughtful tone. "I tried like the devil to find reasons not to like you. I let myself believe the diva stories."

"Well," she fessed up, "they were sort of true."

He winked at her candor. "But not as much as I'd been told."

She found his defense of her honor charming.

He went on. "I told myself you'd never like a guy like me, anyway. I even had myself believing that someone like you wouldn't be good around the kids.

"Then when you told me that you have regular visits from your dead ancestors…. Well, that just gave me one more big excuse to push you away. I mean, I was surprised that you trusted me enough to tell me, but at the same time the story was spooky."

"You think it's weird, don't you?" she asked.

He considered that for a moment. "No, not really. With a mom like mine, I can't help but believe in the supernatural. I just don't want those dead people visiting me!"

She nodded, understanding completely. That's exactly how she'd felt in the beginning. "They won't," she assured him. "They like you but they won't bother you. In fact, I think that now that my wedding is off, and you and I are together, they'll turn their attention to other things."

"Good. I mean, I appreciate them liking me and thank my lucky stars if they helped get us together. Thanks." He waved toward the ceiling at the invisible colluders.

He had no idea how correct he was when he said "lucky stars," Jessie Belle mused, picturing Star. She'd tell him about her spirit friend some other time.

"But then," Dray said, "even ghosts couldn't keep my mind off you! I had to work harder than ever not to want to ravish your body every time I saw you.

"Besides, there was Robert at first and I would never go after another man's girlfriend. Then, all of a sudden, Robert was out of the picture and you were broken-hearted. My god! That night you came to my room it took everything in me not to accept your in-vi-ta-tion." She giggled at how he stretched out the word in jest. With his accent it came out as in-vee-tay-see-own. "That is, until you puked. That pretty much killed the appeal, at least for that night."

Jessie Belle buried her face in her hands in exaggerated chagrin as Dray laughed. "I was so-o-o embarrassed," she groaned.

He grabbed her hands so she'd have to look at him and continued. "But that attraction was back in full force the next morning when you walked into that coffee house so assured and so beautiful. Good lord! My heart almost stopped." He slapped his hand over his chest, as if protecting his heart. "I thought, *I could have had her last night! Clearly, I'm the biggest idiot who ever lived!*

"Really, though," he said after taking the last swig of his Coke, "no guy with any scruples would ever take advantage of a girl as vulnerable as you were that night.

"But once I finally got up my courage to ask you out, I'd waited too long, and that damned Robert was back. And the next thing I knew, you were engaged. I decided I had to forget you. You were a big girl who knew her own mind and it was none of my business."

"Well, it turns out I didn't know my own mind. And now, especially after what just happened in there," she said, pointing toward the bedroom, "I'd say it is your business."

"To us," Dray said, clinking his Coke bottle with hers.

Within minutes the empty bottles were left forgotten on the kitchen island and the two lovers were back in bed. When they finished their third round of romping in-between the sheets and the late afternoon turned into evening, casting streetlight shadows about her bedroom, he gently traced her naked body with the tip of his finger, titillating her skin until it tingled with joy.

"I've loved your body ever since the first time I saw it all tangled up on the floor of the airplane and helped you up," he said, following his touch with a kiss to her tummy. His finger meandered all the way up to her forehead. Planting a kiss there, he said, "I've loved your mind ever since I realized how smart you are as a professional journalist and newscaster." He drew his finger down her body until it reached her heart and kissed that spot on her chest. "I've loved your heart ever since you saved that little girl in Ethiopia." Then he took her hand in his and touched her palm as lightly as if his finger were a magic feather. "And I've loved your soul ever since…." He paused. "Ever since discovering that you are *you*."

I am me, Jessie Belle thought happily. *At last.*

"I love you, Jessie Belle." Dray's dulcet voice enwrapped her in joy.

She caressed his cheek and kissed him deeply. When their lips parted she whispered, "I love you, too, Dray." This time she knew that those words were true, even though she'd said them before to another, because this time they were spoken by the real Jessie Belle Church.

"Hi, Star!" Although groggy from deep sleep, Jessie Belle greeted her friend enthusiastically. "It's so good to see you!" She sat up, rubbed her eyes, and looked again. Yup, Star was right beside her. There was no mistaking the flamboyant lavender antebellum ball gown with the hoop skirt that poofed out all over the bed. "You going to a ball at Tara?" Jessie Belle joked.

"Oh, no! Not in years," Star said, plucking at her skirt. "You know, there really was a plantation like Tara and a girl who was every bit as bitchy as Scarlett! She wouldn't pay a bit of attention to us. Unlike you, my dear." She beamed at her protégé.

"I've missed you!" Jessie Belle said. "It's been two weeks since my wedding. Well, you know, that little sideshow that was supposed to be my wedding. I've been waiting for you to come see me so we could talk."

"Pfft! Really, now?" Star chided. "It's been a little hard for me to drop in, what with you and that big hunk of a man thrashing around at each other every night. This is the first night he hasn't been here."

"Do you watch us?" Jessie Belle squealed, embarrassed at the thought.

"Oh, my, no! I know when to take my leave. I peek in every now and then and if you're, ah-hem, busy, I scoot right outta here. I may be nosy and pushy and intrusive, but I'm not a voyeuristic pervert!"

"Ha! That's good to know!"

"Now, I've been wanting to ask you something: did you know all along that I shouldn't marry Robert? Why didn't you tell me?"

"Well, the girls and I suspected that you were feeling pressured by family issues. That problem is as old as dirt, let me tell you! I couldn't even begin to guess how many times I've had to deal with that. Anyway, we weren't convinced you loved Robert like you should. Of course, dear, that was for you to decide. But, frankly, we were afraid you were totally screwing up. So we cheated just a smidge," she gestured with her thumb and forefinger about an inch apart, "by making that last visit. We figured if you could marry Robert after being reminded of all that you'd learned from your ancestors' life stories, then you really did love him and we should butt out.

"But, of course," she giggled and smacked her thigh, "you burned rubber getting out of there!"

"I know, I know. I let being penniless cloud my judgment. I thought I'd broken through my denial about my life; I thought I was finally thinking for myself. But I wasn't, not completely. My mama's voice was still playing in the back of my thick head.

"'You can never be too rich or too thin,'" Jessie Belle said in a gooey Southern drawl, imitating her mama.

"'Denial is as deep as the middle of the ocean,'" Star said, quoting another of Jessie Belle's progenitors, "'as overpowering as an autumn typhoon in the southern seas, and as blinding as an avalanche on a fjord that buries you under a mountain of snow.' But now your denial has melted away."

"Erik Bloodtooth."

"Yes."

Jessie Belle fingered the soft fabric of her spirit friend's dress while she thought.

"I love Dray," she whispered after a few moments. "He makes me so happy! I don't know yet if we'll ever end up married. We haven't talked about that yet. And if we do, we'll probably never have much money. I may never be rich again."

"That's true."

"And I still don't know if I want children. But I do know that every time little Lily takes my hand, I don't want to let go."

"Did you notice in all of the stories of your ancestors how many children there were who were raised by someone other than their biological mother? Being a mother means more than giving birth."

Jessie Belle nodded. "Dray's mom would be great to be around. She's so young acting and free and fun. Not like my mama."

"Your mama has had her own burdens to bear. Don't blame her too much."

"I won't, if she ever talks to me again. She still won't take my calls. Ida fills me in, though. She says she thinks Lawrence Davidson, the lawyer, is going to propose to Mama soon. Ida says they sit in the front parlor and get totally schnockered together every evening, so they're a perfect couple."

"To each their own," Star observed.

"Dray and I have our own unique relationship, that's for sure. We spend half our time coming up with ideas about programs we'd like to do together. We've filled up half a notebook. Harry put him and Joe on my 'Women's Worth' series with me. It's so exciting! But every time I think of something for that series it uncovers another idea for something else I'd like to do in the future. It's like kudzu on the brain!"

Star reached up and stroked Jessie Belle's hair, as if petting her brain. It felt to Jessie Belle like bubbles of energy shooting through her scalp.

"Your mind is free now," Star proclaimed. "And you did it yourself! Your ancestors and I just showed you new possibilities. But you are the one who opened yourself up to those possibilities. There's no telling where you will go from here! But knowing isn't the point. The point is to explore and discover and journey into the unknown. You've opened your body, mind, and spirit to the woman you are and will forever become!"

Jessie Belle let Star's words slowly sink into her heart. "Forever become," she repeated in awe. "Thank you, Star! Will you thank all of the others for me, too?"

"Of course, dear."

"They were wonderful, weren't they? They lived such amazing lives! I'll always be grateful to them for sharing their stories with me. It makes me think about all of the others. You know, there are so many others who made me, too!"

"Ah, well, you don't need to worry about them right now." Star leaned in conspiratorially. "If there's ever a need for you to get to know some of the men, it'll be quite an adventure! There's the gay Mesopotamian monk who lived in a cave and was a scribe for the princess. When her husband the prince couldn't perform his, ah-hmm, manly duties, our monk rose to the occasion long enough to provide the empire with an heir that everyone thought was the prince's! And then there's the Mongolian who through this whole thing has been barreling in and bellowing, 'Tell her to grow some balls!'" Jessie Belle giggled. "I have to keep shooing him away!" Star said. "Why, the man had a hundred and thirty eight children all over China! You're related to a good third of the country! And then there's our poor lad from an American colonial fishermen family, who was kidnapped by pirates but ended up liking them better than he'd ever liked his boring parents. The pirate life was for him! It goes on and on, of course, but the women who came to you this time were just the right ones for you to get to know for now."

"Star, I just thought of something. In the beginning, you told me there would be nine women whose blood flowed in my veins who would help me become the best possible me. But there were only eight. Who's the ninth one?"

Star's smile beamed, lighting up the night. "It's you, Jessie Belle. It's you."

Jessie Belle's lips slowly curled into an arch of pleasure that matched that of her spirit friend. She lay back down, nestling her head into her feather soft pillow, and closed her eyes to revel in the pleasure of Star stroking her hair.

Her eyes still shut, Jessie Belle whispered, "Star, will you come to me if I ever need you again?"

"Of course," Star said softly. "All you need to do is pray and I'll come to you as soon as I can. And I'll always check in from time to time to make sure you're okay. So will your ancestor spirits, the ones who have come to know and love you. But even when you can't see us, remember that you're never alone. Our love will always be with you. We will love happily ever after."

Jessie Belle's closed eyelids fluttered peacefully as she fell into a bliss-filled slumber.

Star gently withdrew her elegant fingers from Jessie Belle's silky hair, lightly ran a thumb across her unfettered forehead, and delicately placed a kiss there. She sighed, knowing that she would miss this soul whom she loved so dearly. But it was time to go. She smiled down at this glorious young woman named Jessie Belle Church who had finally begun to come into her own glory.

Then the enchanting spirit dwindled into a dazzling mist that trailed off into the eternal night.

About the Author

Becoming Jessie Belle is the culmination of many of Linda's interests, experiences, and beliefs. Being a college professor, she used her research skills to make each tale as historically accurate as possible. The present-day location descriptions come from her years of traveling the world for her former job as a trainer. She has also spent a lot of time delving into her family history, including participation in the National Geographic Genographic project. Jessie Belle's DNA trail is Linda's own. And the concept for this book came about when a psychic friend suggested that Linda do "past life regressions." Linda doesn't believe in past lives, and gave it a try to prove that it wouldn't work. Two hours later, after receiving insights into the lives of amazing women from the past—some of whom are in this book—Linda was stunned at the results. She still doesn't believe in past lives, but she does feel that somehow these women's stories were passed on to her to share with you. No matter what you believe about how these tales came about—past lives, ancestor spirits, or the author's wild imagination—Linda hopes that you will see that you are not alone in your trials and triumphs as a woman. May you feel the love of your ancestor women and live in the warm embrace of their understanding, just like Jessie Belle.

CPSIA information can be obtained at www.ICGtesting.com
Printed in the USA
LVOW11s1404020314

375702LV00001B/1/P